Anneke

The Immigrants

A NOVEL

Gesina Laird-Buchanan

MillCreek Press

In appreciation:

With thanks to author Judy Steed who, in collaboration with librarian Cate Giroux, started a writing group in Coe Hill, and got the ball rolling.

Thanks to all of those who provided encouragement along the way, including: Judy Hatton, MargaretAnne Gorham, Leslie Lewis, Bunny Singer, Barbara Fear, Alice De La Plante, Elaine Vaughn, Karen Richardson, Helen Breslauer, Mary van Baal... and the many others.

Particular thanks are in order to those who helped by editing at various stages: Mary Burbidge, Sheila Round, Marni King, and my daughter Leona Laird.

I would like to dedicate this book to my mother, Henny Legg, 1914 - 2014, from whom I got my love of story telling.

C 2017 Gesina Laird-Buchanan/MillCreek Press
All rights reserved.

Index

Chapter One – The Wooden Crate   page 1

Chapter Two – In the Land of Milk and Honey   page 90

Chapter Three – That Perfect Lipstick   page 155

Chapter Four – The Plymouth Belvedere   page 249

Chapter One – The Wooden Crate

The huge wooden crate sat on the cobbled street in front of the red-brick row house. Workmen were bustling about filling it with the family's possessions: father's pendulum clock, mother's treadle sewing machine, the sturdy table and chairs from the *huiskamer, and* the delicate Delft-blue pottery, wrapped in bed linen and tea towels. As the crate filled, the house emptied of all that made it home, of all that made it different from every other red-brick row house in the Doesburgstraat. Anneke's mother looked sad, frightened even, as the transfer of each piece of furniture, each article of clothing, every pot and pan, brought them closer to the end of life as they knew it. And all of the neighbours had gathered to talk about the goings on, to savour the drama, and to scavenge what the family must inevitably leave behind.

Bursting with excitement, Anneke skipped along the cobblestones, chanting, "We're going to Canada! We're going to Canada!" Anneke knew all about Canada – it was in America – and she'd seen enough westerns at the town hall to know that *she* was going to like America, *a lot!* There would be cowboys racing around on horseback shooting their pistols into the air, saving stagecoaches and lassoing cattle. *She* would even have her own horse! She was sure of it! She was so excited she could hardly wait. She stopped skipping, when a sudden hush fell over the crowd. Perplexed,

Anneke looked at her parents. Her father seemed stunned as he stared blankly at the wooden crate filled to overflowing, and the large pile of household goods, still waiting on the sidewalk. Mother began to sob quietly.

"All right boys, we'd better try this again," said the foreman briskly, and the workmen proceeded to empty the crate unto the street, and try different ways to make everything fit. It finally became obvious that this was hopeless. There was only one thing to be done.

"Mama, we can't leave that! That's our *best* furniture!" Anneke protested. The darkly ornate table and chairs from the front room were being separated from the rest of the family belongings. "Those are the good chairs we only sit on when the minister comes to call!" Anneke recalled years of being forbidden to enter the front room. The sliding wooden doors remained closed except for very special occasions. Yet, once a week, mother would enter the room to lovingly polish the ornately carved arms and legs and the table top, to a high, dark sheen. To Anneke, the front room was a revered place, next only to the church, and the objects in it were sacred. Her eyes grew wide as mother spat out,

"That old junk! It's so rickety it will fall apart on the trip!"

"But, but..." and Anneke withdrew silently, to sit alone, waiting, on a neighbour's stoop.

Finally the packing was finished. Their home, their life as they had known it, was now within the confines of this square, wooden crate. The house gaped emptily. The workmen were ready to put the top on the crate. And as they hammered the lid into place, the mother felt each nail as if it were being driven into her coffin.

And Anneke sat on the stoop pondering the inequities of life, the twists and turns of fate, and what a terrible liar her mother was, telling her all those years that furniture was valuable, when in fact it was only junk.

The truck rumbled off with their crate, and it was time to leave. A neighbour had offered to drive the family to the train station in his small autobus. They placed suitcases, coats and other paraphernalia in the back, and after hugs and tears and promises to write t hey piled into the front: Piet and Johanna Verbeek and their children, seventeen-year-old Mieke, twelve-year old Henk, and ten-year old Anneke.

When they reached the station and boarded the train, Johanna went directly to a corner of the compartment, where she sank back in her seat and closed her eyes. Opposite her, Mieke sat down, sniffling and sobbing disconsolately into her handkerchief. Even the kids were quiet and subdued. Piet stood looking on with a worried frown. He walked to the window, "Come over here," he gestured his younger children, "and look carefully at everything, so you'll remember." They came and stood on either side of him, and he rested his hands on their shoulders. The train started up with a jolt and a squeal of metal on metal. Soon, red-brick houses began sliding by their window. Towering over these houses was the enormous factory complex of Philips Electronics. "Later," said Piet, "when we're living in Canada, somebody is going to say, 'Anneke, what did Holland look like,' or 'Henk, what was the town like where you born?' And what will you tell them?"

"Eindhoven is Philips, and Philips, Eindhoven," said Henk, repeating a mantra he had heard.

"You're dead on," said Piet. "Why, Eindhoven wasn't much more than a village when Philips came here and started making the light bulbs. That was in 1891, right after they were invented. And do you know who got the first ones?"

"The queen?" asked Anneke.

Piet scratched his head. "Well maybe." He lit up a cigarette. Blew out some smoke, "*Ja,* anyway Anneke, it was really rich people who bought the first light bulbs. People who wanted to show off that they owned the latest invention. But before long everybody else wanted light bulbs too! More workers were needed to make them, like glassblowers with powerful lungs to blow the glass bulbs, and young girls with slim flexible fingers to put the filaments inside those bulbs. Glassblowers came to Eindhoven from Austria, France, Germany, even all the way from Italy. But when it came to girls, well there had to be lots of young girls in Holland who were suitable. So Philips sent out scouts throughout the country to find those girls, in fact to find whole families of girls."

"Scouts?" asked Henk. "Like soccer scouts? Like to find the best soccer players?"

"Same idea. They went especially to poor rural areas where people might be keen to move, like the Province of Drenthe."

"Where mama's from," said Anneke.

"Right. They looked for families with at least three daughters who could start working in the factory right away. But first they had to test them, and you would have been good at this Anneke, because they made them cut paper into shapes, bend wire a certain way, sort screws and so on. If the girls passed the test, then the whole family got to move to Eindhoven – train tickets for everybody and a brand new house just waiting for them." Piet nodded in the direction of his sleeping wife, "And that's how your mother came to be here. It was 1925, and she was your age, Anneke, and she had older sisters who could start working in the factory right away."

Henk creased his forehead, "So mother's family came to Eindhoven by train thirty years ago, and now we are leaving by train." He looked around, "Think it's the same train?"

Piet grinned, "Could be!" The factory had vanished, but streets of red-brick row houses continued to whiz by. "See all those houses? All built by Philips. Built for the workers. They couldn't just keep bringing more workers to Eindhoven, without providing houses for the families to live in. So an architect was hired and he built an entire neighbourhood of houses like ours. When your mother's family came from Drenthe, one day they were living in an old house with oil lamps for light, turf for cooking, and an outhouse out back for a poop; and the next they were in a brand new house with electric lights, gas for cooking, and, oh what a miracle... a flush toilet! What a change, eh? Why, your grandmother thought she'd died and gone to heaven!"

"Mama said she can still smell the fresh cement," remembered Anneke, "the most wonderful thing she ever smelled!"

Piet nodded, "And along with all those houses, Philips built parks..."

"Gelderlandsplein!" interrupted Anneke.

"Right, the park you walked through to go to school was built by Philips. And there were schools, and a hospital, and a sports complex..."

"PSV soccer club!" yelled Henk.

"The best there is," Piet smiled, then added, "but quiet down you two. Don't wake your mother."

The train was leaving the city behind, and as the kids were pointing things out and elbowing each other for the best view, Piet sat back in his seat and smoked and ruminated on why a capitalist like Philips would provide to that extent for his workers. Must be the communist connection, he decided. He remembered hearing that the mother of Carl Marx was sister to whoever was head of the Philips family in the mid-1800's, and while the mother disapproved of her son and had little to do with him, uncle and nephew were close. In fact, while in London working on his Manifesto, Carl Marx frequently got financial aid from his Dutch uncle. Well, thought Piet, it was all rather beyond him, but, maybe that was the reason.

"Look how pretty, papa!" There were fields of heather punctuated by clumps of white birch and ponds reflecting scudding clouds. Anneke had her nose pressed to the window.

"Yes, a beautiful land," Piet said softly as he gazed out at the landscape. They passed a thatched farmhouse with brightly painted shutters. "Remember this one kids," he told them. "You can tell them all about it in Canada. See how wide it is! It's called a *langgevelboerderij.* One end is the house and the other the barn. Very practical. When it rains you don't have to go outdoors to look after the cows, you just step through the doorway, and in the winter the heat from the cattle helps heat your home."

The train rumbled by a cluster of houses punctuated by a church steeple and a windmill whose arms turned reluctantly with the wind. Ditches divided lush green meadows where black and white cows grazed. Lazily they turned their heads and observed the passing of the emigrants.

The retching woke her. Anneke lay quietly in the semi-darkness and listened to the gasping intake of breath, followed by even more violent retching, and the sound of vomit splattering in the seasickness bag. The stench filled the tiny cabin, the sour smell searing her nostrils. To escape it she rolled unto her stomach and buried her face in her pillow. She felt herself being jostled, back and forth, back and forth, and she clutched her pillow in an effort not to be tossed against the sides of the metal bunk. When at last the retching sounds died down, Anneke could hear her father murmuring softly, and she raised her head slightly to locate the comforting sound. Across the narrow cabin in the circle of dim yellow light she could see father, wearing his pajamas, sitting on the edge of mother's bunk. Anneke watched as he held the gray-paper bag in front of mother's face, one hand supporting her back. Then finally he put the bag on the cabin floor, and with a soapy-fresh washcloth, tenderly washed mother's ashen face. He murmured a few more words, brushed his lips against mother's cheek, and departed for the ship's deck to throw the bag overboard. Anneke continued to clutch her pillow, to resist the rolling motion of the ship, and to fight the queasiness now in her stomach. At last father was back. He threw open the porthole. An icy ocean wind whooshed into the cabin and Anneke burrowed deep down in the blankets until just her nose protruded. She breathed in the fresh, salty air; then, content, drifted off to sleep.

Dawn stole through the salt-pitted porthole, touched her face, burnished the copper-penny hair. Anneke yawned and stretched... and felt her fingers touch something. What the heck? She looked up and saw the ceiling at arms-length from her face, then looked over at a sink, metal locker, and bunk-beds. Directly across was brother Henk, splayed on his back, snoring. Anneke snorted derisively, but then a slow smile began to spread across her face as the full implications of her situation hit her. She was in their cabin on the ship, and might be... the only one awake. It was her chance to go exploring! She crept quietly down the ladder, pulled on the red dress with the black polka-dots, and her knit socks and leather sandals, and stepped into the hall, closing the door soundlessly behind her. And then she ran! Up the metal stairs she flew, sandals clanging merrily. She pushed open the door to the deck... and came to a sudden stop. There was nothing to be seen, no deck, no ocean view, just fog. She thought for a moment, then stretched out her arms in front of her and started across the deck. After four or five paces, the ship bucked! She fell, skidded across the slick deck, and came to a crashing halt. Steaming coffee narrowly missed her! Dishes smashed to smithereens around her! *"Godverdomme!"* cursed a deep voice. Legs, she realized. She'd crashed into legs! An enormous drooping mustache neared her face and growled, "Ya burnt?"

In a tiny voice, "No."

"Right!" and the sailor picked her up under his arm and marched off with her. "What were ya doing on the deck anyway? Do ya want to go overboard?"

"No-o," whimpered Anneke.

"Sit!" he commanded, as he dropped her in a deckchair. "And don't you even think of moving off that chair until your parents turn up!" Grumbling to himself he walked away, *"Net een gekkenhuis!* Kids running wild all over the decks while their puking parents stay cooped in their cabins. It's a wonder we don't lose half them little buggers overboard. Pulled one right off the railing last week. Seemed to think he was walking a tightrope. Stupid little bastard! Nearly became fish food. Damn, I miss the navy. Discipline! Order! That's what I miss!" Anneke heard him muttering even after he'd vanished in the fog.

She curled up in the chair, hiding her face and sobbing quietly, terrified the sailor would return. She was shivering from the damp cold. At long last she dared to peek round her fingers, and saw that the fog was lifting. Still she stayed, both from fear, and because she no longer had any idea of how to get back to the cabin

"Anneke!" She perked up her ears.

"Anneke!" It was her brother's voice. Quickly she wiped her face on the back of her arm as Henk came striding across the deck. "Are you ever in trouble!" he said with relish. He observed her more carefully and added, "You been bawling, ain't ya?"

"N – no," she snuffled.

"Well, you will be," he chortled, "when you get back to the cabin! Ma's having a fit sure you've fallen overboard and Pa's trying to calm her down and he told me to tear around the ship and find you and tell you to get your sorry ass back before he booted you from here to Canada."

"Papa said *that?*"

"Well… not *exactly*."

Anneke uncurled herself from the chair, and followed her brother below deck. They walked into the cabin. "Agh! Agh! I thought you were dead! I thought you drowned! I thought…" and mother grabbed Anneke's shoulders and shook her. "What were you doing going out by yourself! You scared me half to death. I thought you were in the ocean. I thought…"

Henk said derisively, "She was sitting all dozy in a deckchair like she didn't have a clue." He added in a jeering tone, "That dumb-ass girl got lost."

Anneke's eyes narrowed.

"That's enough Henk!" said father. "And from now on, Anneke," he said, shaking his finger at her, you will not go anywhere without you brother. Understand! Nowhere!"

"What about the toilet?" she said mutinously. Their cabin had only a sink. Toilets and showers were down the hall, separate for men and women.

He sighed in exasperation. "All *right*! The toilet, but that's *it!*"

The ship plowed on through the rough Atlantic. At night they were jostled in their beds, and sometimes there'd be a crash in the hallway, when some half-asleep soul traversing the rolling ship lost their footing enroute to the toilet, and then the Verbeek family would grin with *schadenfreude*. But it was less amusing when one of them had to go pee in the middle of the night! And it became another job for father Piet – along with tossing pukebags overboard – to walk his womenfolk down the dimly-lit hallway to the WC. He was glad when morning came.

Piet lit up a cigarette and leaned against the railing. The wind whipped his gabardine overcoat and he crushed his fedora more tightly to his head. He was a handsome man, in a rugged, Humphrey Bogart sort of way, but now he had a haggard look about him, and there were circles under his eyes. He let out a deep sigh. My God, what had he done? To leave a home and a steady job, friends and family – and to strike out for what? What *really* awaited them on the other side of this god-forsaken sea? What information did he have anyway? He knew what Theo had told him. In the year since Femke and Theo had emigrated, they'd sent back glowing letters about life in Canada. There were so many opportunities that Theo could take his pick from any number of jobs. They were doing so well that they'd already bought a house, and paid for it, and in less than a year. That could never happen in Nederland! But, Piet pondered, could he really trust Theo? Bit of a peacock, that man. Liked to make himself look good. On the other hand he *was* family. Piet sighed again. That bastard of a brother-in-law better be telling the truth.

Toward the stern, Anneke was watching the dolphins. She was lying on her stomach, pencil poised over grey paper bag. Every morning when the sailors dumped barrels of kitchen waste into the ocean, the dolphins turned up. Where they were the rest of the day was anybody's guess. Must have a great love for potato peelings, Anneke thought, to find their way back to the Groote Beer from wherever they were in that huge ocean, just in time to get fed. Awe-struck she watched as they leapt high into the air to catch the offal. The sailors brought more and more barrels and the show continued. Finally it was over, and Anneke started to draw. She drew their sleek bodies as they sailed through the air, and, her tongue protruding slightly, she drew the splashing water as they re-entered the ocean. Caught up in her drawing she barely heard the sigh as it wafted along the deck. Then she glanced over, to where her father was standing at the railing, staring blankly at the distant horizon.

Piet shook his head and blew out a smoke-ring. He was remembering how tough it had been convincing Johanna to emigrate. Many nights they'd talked until well into the morning. "I don't want to leave my family behind," she'd protest, tears in her voice. They lay in bed, the door closed so as not to disturb the children.

"But you already have *one* sister in Canada!"

"*Ja. Ja.* But I have a lot more family here. And if I leave the *ouwe mensen*, I'll never see them again. You know how old they are, over the seventy! And my mother. Isn't it enough heartbreak for her to lose one daughter to Canada, without losing two?"

Piet had no answer for this. But he tried, "You can come back to visit."

"Huh!" she snorted. "Nobody ever comes back. Has Femke been back? And others, friends who emigrated years ago, have they been back?"

"They're busy building a new life. Once they're established, they'll be back. You'll see your mother again. I promise."

"To do that I'd have to travel over the ocean twice. I'm scared to death to go even once! You think I'd do that again? To go on that water? You know how afraid I am of water. It makes me shiver just to think about it."

"Johanna, we'd be going on a huge ship, so big you'd barely know you were on the ocean. You can relax on board and have nice meals," with a twinkle he added, "that you wouldn't even have to cook. It would be like a holiday."

"Then there is that language. I don't want to go to a country where I can't even talk to the people. You already speak a little English. I can *never* learn it! It is too difficult for me." Piet rolled his eyes but in the dark Johanna couldn't see it. "And besides we're too old. In the forty we are. Too old to start new."

"*Just* in the forty. *Kom, kom,* Johanna, you are still a young and beautiful woman, and I'm a lucky man. Out of that nest of sisters of yours, I got the prize hen." He pulled her toward him. Nuzzled her neck. Reached for her breast. But she rolled back.

Her voice continued on in the dark, "Here, we know what we have. We have a good house, and you've been working for years for the same company. We have security."

"We have a house, but it is not *our* house. We only rent. And if we stay here we will always rent. We will never own our own home. Johanna, you know that!"

"*Ja.* I know that. But is it worth uprooting the family so we can own our house?"

Piet decided it was time to play his trump card, "Johanna, we're not doing this for ourselves, we're doing it for the children. You saw the government films about immigrating to Canada! All that empty land! Everything is wide open there! Immigrants start up farms and businesses and make a big success of their lives. And you know how it is here! In Nederland everything is so crowded, so regulated, you have to wait months and even years for a permit for this, a license for that, a document for something else. Young people can't even get married when they want! Their names go on a waiting list, and they have to wait *years* for a house to become available."

"Of course there's a housing shortage Piet! It's only ten years since the war, when all those houses were flattened by the bombs!"

"*Ja,*" said Piet, "but on top of that, the land itself is in short supply. Too many people on too small a patch of land. They keep building dikes and draining *polders,* and *still* there isn't enough land. The point is, Johanna," and he softened his voice, "that if we emigrate our children will have opportunities they could only *dream* of in Nederland!"

"The bombs," said Johanna, "the bombs…" and he could see that he'd lost her. "Remember Piet, those planes, the Beukenlaan…" Of course he remembered. How could he not remember? The date was burned into his memory: September 19, 1944. It was the day after the Allied Forces had liberated Eindhoven. He and Johanna went with their small kids to her parents to celebrate. When they got there the house was already full of noise and smoke and relatives. A bottle of gin stood on the middle of the table and was poured all round neat. *"Proost!"* everyone chimed. They belted out patriotic songs; told off-colour jokes about Germans and roared with laughter. After much back-slapping they left to go home. The streets were full of celebrants. Red, white and blue flags flapped merrily from upstairs windows. There was singing and dancing, and everywhere folks joined hands to create swaying garlands and circles of dancers. Suddenly, over the laughing and singing, Piet and Johanna heard the distant droning of bombers. Wide-eyed, they looked up at the sky. My God, were they back? Pandemonium erupted on the street as people ran in every direction. Piet and Johanna grabbed their children and dashed into an alleyway, as the bombs began to whistle down. Deafening blasts shook the ground, filled the air with smoke and debris. There were more and more bombs and the children were screaming in terror. Johanna went hysterical, "We're going to die! We're all going to die!"

"No!" he'd yelled back. "We'll be all right! Hang on, we'll be all right!" And they *had* been. Finally, the bombs had stopped falling, the droning faded, and they picked their way home through the rubble. The next day they saw flattened houses very near the alleyway where they had been sheltering. As if... he could ever forget *that!*

"The bombs," Johanna had said again. "The bombs. If another war comes to Europe… the children…. must be safe."

Piet gazed out on the turbulent ocean. That *had* been the deciding factor for Johanna: her fear that another war might break out in Europe. *His* reasons had been different – it was opportunities he was after. He smiled somewhat ruefully. In remembering his arguments with Johanna, he'd even managed to re-convince himself. He blew out a ring of smoke. He was starting to relax. He'd made the right decision. "All right!" he said aloud, and pounded his fist on the deck-rail. He flicked his cigarette butt into the ocean. "Anneke! *Kom!* We're going inside. We'll get the rest of the family and go to breakfast."

"*Papa*! Wanna see what I drew?"

"*Mooi. Heel mooi*," he praised absently and took her hand to descend the stairs. There was the clanging of leather soles on metal, then Anneke's ears perked, as her father mumbled, "All those glowing letters. That bastard of a brother-in-law better not be lying!"

"Don't you at least want to come for coffee?" he asked his wife, but Johanna just shook her head. The last thing she needed in her stomach was coffee. She just wanted to sleep, and with the kids gone, it might just be possible.

"I'm starving!" Henk complained, and Piet thought ruefully that the boy was always starving. "I'm so hungry I could eat a horse. A *whole* horse!"

"Mieke, are you ready?" They left for the dining hall, with Mieke trailing along morosely, dressed to the nines in a frilly white blouse, pleated wool skirt, and – proof of her near-adult status – nylons. *She* had not wanted to emigrate. In Eindhoven she'd had her friends, her social life, her clubs… and *most* important… she'd had Tim, and Mieke was madly in love with Tim. *She* had wanted to stay, had even arranged with a girlfriend to board with that family. Mieke had cried and she'd pleaded, but Piet had absolutely refused to leave his daughter behind. And so she'd come, but it was under protest, and just as soon as she could manage it, she'd be heading back to Tim!

It was a huge dining hall and the long tables were dressed with white tablecloths and flowers. Piet wondered idly how long those vases would remain erect. Henk got his wish, and *rookvlees*, smoked horsemeat, was indeed on the menu. Across from him, Mieke sat scowling, poking at her food, pushing it around. "If you don't want it…" said Henk, reaching with his fork for her *rookvlees*, but a frown from his father made him pull back.

Piet was relaxing with several cups of coffee followed by a cigarette. Finally, contentedly, he asked, "Everybody finished?"

"*Ja*, papa," said Anneke, while Henk quickly jammed more food in his mouth and Mieke stared morosely into the distance. "Can we go explore the ship?" Anneke asked.

"I have to get back to the cabin to check on your mother, but yes, the three of you can go."

"I am not going anywhere with those children!" spat Mieke. "I am going to the lounge, and I'm going to write a letter to Tim!" and she flounced from the dining room.

Piet sighed and rolled his eyes. He started walking toward the door, then turned his head, "Anneke, Henk, don't forget what I told you two earlier about staying together!" Anneke pulled a face, but thought better of it and nodded, while Henk mumbled something through a mouthful of food. He finally polished off his plate, then waited until the steward's back was turned to stuff extra rolls down his pants. Knickerbockers were ideal for contraband – very baggy, with tight bands below the knee which kept stuff from falling out. In Dutch colloquial they were called *drollenvangers,* or turd catchers.

Just outside the dining hall were signs for a doctor's office, pharmacy, nurse's room, even an infirmary. A youngish man was sitting on a bench outside the doctor's office. "Now why do you suppose," he said to the kids, "all of these medical facilities are located right next to the dining hall?" and he looked meaningfully at the children from under a worn leather cap.

Henk blanched, stammered, "F- f- food poisoning?" and he put his hand on the stomach he had so recently overstuffed.

"Ha, ha, ha! No sonny, that's not what I meant. I was talking about sea-sickness."

"Yeah," said Anneke, and gave her brother a patronizing look, "our mother is really sick, and our father, he just runs around with these little bags of puke and…"

"Right," said the man, "well you just wait 'till we get further out to sea and there'll be a whole lot more sick people. And do you know why?" They shook their heads. "Because this ship, the 'Groote Beer,' was not built for the comfort of passengers; this ship was built as troopship!" Henk's face lit up. "Really!?"

"She was built by the Americans in '44 with an extra-thick, steel hull in case of German U-boat attack. Come here and sit down," he invited the kids, "and I'll tell you all about the Groote Beer." Henk hurried over and sat. The man leisurely filled his pipe and sucked at it as Anneke remained standing, mouth pursed, arms crossed.

"S'posed to go exploring," she grumbled.

"Yup," said the man, "lots of exploring to be done. Do you know, little girl, this ship, she's got six decks, and she's as long as one-and-a-half football fields? Lots of exploring and easy to get lost!" Anneke went to stand a little closer. "During the war, she carried a lot of American boys to the front, and after World War 2 ended," he turned back to Henk, "she brought them back home, that is, the ones who survived," he said meaningfully. After that the Americans didn't need her anymore and they sold her to the Dutch. And that," he said fondly, as if speaking of a girlfriend, "was when I met her, when she carried our soldiers to the Dutch East Indies to fight the rebels."

"Were you a soldier?" Henk asked, eyes shining.

"Sure was! They shipped us to Batavia packed like sardines, sleeping in hammocks four deep! I remember I picked the bottom one 'cause it was tricky climbing up, but let me tell you son, when ya got three guys sleeping above you and they're seasick, you are living in hell!" and he grinned wryly. Henk grinned back. "And there's lots does get seasick on the Groote Beer. She's a hefty girl at 10,000 tons, and she rides mighty rough if there's stormy weather."

"Is that how she got her name, the Groote Beer, because she's so big and heavy?"

"No, my boy!" "She was named after the stars! Great Bear! Ursa Major!" He continued on, "When we lost the war in '49, I was mighty glad to get out of there – the heat, the malaria – and the Groote Beer, she brought me home." His eyes were far away as he sucked on his pipe.

"Finally, when that was all over, she was refurbished as an immigrant ship, and I'm proud to say she's one of the few ships in the Holland-America Line sturdy enough to sail year-round – to Canada, America, Australia, New Zealand and even South Africa. But," he grinned, "this ship was definitely not built for comfort, and there are many tales told by emigrants now settled in far-flung places, of a bucking ship, crashing waves, and ever-lasting seasickness."

The doctor opened his office door. "Just something for the baby," the man said as he went in. "Freddie's teething."

They went down a flight of stairs and peeked into a dormitory which held a huge number of beds, then they followed the sound of sobbing to a small lounge, where a young woman was crying as if her heart would break. On his knees in front of her, a young man asked beseechingly. "Now Suzie, don't cry! It's not so bad. It's only for a few nights. The dormitories are so much cheaper honey, and we need all our money set up house in Canada. Please don't cry!"

"But we just got married," she sniffed, "and now I have to sleep with all those strange snoring women and…and other couples have cabins!"

"Other couples are older and already have their household goods with them. We are just starting out. Remember *meisje*, we have nothing. We have to buy everything when we get there. Suzie, we talked about this already, honey, that we need every penny to set up house in Canada!"

"But I'm so lonely and so homesick and… " and she burst into loud wailing.

But Anneke and Henk had lost interest, and ran back upstairs, They found a group of kids at the stern of the ship, looking intently over the railing. Dolphins maybe? They hurried to stand beside them. Didn't see a thing. "What are you doing?" Anneke asked a little dark-haired girl.

"Just playing a game. Puke in the Ocean."

"What kind of a dumb game is that?" sneered Henk, and the little girl stuck out her tongue.

Anneke was intrigued, "How do you play it?"

"Lean out as far as you can, and look straight down. Just keep looking." They stared through wisps of fog into the raging whirlpool of foam and water churned up by the ship's massive propeller. They became hypnotized by the whirlpool, and as their eyes rolled with the motion of the water, so did their stomachs. And then, one after the other, the kids heaved into the ocean. "Is this a great game or what?" the little girl enthused. "Just by looking into the water, you can *make yourself puke!*"

"Yeah, that is pretty good," Henk had to admit, wiping his mouth. "Make yourself puke! Just like that! Neat trick. But now I'm hungry again," and he unbuttoned his knickerbockers below the knee, and pulled out a roll.

The Groote Beer sailed further out into the Atlantic, rough seas keeping more and more adults in their cabins. Meanwhile, on the top deck teenagers played shuffleboard and howled with laughter when the bucking ship sent the pucks flying. Small boys with cap pistols chased each other around and around on the decks. Girls crafted dolls from yarn, tossed them into the ocean and watched to see how long they took to drown. And kids had once more gathered at the ship's stern. Tall skinny Jochem, said he had an idea for a game. Henk said derisively, "That puking game again?"

"Nope. A contest."

"Yeah? What kind?"

"A contest to see who can piss the farthest over that railing."

"No contest there," bragged Henk, "that'll be me!"

"Not bloody likely!" said Jochem. "All right! All you guys get over behind that line." There was lots of shoving and bravado, as the boys clamored to line up.

Anneke was far from amused. Bloody show offs! Another game girls couldn't play! She'd long been annoyed about the unfairness of the whole peeing thing anyway. If a girl had to pee, she had to nicely go indoors and use the WC. If a boy had to pee, he could go stand behind a tree and just piss up against it. Grossly unfair!

As the boys lined up, the girls formed into a clutch nearby. The watched from the corners of their eyes as boys undid buttons and zippers, and pulled their *piesertjes* from their pants.

"Ready?" called Jochem. "One… two…" On the count of three, glorious golden arches sailed high over the railing to vanish into the misty depths below. In full stream, the boys smiled smugly. Suddenly, a wayward wind whipped their golden spray up and around, to fall on them like rain. "Shit! Shit! Holy shit!" The boys jumped around like mad, then danced like whirling dervishes trying to shake the piss from their clothes.

And at a safe distance… the girls howled with laughter.

Below deck, life continued in an agony of illness. Grey and weak with seasickness, Johanna languished in her bunk. The ship's doctor was finally called. After examining the patient, he said there was not much he could do. The wind must die down for the seas to become calm and the ship to stop heaving, and *he* had no control over that. "But it's been days!" Piet almost shouted. "Doctor, look at my wife! She can keep nothing down. She's wasting away!"

"Tut, tut, tut," said the doctor. Then brusquely, "I have hundreds of sick people this trip. The May storms have been ferocious this year. The best advice I can give you is to get your wife some ginger ale and *beschuiten* from the galley, and keep her as comfortable as possible. I'll look in again tomorrow." He walked briskly from the cabin.

His face creased with exhaustion and worry, Piet trudged back from the galley. He fed his wife a sip of ginger ale, a bit of *beschuit*, and within minutes had to hold out a paper bag once more, as she heaved and sobbed with her illness; then he went out to throw her misery overboard.

That evening the wind whipped the ocean into a boil until waves were slamming up on the decks and the captain ordered a lock-down. No one was allowed outside. Johanna went hysterical! They were sealed in this ship, and it would be their coffin, their death-crate! The ship would sink like a stone. They would all drown! *Drown!* Anneke sat on her bunk and watched her mother with huge eyes. Piet felt he had to do something! He finally managed to get some sort of draught from the doctor that put his wife to sleep.

The next day they woke to a creaking, shaking ship and knew immediately that the storm still raged. By now, Mieke was now as seasick as her mother. And all day the storm continued. It was only towards suppertime that it let up enough so that the lock-down was finally lifted. Henk was famished, so Piet sent the boy on ahead. He checked with Johanna and Mieke, but neither was in any condition to go to the dining room. "Anneke, you coming?"

"*Ja*, papa," and she held tightly to his hand as they navigated the halls and made their way down the stairs. When Piet pushed open the dining room door, Anneke was hit by an overpowering stench! She tore lose from her father's hand and went racing up for fresh air! Piet just shook his head, then waited patiently by the door. Finally she came back down with her nose pinched tightly shut. "Awful stink!" whined Anneke in a nasal tone as he led her to the table. Henk was sitting across from her, his plate piled high! There was blood sausage, Gouda and Edam cheese, rolls with real creamery butter, herring-in-tomato-sauce, eggs, stewed fruit, and ginger cake! Anneke looked on with a combination of disgust and queasiness as he shoveled huge forkfuls into his mouth.

A steward in starched white uniform approached. Piet ordered, "Coffee for me please, and ginger ale for my daughter with some dry *beschuit*." The steward nodded and started to leave. Piet added thoughtfully, "By the way, what *is* that odour in here?"

The steward spun on his heel. "Odour? Odour? There is *no* odour in *this* dining hall, I can assure you!" He stared down his aquiline nose at Piet, then stalked out.

"I bet his shit don't stink either!" came a chuckle from the next table. Anneke looked over and recognized the cap. It was the man from the doctor's office! "Kees van Berkel," the man stuck out his hand to Piet, "an Amsterdammer."

Piet shook the proffered hand, "Piet Verbeek from Eindhoven."

"Eindhoven you say. Know it well. Lived there when I went to trade-school. Studied radio technology."

Piet continued, "And my daughter Anneke and over there, behind that mountain of food... son Henk."

"Good to see that boy's got an appetite!" His blue eyes twinkled under the brown leather cap. "How are you kids doing? Not exploring today?"

Henk asked eagerly through a mouthful of food, "Mister, can you tell us some more about the Groote Beer?"

Kees smiled. Told Piet, "Was telling them about the ship the other day. Sailed on her in '49 when she brought me back from Jakarta."

"Heard it was hellish there," said Piet, and settled back in his chair.

"With the Japs driven out they sure didn't want us Dutch back. Nasty jungle fighting." He looked Piet in the eye, confided, "We shouldn't have fought them, you know. Should have just left them to it. *Indonesia!* In the end they got their independence anyway, but we left a lot of our boys over there, buried in that steaming jungle."

"You must have been mighty glad to board the Groote Beer and get off those islands."

"You bet! Love this ship. She might be a rough old girl, but I do love her!"

"Don't think there are a whole lot of folk on this trip who share your sentiments."

"Ha, ha. You might be right about that!" The steward came with drinks, then Kees continued his story, "Loved her so much I decided to live on a boat." In response to Piet's raised eyebrows he added, "Got married as soon as I got back to Holland and we moved into a houseboat on an Amsterdam canal. Converted barge really. Very romantic," he grinned, and sipped his coffee.

Henk said, "But mister, about *this* ship! I wanna know about icebergs. You said it's an extra thick hull and they did that for the torpedoes. But what about icebergs? Is the hull thick enough for icebergs? And do you think we might hit one?"

"This isn't the Titanic. Today there are sophisticated instruments to spot icebergs long before you're likely to hit them"

But Henk wasn't done yet, "How fast can the Groote Beer sail?"

"Top speed is 17 knots – that's about 31.5 kilometers per hour. How is your arithmetic, son? We've got about 5000 kilometers of ocean to cross…"

Grinning, Piet said to Kees "That will keep him busy for a while!" The steward anchored platters of food on the table and the men helped themselves. They enjoyed their meal and were sipping another coffee when

Piet said, "You know Kees, my wife has barely eaten since we set sail. Worried about her! Oldest daughter is sea-sick too, and now it looks like this one," he gestured at Anneke nibbling on a dry *beschuit*, "might be starting."

"It's been a rough sail all right, but... we *might* be over the worst of it."

"Mijn God! I hope you're right! And the sea-sickness is bad enough, but then last night, when that lock-down was ordered, my wife went completely hysterical! Convinced we were all going to drown."

Kees shook his head sympathetically. "Oh, oh."

"Finally had to get the doctor involved."

"Guess I'm lucky. My Liesje doesn't mind a storm. S'pose living on a houseboat helps."

"Even last night she didn't mind? It got just wild in our cabin!"

Kees furrowed his brow, "Come to think of it Piet, it *did* get a *bit* wild in ours too. See, Liesje and I, we've got five little kids including a baby, so the bunks are all filled up, and the baby's crib is in the middle of the cabin floor."

"What?" interrupted Piet. "You get married after you came back in '49, and you've got 5 kids already? In 6 years? You have been a busy boy, haven't you?"

Kees grinned, "Told you it was romantic on that houseboat! But anyway, last night, as the ship's heaving got worse, that crib started to slide across the floor. Baby Freddie, he stood there clutching the bars of his crib, grinning with those two teeth of his, enjoying the ride. Soon, the crib was sliding from one end of the cabin to the other. The older kids thought it hilarious. They shrieked with laughter as their brother went sailing by. The faster that crib went, the harder the kids laughed! Then the storm got worse! I was afraid Freddie would get hurt from the crib crashing around, so I looked for something to tie it down with. I finally took off my leather belt and used it to tie the crib to my bunk. After that, we managed to go to sleep. Until, *Crash!* I jumped up, and flicked on the light. Saw my broken belt dangling from the bedpost. Saw the crib up against the far wall, a wide-eyed Freddie pulling himself up on the bars, peering over the top. Then the ship bucked and the crib came thundering back! I thought he would knock his teeth out, so I grabbed the crib, but lost my footing and fell on my ass. I hung on, though! One hand on the crib and the other on the bedpost, sliding with the bucking ship, butt skidding across the cabin floor! The children woke at the commotion (I may have uttered the odd curse word) and shrieked with laughter as Freddie and I thundered across the floor. Even my wife, normally a sympathetic woman, laughed until the tears ran down her face."

Piet roared! Finally, as he wiped his eyes, he said, *"s'Jonge, jonge!* I needed a good laugh!"

Anneke laughed as well She even stopped pinching her nose. "*I* have a question about the ship Mijnheer van Berkel. Why does it *stink* so bad?"

"Well, Anneke, some say it's the consommé, you know, that clear soup, but I was told by one of the fellows in the kitchen that it's the powdered eggs."

"Whatever the cause," said Piet, "you'd think they'd do *something* to fix the problem. Just look around this dining hall! It's almost deserted!"

"You're right. People who feel the least bit queasy steer clear of this place. The Holland-America Line must be saving a bundle on food! Hmmm," Kees pondered. "You'd almost think that smell was part of a conspiracy wouldn't you – that stink – the empty dining hall... It's a good thing young Henk there is doing his best to make up for the other passengers!"

Piet looked at his son and shook his head in wonderment. Henk's left arm was wrapped protectively around his plate to keep it from sliding with the motion of the ship. He was having a *grand* time. Had never *tasted* such wonderful food! He'd refilled his plate several times, and still it was piled high! Henk was in heaven. He'd be happy to cruise on this ship forever – especially if the other passengers continued to stay in their cabins and he got to eat all their food too. Henk had never felt so totally satisfied with life.

"Does my heart good," Kees said, "to see that boy eating into the ship's profits!" and he gave Henk the thumbs-up.

Henk grinned proudly. As he did so, his mouth opened to reveal the blood sausage between his teeth.

Anneke bolted from the room.

Finally, Johanna managed to venture on deck. She was a slim, attractive woman with soft, brown, permanented hair. She looked wan from her illness, but today, for the first time in days, she had managed to eat lunch, and even keep it down, and she felt much improved as a result. Also, this interminable boat ride would soon be over, and it couldn't be soon enough for her. She was afraid of water, and just the thought of being on this floating cork on this endless ocean could make her ill. As if that weren't bad enough, the storms had come, and had tossed her with gut-wrenching vigour back and forth, back and forth, until she wretchedly threw up everything that was inside of her, and then she retched some more, then painfully, exhaustedly, retched again. And then this morning, when she had finally left her cabin to appear at the breakfast table, the captain had euphemistically said, "The ocean, she's been a bit capricious this May," as if that gave any consolation.

Johanna raised her eyes to look at her enemy, the ocean, and felt a sudden surge of panic. She grabbed the nearest thing, a deck chair, and sank into it; ferociously gripping the arm rests. She closed her eyes to block the view, but when she did, she became again that small girl who had been looking for frogs along the ditch. A sudden misstep, and she tumbled in, mouth filling with slimy, greenish water as she sank. She bobbed to the surface, spitting, filled with slime and terror, managing one weak yell before she sank once more. And again she rose, and broke the surface, and this time, as she did, she felt someone grab her hair, and pull mightily, as her mother yanked her crying, choking, dripping, from the slimy green clutches of the ditch.

Johanna shook her head; opened her eyes, and was back in the present. The enemy was still there, staring her in the face. And she cursed Piet for bringing her here. She could be at home, where she awoke every morning to the sound of milkman Holman's horse clomping along the cobblestone street. She'd get up and make the coffee and take the bottle of sweet, fresh milk from beside the front door. She could be there still, in her tidy brick house with the red-tile roof and the white lace curtains behind sparkling windows. Every week she'd wash those windows. Friday, that was the day all the women on the street were out front washing and polishing their windows, and socializing, and chatting and.... What day was today? Monday. It was Monday. Monday was laundry day. By now, her electric washing machine with the wooden tub would be filled with hot soapy water; water she had heated in a big copper kettle on the gas burners in the kitchen. She always did the whites first, when the water was hottest and cleanest. Then she'd do colours, and finally the darks. When all the laundry was done and flapping merrily on the clothesline, she would take a pail of the soapy water out front, and with the scrub broom she'd scrub the sidewalk in front of her house. And all the other housewives would scrub their sidewalks on Mondays, and they would chatter, and gossip, and then the whole street would shine, and smell fresh, from the soap, and from their industry. Tuesday was ironing day. Wednesday she cleaned the upstairs, Thursday the kitchen and *huiskamer* and Friday the *voorkamer* and front window and the brass doorbell and mail slot and, and... And today was Monday... Monday... her mind trailed off.

Why had she left her neatly organized life, her pleasant life, to find herself here, on this ship, on this god-forsaken ocean? Why had Piet come up with this emigration idea, this stupid idea, and why in God's name had she agreed? But she knew why! It had to do with the past. The past.... the war... Johanna was once more crouched under the table that she'd pushed against the wall, covering her small children with her body. High-pitched whistling seared the air, and with racing heart she clutched her children more tightly, as the bombs exploded with ear shattering, heart stopping blasts. With utter random chance they blew up houses, churches, hospitals, and schools. A distant explosion provided relief; the bomb had not landed on *them*. *They* were still alive. *Their* house was still standing. She relaxed her vigil. Loosened her hold. But she had no more than caught her breath when the whistling started again. And again. And now the whistling sounds were overlapping and the explosions getting closer. In her terror she squeezed baby Henk until he screamed. A final thundering boom rattled the windowpanes. Then there was a brief eerie silence, followed by sirens. When she let go of Henk, he raced about the house like a mad child, bumping into furniture, falling down.

And then, after the war, when the men came back from Germany, from the forced labour camps, and Piet's brother Geert barely made it home because his body was so wasted by tuberculosis. A short time later he had to have a lung removed. Johanna feared a similar fate for her son. Within a few years *he* could be called up for military service. The radio had told her there was a 'cold war' going on. Johanna wasn't quite sure what that meant, but she knew there was much threatening behaviour between the east and the west; between Russia and America. And Holland, vulnerable little country that it was, was located right in the middle. Before another war broke out, she had to get her children to safety. She remembered it was Canadian soldiers who liberated Holland, and that Queen Juliana and the princesses had found a safe haven in Canada. That same country, Canada would also be the place of safety for Johanna's children.

My but it was getting foggy! She heard a raucous sound, and looked up to see ragged gulls hovering overhead. Where had they come from? Suddenly an ear-splitting blast rent the air. Johanna screamed! More blasts followed! A seaman approached, smiled at her concern. "It's all right, missus. That were only the foghorn. We're in the shipping lanes here, close to land, and there's that bit of fog. Nothing to worry about." He continued, "Oh yes, and you might like to have a look over there," he pointed, "we've spotted an iceberg." He winked, and quickly moved on. Black panic filled her mind.

She spotted Piet, and screamed, "Icebergs! We're going to sink!"

"Wha-at?' said Piet slowly.

"We're going to sink! Get the lifejackets!"

"Have we hit something?"

"Icebergs!" She shouted at him as if he were deaf, "There - are - icebergs - in - the - water!" Piet looked around, puzzled.

Anneke came running, "Icebergs! Wow!" and dashed for the railing.

"Piet, get her. She'll get killed. Grab her Piet! Now!"

"Goed, goed" said Piet calmly. "Anneke, come here. You've got your mother all upset."

"Papa!" yelled Anneke, "I can *see* it! If you stand over here, you can *just* see it. And it's blue and green and *huge! Look* papa!"

"You can really see it?" Piet walked to the railing for a better view. Johanna stared at him, burst into tears, ran for the stairs and disappeared below deck. Piet turned, looked thoughtfully after his wife, then, with a rueful expression, followed her below.

Piet opened the door to the lounge. In a far corner he spotted a cap, and under it, his new friend Kees nursing a beer. The younger man's face lit up when he saw Piet. *"Ober!"* Kees rang out. *"Bier voor mijn vriend!"*

Piet sank down in a chair, lit up a cigarette, half-drained his beer as soon as it arrived. He smacked his lips. Nodded appreciatively at Kees. "Needed that!" He confided, "Wife not amused."

"Tell me about it! My wife's not so friendly either these days." He frowned and grumbled, "Why we've hardly had sex since we boarded the ship!"

Piet grinned, "Maybe she doesn't want another ankle-biter."

"That's why I bought a condom for the trip."

"One? You brought one for the whole trip? Well that explains that, doesn't it. You ass, why didn't you bring more?"

"I always rinse it out in the sink and hang it on the tap to dry. Should have been fine for the rest of the trip, but then the kids woke up early one morning and were trying to blow it up for a balloon. They were fighting over it – who got to blow – that's what woke us." As Piet roared with laughter, Kees said ruefully, "Wife was not at all amused. In fact she threw it overboard" He added sadly, "No more nightly *neukie* on *this* trip." Piet laughed even harder.

"Won't be long now at any rate," he consoled Kees. "Icebergs mean close to land, right?"

"Yeah, right," Kees still looked gloomy.

"Anyway, you've just got your wife to contend with. I've also got Mieke. Didn't want to emigrate, our Mieke. Pouts and cries. Cries and pouts. Didn't want to leave her friends. Planning to go back to Holland first chance she gets."

"Well, Piet, could be worse! When we were boarding in Rotterdam, a couple of teenage lads came on board with their family, and immediately took off for the far end of the ship, and there... they disembarked. They just mixed in with some folk who'd come on board to say goodbye to relatives, and then they calmly walked off with them." Kees grinned admiringly,

"They just got on at one end the ship, and off at the other! We were well out to sea before the parents realized their sons were missing. At first they thought the boys were just off exploring, but then finally…"

"They must have been frantic! I know Johanna would have had the boys long drowned and at the bottom of the sea. How did they even find out what happened to them?"

"They sent a telegram back to the ship. At least they had the decency to do that! But they must have had their escape well planned to even know there was a telegraph office on board."

"Hmmm," said Piet, downing his beer. "Yeah, I guess it could have been worse. Mieke might be a pain in the ass but at least she's still on the ship!"

Anneke came skipping into the lounge. *"Hallo papa! Dag mijnheer van Berkel!* Brought my art stuff. Gonna draw Canada!" She sat down at an empty table by the window and looked out expectantly. She stared for some time, then, chagrined, sat with her head in her hands.

Piet suggested, "Why don't you draw what you're going to see when we get there. *Ja?"* Anneke nodded reluctantly. *"Ober!"* Piet called out, *"Oranje limonade* with a straw for my daughter, and two more Heineken, please." The drinks delivered, Anneke was soon happily sipping lemonade as she drew. Watching his daughter, Piet confided in a low voice to Kees, "When I was her age, I was drinking gin."

"How did you get your hands on that?"

"It was given to me. You see were a huge family, 16 kids, with little money, so everybody had to work at whatever job they find. I dredged ditches and picked berries, and along with my brothers and sisters I harvested flax. You had to take your *klompen* off and do it in your sock-feet so you didn't crush the flax. Guess that's why they preferred kids – lighter."

Kees raised his eyebrows and said, "Cheaper?"

"Late in the season we'd work the harbour. Farmers would bring in wagons piled high with sugar beets – sometimes there'd be a huge row of these wagons waiting – and it was the job of us kids to load those muddy sugar beets into canal barges for transport to the sugar factory. It was heavy work, and it could get mighty cold there out in the open right by the ocean. The damp wind blowing in off the sea could plaster the freezing clothes to your body. At noon we got to go home for a hot meal, and mother would hang our frozen coats up near the stove from ceiling hooks, but they'd never dry that fast, so after we ate we'd pull on other old coats and go back to work. When the coats were finally taken down from the ceiling, they were so stiff from the dried mud they stood up by themselves, and would have to be beaten before they could be worn again. We'd just keep loading beets, in the sleet and the wind and whatever weather conditions there were, until we started to stumble from the cold and the exhaustion. Then the boss would pull out a bottle of *jonge jenever*, and give us each a shot. I'll never forget that feeling of heat, when that gin hit my belly! And after that shot of gin, we'd buck up again, and keep on working. We stopped only when it got too dark to see."

"Good Lord!"

"But at the end of the week, Kees, I'd take the few *stuivers* I'd earned home to my mother, and I'd feel like a man."

Spitting out her straw, Anneke said incredulously, "You *worked* when you were ten?"

"Small pots with big ears!"

"When you were *ten!* You didn't go to school, and you drank *gin*."

"Oh, oh!" said a grinning Kees. "I can see where this is going!"

"It was a long time ago," explained Piet. "And we were a big family."

"Well," said Anneke, "when we get to Canada, *I'm* gonna get a job. I'm gonna be a cowgirl! I'll have my own horse and I'll call him Patches and I'll ride around on the prairie lassoing cattle and saving stagecoaches. No more school for me. No siree." The men burst out laughing. Anneke ignored them and carried on drawing.

The men puffed on their cigarettes, drank their beer. "I can see her point though," Kees finally commented. "That bit about horses and cattle sounded pretty good to me! I'd really like to get me a farm, or some land at least, and there's lots of land to be had in Canada."

"True!" said Piet. "It's a huge empty country."

Anneke called over. "Not many people there, but there's lots of horses and cows! Wanna see what I drew?" She came over holding out a grey seasickness bag. On the back was a red-headed girl on a piebald horse in the midst of what might have been cattle – or perhaps deer – or...

"Heel goed!" said Piet.

"Mooi zo," said Kees, and with a satisfied grin Anneke gathered up her art supplies and departed. Kees blew a smoke-ring, mused, "Her picture makes me think of that government film, '*Mijn neef uit Canada.*' They showed it in our town hall. Did you see it as well?" Piet shook his head. Kees said, "I saw it at an information session. The film takes you on a journey across Canada to meet successful immigrants. There are guys on horses and everything. They talk about the ready availability of good arable soil, and about farms that are on the market at reasonable cost, because the farmers don't have sons to take over."

Piet said, "It kinda warms your heart doesn't it, how keen the Canadian Government is to get Dutch immigrants over there, making those promotional films, and in Dutch even! *Really* gives a welcome feeling!"

Kees rubbed his forehead. Took a tug of his beer. Blew another smoke-ring. Finally said, "Uh, Piet, I don't want to burst your bubble, but those promotional films, they weren't made by the Canadian Government."

"What? What are you talking about?"

"Well..." said Kees, and he proceeded to count things off on his fingers, "there's the post-war housing shortage in Holland, *and* the unemployment crisis, *and* of course the country is still financially strapped from all the reconstruction..."

"Yeah, so…" Piet frowned.

"What better way," Kees said, grinning sardonically, "to solve a host of problems, than by shipping a bunch of good Dutch citizens overseas. For every family that leaves, they can build one less house, create one fewer job."

"Come on!" Piet burst in. "What are you saying? That the *Dutch* Government made those films? To get rid of us? I don't believe it!"

"We-ell……"

"Shit!"

The Groote Beer nuzzled her way into the mouth of the St. Lawrence River. "Land!" the shout rang out, and it echoed throughout the ship. "Land!" Suddenly the decks were swarming with immigrants eager for their first glimpse of Canada. "Did you see it yet? Which way? Where?" As Canada came into view, they stared with apprehension at the outcroppings of bleak, coal-black rock, slick with Atlantic spray and encrusted with spare, wind-mutilated fir trees. Sea gulls squawked and screeched a raucous, 'Welcome to Canada.'

Johanna's face crumpled and tears formed in her eyes. "*This* is Canada?"

Piet put his arm around her, "Canada*, ja*. But we are going to a much nicer part of Canada. It's a huge country, Johanna, with every part very different."

"A huge country!" she scoffed. "That's just what you said about the Groote Beer. A huge ship! So big you won't know you're on the ocean. Just like a holiday. *Ja,* I've heard that story before, Piet. How wonderful it is just because it's huge. *Ja, ja!* You can talk!" She nodded her head, and added, "I have to see it first!" She pulled away from him. "Well, enough about that; I'm going to pack the things in the cabin." She marched off.

"It'll take another day," he said to her back. Then in a louder voice, "We'll be sailing on this river for a whole day yet!" but she just kept walking. Piet shook his head. "That woman just can't wait."

"There are lots of others going below deck already," Kees answered. Off to pack their suitcases so they don't waste any time when we disembark. Look, the decks will soon be clear."

Piet's eyes returned to the shoreline. How wild and raw it looked! He reflected that there had been other countries they could have immigrated to: South Africa, New Zealand, Australia...but Canada had seemed so welcoming. Sure didn't seem so welcoming now!

"Papa!" Anneke pulled on his jacket to get his attention, and he turned, frowning. "Papa, how can those trees grow on top of those rocks? Don't they need roots?"

Piet scowled, impatient to get back to his thoughts, "Anneke, I don't know!"

"If they don't have roots, how come they don't just blow in the ocean?" She'd had lots of experience lately with stuff blowing into the ocean, particularly gray-paper bags she was trying to draw on. "How come papa?"

Grinning at Piet's scowl, Kees told Anneke, "You're right! Can't have trees without roots! See those dark lines? Those are the cracks in the rocks, and that's where the roots are."

"Oh yeah?" and she stared more intently.

"Roots," said Piet morosely, "roots. Well we've certainly left those behind, haven't we, and with it our lush green country."

Kees slapped Piet on the back. *"Jongen,"* he said, "we'll grow new roots here."

"I hope we'll have more than rocks to grow them in, or we'll end up as stunted as those trees! I've never seen such rocks!"

"Too late for second thoughts *jongen.* "

Piet let out a sigh, "You're right of course. We're into this adventure now!" Then he thought of something. Grinning sardonically he added, "So Kees, you think you want to be a farmer here?"

The Groote Beer chugged on, churning up water in her wake, creating waves which rippled to the banks of the St. Lawrence River. And now those banks began to change as grassy slopes appeared between the cliffs. Suddenly the sun broke through, sparkling golden on the deep green river, and with it, the gloom that had enveloped the ship began to lift.

Anneke looked on, delighted. How beautiful! Suddenly she spotted it, caught in the glint of the sun. *'Look"* she yelled, *"a house!"* Excitedly everyone gathered to see where her finger was pointing."Over *there,* and it's *blue!* Did you ever see anything like that? A blue house?"

"No," said Piet, shielding his eyes as he peered. "No, I haven't."

"Another one," said Henk, "and it's white. And there's a green one and..."

"Look *there!*" yelled Anneke, virtually jumping up and down. "Look at that *yellow* house! Yellow as a dandelion!"

"Ja!" said Piet, shaking his head, *"ja,* and not a red-brick house to be seen!"

Anneke took off running. "Gotta get a paper bag!" she yelled over her shoulder. She was back in a flash, lay down on the deck, and started drawing. With her pencil-crayons she created a lush green hillside, where brightly coloured houses were scattered about like flowers.

"Ahhhh!" said Lies, stretching her arms, arching her back. "How wonderful to relax and get some time to myself. And look Johanna, what a great view of the shoreline!"

"Ja! And I can relax too. Finally away from that ocean! And I'm already packed. So until we get into port, nothing more to do. *Proost!"* They clinked glasses.

"High time Kees looked after the kids!"

"High time we were in the pub instead of the men!" said Johanna.

"But, *ja*, I know how you feel. Piet was insurance agent and when he had to go out in the evening to catch clients at home, I would be left with the children. They'd play in the street with the neighbourhood kids, and I would be sitting inside all alone."

"When we met, we both worked in the same factory. Every day at closing we'd cycle home holding hands, as thousands of other workers poured out of the Philips Factory. We got married, and of course I stopped working, but Piet was still in the factory and home with me every night. When the factory was bombed, it seemed to change him. After that he got out of there as soon as he could. Said he had enough of being cooped up. And as insurance agent, Piet would head out in the morning on his bicycle, saddlebags full of insurance papers, and cycle throughout the countryside collecting monthly premiums from farmers' wives. They'd make him a cup of coffee and bring out the cookie tin. He was good with the clients, and good with numbers. Why he could do all that math in his head!"

"Does he plan to be insurance agent in Canada?"

"Can't," Johanna said, shaking her head. "Doesn't know good enough good English. We both went to night school, but what a difficult language! Well, maybe there is one good thing about emigrating – maybe I'll have my husband home more. But, Liesje, what about Kees?"

"Kees wants his own farm."

"So that is his work? Farming?"

"*Ja.* That's what he wants to do, and as for myself, I grew up on a farm. It's a good life, a healthy life. At dusk my sisters and I would go out for the cattle. Very early in the war, Johanna, there was a German encampment across the canal at the back of our farm. We'd see their campfires, and the most beautiful haunting songs would come wafting across the canal as those German boys sang about their homeland. Some of those boys were very young, Johanna, away from home for the first time, and they were terribly homesick – you could tell from the songs, there was that sad longing in them. My sisters and I would sit in the grass and watch the sunset while we listened to the songs of those young German boys, there, in that still land. And I would be carried away by that beautiful haunting music, and feel their longing. Later on, of course, the occupiers got increasingly harsh and repressive, and manic even. But in those early days there was still an innocence, even a beauty about them."

"Maybe you thought that," said Johanna, "because *you* were still innocent in those days."

"Maybe," she admitted. Suddenly she smiled, "A good thing there was that canal between us! When my sisters and I finally got home, my father demanded, 'Where have you been so long?' 'Oh, those cows tonight! Just didn't want to co-operate!' He'd stick his face back in his newspaper even as my sisters and I winked at each other. Then mother poured coffee as we got out our knitting, and we'd sit around the kitchen table drinking coffee, and knitting, and chatting." Her eyes were distant, as she smiled at the memory. "*Het was zo gezellig!*"

"*Ja,*" said Johanna, "sounds wonderful. And your family must be rich to own a farm."

"Land rich," answered Lies, "not in money. Mind you, in the war, having land and growing food was a whole lot better than having stacks of money. You couldn't eat money. That's when I met Kees, in the war. He'd gone underground to avoid the labour camps in Germany, and was living in our barn. That was when he got hooked on farming; he'd been a city boy up to that point. Later, after he completed his military service, we got married." She called to the waiter, *"Nog een advocaatje ober! Ook voor mijn vriendin."* The drinks were brought – the bright yellow advocaat so thick it required a coffee spoon. "But what about you, Johanna, have you always been a city girl?"

Johanna didn't often talk about her early days – found it embarrassing, the rough life, the poverty. But, another spoon of Advocaat and she might just open up! Besides, she and Liesje were just ships passing in the night. They'd never see each other again.

"Liesje, I was born in the peatfields of Drenthe. We lived in a house with a thatch roof along a canal. It was rough living. We got our washing water from the canal, drinking water came from a rain barrel, and from the outhouse out back we got the fertilizer for the vegetable garden – once a year it got dug up and spread on the vegetable plot."

"But your story about the singing of the German boys, made me think of something. My mother was a girl of 18, walking across a field to another village. Suddenly she heard singing – faintly at first, but as she walked on it became louder and it was the deep, rich sound of a men's choir. She stood still, looking around. She was out in the middle of a field, and it seemed like the singing was coming from the very bowels of the earth. Then she noticed up ahead, there were freshly dug long, earthen banks… and she realized what she was hearing – it was the song of the canal-diggers. It was so powerful, my mother said, the sound of that huge male choir just pouring from the earth, out there in that open field. When she got close enough to look over the edge, she saw a tall, handsome man, singing full-chested as he heaved shovels of earth up on the bank. My mother said that she fell instantly in love!"

"Sounds very romantic!" smiled Liesje. "But is that really how they dug all those canals up there? By hand? Unbelievable!"

"Isn't it! And you know people look down on ditch-diggers, but you have to be very fit and strong for that job. My father told me that as a *wijkgraver,* or canal-digger, he worked in a crew of 100 men, organized 20 across and 5 deep. The man lowest down stuck his spade into the ground and dumped the earth on the shovel of the next man and then the next so on, until the last man threw the dirt all the way up on the bank. That was my father's position, a key position, last man. Because of his strength and height he could heave the earth a long way! And they sang to keep the rhythm, their songs punctuated by the percussion of their spades."

"How totally romantic! To follow that mysterious singing, and find yourself a handsome young man."

"I think the romance soon wore off," Johanna chuckled. "He was a handsome devil, but not the brightest. Our house had a mouldy thatch roof that was full of mice, and there were wild cats in the attic who lived off them. That roof was forever leaking. One day when my mother wasn't home. my father decided to repair it. There was a trapdoor in the living-room ceiling. My father climbed a ladder, pushed it open... and with hellish shrieks the cats attacked! My sisters and I ran screaming from the house as my father tumbled off the ladder and then came racing after us. What a sorry mess he was! When my mother came home she laughed at him. 'Yo patch it on th'outside, not th'inside yo twit!'"

They laughed, then Johanna continued, "My father was not only strong and handsome, but illiterate. One time he tried to go back to school. That was before they were married. He and a bunch of other young fellows went to night school with a very pretty teacher. While they were in the classroom my mother, with a gang of girls, stood outside the classroom window chanting, 'A, B, C... A, B, C!' Needless to say, the red-faced fellows didn't stick it out for long. Anyway, not being able to read or write didn't mean much working in the peatfields, but when we moved to the city, it sure limited the jobs he could get!"

Johanna took a spoon of advocaat. The liquor had indeed loosened her tongue and she was on a roll. "My whole family worked in the peat fields. They'd cut the turf from the boggy ground and stack it, and when it was dry they'd haul those dusty turf slabs by wheelbarrow to a waiting barge. Whenever a new baby was born – and that happened every two years like clockwork – my parents would take the baby along to the peat fields in a wheelbarrow with a hooped cover like a little covered wagon, so it could be nursed when it got hungry. That's how I started life, Lies, in a wheelbarrow!"

Lies grinned, but the smile faded somewhat when she saw her companion's set expression. She leaned forward, "You know what, Johanna, I think you must have a very strong constitution to have survived a rough start like that. Johanna, I think you will probably live to be ninety!"

"Ja," said Johanna, "maybe, especially since we didn't drown in the ocean already! But Lies, tell me, why did you agree to go to Canada, when you were so close to your family?"

"Well, it was like this. Kees was working in a greenhouse. Loved the work, getting his hands in the dirt, growing plants from seed. But Kees had a dream – wanted to grow things on a larger scale, wanted land, wanted his own farm, and there was no way we could ever afford that."

"What about your family farm?"

"Goes to my oldest brother. Kees knew the only way he'd ever get his own farm was to emigrate, and well, I do love that man and want him to be happy so… When I told my mother, she cried as if her heart would break. 'I'll never see you again!' she wailed. 'Don't go *mijn Liesje*, I can't bear to lose you,' and she set up a keening as if I were dead. It was heart-breaking,

Johanna, to see the old woman like that, absolutely heart-breaking," Lies sobbed with the memory. "I was so torn up inside! I'd promised Kees that I'd emigrate, but it broke my heart to leave my family. He didn't seem to notice. He was so busy with the emigration plans, researching what country to go to, wading through the red tape. He decided on Canada because I have an old friend who lives there, Molly. She could connect him with a farmer to work for until we got properly established."

"Is your friend in Canada on her own?"

"No she married a Canadian soldier." Lies smiled, reflecting, "We sure had a lot of fun with those boys in '45! You know how crazy things were. Everybody just cutting loose. I still have a photo of Molly and me dressed in Canadian soldiers' uniforms."

Johanna grinned. "And what did you do with those naked soldiers?"

"Well... those boys, they deserved to be rewarded!"

"Ha, ha!"

Lies smiled with the memory. Then she took a deep breath. "I don't normally even think about those boys any more. Kees keeps me happy. But lately I've been forced to be celibate! Kees only brought one condom for the trip, and the darned kids used it for a balloon."

"Wha-at?"

"Never mind. Have a drink. Anyway, I started telling you about Molly. She ended up marrying one of those Canadian soldiers, Stanley Whittaker, and went to Canada as a war bride. We've been writing letters back and forth ever since. Molly helped Kees get a contract with a farmer, and everything was set. Kees gave his notice at the greenhouse. And you knew we lived in a houseboat – well we gave our notice to the housing authority as well. One Monday morning there was a knock on my door, and an official looking man stood there with a clipboard in his hand. Must be from the housing authority checking that we were leaving the houseboat in good shape. 'Are you all ready for your big move, Mevrouw van Berkel?' he asked pleasantly. Well, I was pregnant and moody and I just exploded. I yelled at him, *'I don't want to leave!'* and promptly burst into tears. The poor man was quite taken aback. Got out his handkerchief for me and everything. Well!" said Lies. "As it turned out, this man was not a housing inspector at all but... an emigration inspector! He wrote up a report that Kees was trying to take me out of the country against my will. The authorities withdrew permission for us to emigrate. Kees was fit to be tied! And... he no longer had a job. He ended up working for my father on the farm – and those two don't get along."

"I thought your father allowed him to hide there during the war?"

"True. And all was well 'till the day he caught us rolling in the hay. *Potverdomme* he was livid! A miracle he didn't hand Kees over to the Germans! Kicked him off the farm though and he had to find another hiding place." Lies took a sip of her drink, continued, "But Johanna, when permission to emigrate was withdrawn, it wasn't long before I was just as upset as Kees. Even though we were no longer emigrating, we were still supposed to vacate that houseboat; it had been already been allocated to another couple. We wound up sharing the space with the people who were supposed to move in. What a nightmare! No privacy whatsoever and it was a year before we could re-apply. *What* a long year it was! By then, when asked if I wanted to emigrate, I said, *'Yes!'* and you'd better believe I meant it!"

Mieke sat on a bench on the highest deck. In front of her was the wide expanse of the Saint Lawrence River. Behind her other teens were rambunctiously playing shuffleboard. But Mieke had no interest in the view, and although she'd been invited to join the shuffleboard, she had no interest in that either. Mieke was only interested in the small photo she held in the palm of her hand. It was a picture of Tim. She let out a dramatic sigh. Life was so unfair! Tim, Tim, Tim! It was just plain mean of her parents to drag her away to some god-forsaken wilderness! She almost thought they were doing this *whole* emigration thing… just to break up *her* relationship. Just because they thought she was too young. Too young. Huh! She was seventeen already!

She thought of when she'd first met him, at the MULO, the high school she went to after six years of elementary. He was just a little runt then, and he was a pain in the ass. Who was to know he would grow into such a gorgeous hunk! At any rate, back then she was too stressed about school to think about much else. She'd never really thought she was smart enough for the MULO, because it was an academic high school, meant for kids going on to university. Mieke wasn't that keen on learning, but her father was. He told her that he'd never had the chance for an education, and he was going to make darned sure his daughter got the opportunity. For Mieke, the biggest problem with the MULO was, that they had to learn four languages, and she had enough trouble with one. Along with Dutch, they had to learn English, German, and French... and she kept mixing them up. No matter how hard she studied, she couldn't tell a *hund* from a *chien*. And who could possibly remember the different spellings of: *cat, Katze, kat, chat?* When despite her best efforts, she didn't pass at the end of her third year, her father said, "Enough! You've had your chance. It's time to start earning your keep." Mieke went to work in the Philips Factory.

She'd felt like a failure at fifteen, going into the factory, and she felt terrible about disappointing her father. But, after a while, she adjusted. And it did feel good to bring home a pay-packet to contribute to the family finances. Made her feel quite grown-up, in fact. And once the stress of school was off there was no more homework either and her evenings were free. Mieke now joined different clubs. At *Philips Fietsers,* a youth club for cyclists, she reconnected with Tim. Hardly recognized him at first! How tall and handsome he'd become! They started cycling side by side, then holding hands as they cycled, then there was that first kiss, then...

Sunday afternoons, the *Philips Fietsers* would cycle out to the countryside. Mieke vividly remembered the last time she went. It had been a mild sunny day, and she'd worn her new spring coat. Once they left the city they cycled on the sandy paths which ran through the pungent heather. Had to pump hard in that sand, so they took a rest break, lying back in the prickly vegetation, and the aroma of the heather clung to their clothes for hours. Then they carried on pedaling until they reached the lush verdant banks of the *Wilhelmina Kanaal*. Bicycles were laid down against the bank and some stripped to their underwear and dove into the chilly water. Mieke shivered just to watch.

Tim found them a secluded spot and they seated themselves between the bushes. They'd never done much more than kiss before, and she wondered idly why their spot was so far from the others, but she didn't care, as long as she and Tim could be together. They ate the fresh rolls with Gouda that she had brought, and then took turns drinking from Tim's liter of Heineken. The bottle half-empty, they sat there in the bushes gazing into each other's eyes. He kissed her tenderly, then asked, "What did I hear about your family going to Canada?"

She'd been avoiding telling him, was afraid he might break up if he heard she was going to leave, and now he'd heard anyway. "My father wants to go, but not my mother, and I sure as heck don't want to!" and she started to bawl. Great tears rolled down her face.

"Oh, oh, oh! Don't cry *meisje,*" he soothed, "Maybe it won't really happen." He took her face in his hands, and kissed it all over. "We love each other, right?" She nodded through her tears, and he said, "Nothing will ever change that," and now he kissed her mouth, a long lingering kiss. He started to unbutton her coat. "I'll keep you warm," he promised. You *are* my girl, aren't you?" And he'd said it so possessively that it was making her feel good, cherished even, and all she could do was nod. The coat now open, he reached inside and cupped a hand on her breast, and her eyes opened wide.

"What....?"

"It's OK, *meisje*. It's all good." And he put his other hand behind her head and kissed her urgently as he caressed her breast. She could feel a tingling begin deep inside her. Finally he pulled his mouth away briefly, "Good?" he whispered, but didn't wait for a reply, clasped his mouth back against hers, caressed, massaged, manipulated her other breast. And he hugged her close, kissed her, rubbed her shoulders. "Little problem," he whispered, "Can't really *feel* my girl," and he cocked his head sideways as if thinking, then reached behind her to unhook her BH. She started to squirm, her eyes flitting about. "It's OK, meisje. No one can see us. But if you're worried – here, you can lie down." And he laid her back against the grassy berm. And with her stiff cotton bra now loosened, he pushed both bra and blouse up, his eyes feasting on her breasts. She watched his eyes; her head in a turmoil. And now he kissed a long lingering kiss as his hands, his fingers manipulated her breasts, her nipples, and she began to move in response. "Want to touch our chests together," he said, and he pulled up his shirt, and then he stretched his body fully on hers. When her nipples touched his naked chest, he shuddered. And now he kissed her, and caressed her, and then he started to move his body in a circular motion. She kissed him back and clung her arms tightly around him. He reached his hand under her skirt. She tried to pull away but she was firmly pinned under him. His hand slid under the elastic of her white cotton briefs. and she felt his hand caressing her belly and slowly moving down, caressing and moving, slowly, slowly.

"No," she finally found her voice. "No!"

His hand didn't stop. He said huskily, "You're *my* girl, aren't you?"

Mieke's head was in a turmoil. It felt so good, so wonderful. And she *was* his girl. She groaned softly, "No..."

"You *are* my girl! And now you can prove it." He clamped his mouth back on hers, and now she felt the caressing hand move between her legs, touching, caressing, and she shuddered.

Then, "No!" she yelled.

"Damn!" he exclaimed and vanished into the bushes.

As Mieke was trying to straighten her clothing, her mind was a whirlwind. Would he still love her now that she hadn't... And really, it had felt so good, she hadn't *wanted* to make him stop. But she *had* to, right! Nice girls didn't... and what if she'd gotten pregnant. But what if he *dumped* her? She did up her BH, tucked in her blouse, put her coat back on. Finally, Tim, whistling, re-emerged from the bushes, reached a hand inside the coat which she still hadn't managed to button, squeezed her breast, and said, "My girl!"

But when she got home later that day, the shit hit the fan. There were grass stains on the back of her new coat, and father exploded! "What were you doing rolling around on your back? Who was it? That *Tim?*" he practically spit the name out. "You are not to see that boy again!" Mieke burst into tears. "If I see him skulking around here, I will break his neck!"

"No, papa! We were just…"

"Enough!" he thundered. "I will not hear another word! I am the head of this house and as long as you are living under my roof, you will do as you're told!" Crying wildly she ran from the room."

As she relived the scene, her tears flowed. Papa had never treated her so harshly! Had never yelled at her like that! In fact, since she started working he'd treated her almost as an adult, and now… And now here she was, on this ship sailing farther and farther away from Tim. She had tried to stay behind, but her father said no, that at seventeen she belonged with the family. Mieke sighed deeply. Tim, Tim, Tim. She was his girl, always! Well, she'd made a decision; as soon as she could save enough money, she would take the ship back to Nederland. Thus resolved, she blew her nose and wiped her eyes. As she leaned back on the bench gazing at the photo, she completely failed to notice their destination when it came into view – the magnificent cliff face of old Quebec City, crowned with ancient ramparts.

Anneke pulled on her father's sleeve. "Come on, papa. Time to go! I've been waiting for a-a-ages!"

"Anneke, settle down!" he said, frowning. "We can't get off. Just because the ship is in port, doesn't mean we can get off," and he resumed watching the activity on the dock. Did seem to be taking a heck of a long time though.

The decks were swarming with passengers impatient to disembark – family units surrounded by suitcases, knapsacks, umbrellas, and other paraphernalia. Although it was a warm day, some had donned coats and hats, perhaps afraid of leaving them behind. They had to wait because goods were being unloaded before passengers. At least there was lots to see while they waited. Overhead were the towering ramparts of old Quebec, the bulwark of their new homeland; while down below on the dock was the bustle of cranes, trucks and longshoremen. On the gang-plank between ship and dock, the crew hustled back and forth. The passengers watched, waited, and waited some more.

Henk stood clutching the railing, totally mesmerized! He could think of nothing more exciting than watching the machinery in this port. It was almost like having his old Meccano set come to life. "Look at the size of those cranes! Wow! Enormous! How tall do you think papa?"

"Hard to tell," Piet said thoughtfully, "maybe the height of a ten-story building?"

"Ja? Think they'll use *that* crane to move *our* crate? It's gotta be really heavy with all our furniture in it."

"Could be."

"Wonder if crates ever break open when they're lifted up in the air. Boy, that would make a heck of a mess wouldn't it!"

"Wha-at?" said Johanna. "That can happen? Our crate could…"

"No, no," said Piet. "I'm sure it's fine. They do a good job building those crates. They're very strong."

"Papa?" Henk started again.

"Why don't you be quiet for a while *jongen*," Piet grumbled.

"Wanna ask about the cables. Those steel ones on the cranes. Do ya think they ever break?"

"That's *enough*!"

"I think if they did break... "Henk said, idly twirling an elastic between his fingers, "they would just go... *snap*!" and he zapped his sister and ran!

"Aaaah!" screeched Anneke. *"Rotjong!"* And she tore after him as he raced away across the deck dodging passengers and luggage.

"Henk!" bellowed Piet. But the noise of cranes and passengers filled the air, and his voice was lost. His eyes narrowed, he told Johanna, "I'm gonna kill that boy!"

"Now, now, Piet. Calm down. Here. Have a cigarette," and she stuck one between his lips. As he lit it she continued, "I'll be so glad to get ashore and get settled back into a normal routine. Those kids have become just wild on this trip!"

Piet puffed on his cigarette. Blew out a smoke-ring. Put his arm around his wife. "You're right, *vrouwke*. At least now it won't be much longer. Soon we'll be happily settled in our own little Canadian house."

"Ja," Johanna joked, "but what colour will it be?"

By the time Anneke and Henk reached the far end of the ship, they'd dodged over and around so much interesting stuff, they'd forgotten why they were even running. "That beautiful case back there. What do you think's in it?" Anneke asked. "You know, the red one with the gold trim."

"I think an accordion. It's the right shape."

"Really? Think that man would let us see it?"

"I dunno. Whyn't ya ask?" She did ask, and the bearded man it belonged to, not only showed it to them, but even played them a song. Delighted, they headed back to their parents chattering about what they'd seen.

"We saw a lot of neat stuff," Anneke shared.

"*Ja?* Like what?" Piet asked."

Henk, without taking his eyes from the scene on the dock, said, "Well some guy brought his toolbox on the ship. Carpenter. Seemed pretty strange he didn't pack it. Maybe he thought he'd need it if we hit an iceberg! Ha, ha, ha!"

"Must be a tradesman," said Piet. "They're in great demand. Probably has a job waiting that he's going to start the minute he gets there. Doesn't want to wait for the crate."

"And we saw an accordion," said Anneke, "and the man even played it for us!"

"That was nice," said Piet. "I wouldn't mind a little accordion music myself. But again that's a big item for hand luggage. Wonder why he didn't pack it? Maybe afraid of damage?"

"Yup," said Henk, "Like if the crate got dropped and everything busted!" Piet gave him a swift kick in the butt. "Hey!" hollered Henk.

"How much longer do we hafta wait, papa?" Anneke whined. "Why can't we leave yet? We're *at* the dock, and there's the *gangplank* and there's the…"

Piet sighed, "They're still unloading freight."

Henk said, "Maybe they'll unload *all* the freight, before the passengers. We could be on board for a lo-o-ong time."

"Do you want another one!" Piet demanded, and Henk scooted out of the way.

"I'm bored," said Anneke. "I'm gonna draw."

"Good idea," said Piet with relief in his voice. "Find a quiet spot and draw." Anneke picked up her small red suitcase and walked off. Johanna threw a worried look, but Piet nodded to indicate it was all right. Anneke wedged herself up against a lifeboat, opened her suitcase, got out her pencil-crayons and dug into her stash of gray-paper bags. She drew the rocky cliff and the fort at the top, and she was starting on the houses near the bottom, when a voice came over the loudspeaker. Her ears perked up. It was the captain.

"Ladies and Gentlemen, we will now begin the orderly process of leaving the ship. Please make certain you have all your belongings, and keep family members together in one group." Anneke threw her stuff into her suitcase and ran for the gangplank. Piet saw her go and yelled her name, but to no avail. Suddenly a hand reached out and grabbed her.

"Whoa!" said a familiar voice. "Hold on, Anneke. Where's the fire?"

"Fire?"

"Why are you running? Captain said something about 'orderly process.' Right?"

"I wanna be the first one off."

"Really?" said Kees. "By yourself?" He grinned, "Do you speak French?"

"French?" said Anneke suspiciously. "This is Canada!"

"Of course it's Canada. But this is the province of Quebec, and in this province they speak French. You don't want to go on shore all by yourself when you can't speak French."

"Doesn't matter," said Anneke, and added. "Don't speak English either."

Piet came over and hauled Anneke back, whereupon Johanna gave her a good tongue-lashing. Finally the family proceeded to disembark, with the reluctant Mieke bringing up the rear. Johanna glanced back at the ship, muttered to Piet, "I've never been so happy to see the last of anything in my entire life! If I'd known ten days ago what I know now, you *never* would have gotten me on that ship. *Never!*"

"*Nou vrouwke,*" he shushed her. "We're here now. We have a new life! We are in Canada, where everything is possible!" Johanna's mouth twisted, but she didn't reply.

They were directed to walk along the dock to Canada Customs and Immigration, housed in a huge warehouse. The immigrants had to queue up in alphabetical lines, separated by sturdy ropes. It was a long wait, and a bored Anneke started to hop from one foot to the other, which landed her a swat from her mother.

"Enough trouble from you! Behave!" Anneke glowered. They reached the front of the queue, went into a screened-in cubicle for inspection. Did they have the proper inoculations? "Show your arm!" ordered Johanna to the still-scowling Anneke. Anneke pulled up her sleeve, showed her smallpox inoculation scars, remembering how sore her arm had been. Sore as heck!

"You'd think we were cattle!" a man exclaimed in the next cubicle, eliciting a wry grin from Piet. Medical inspections completed and papers stamped, they could leave… but only so far as the next processing station, the next queue. Again, they waited, and waited…

"Are you bringing any agricultural products into the country?" the inspector asked.

"No," said Piet, "nothing."

"Can I get you to open your suitcases please?" They started to oblige, when suddenly they heard a shout!

"No, no, no!!!!" Throughout the warehouse, heads swiveled. *"You*

can't have those!" The shouting came from few queues over. *"I need those back!"* Anneke squirmed around to see what was going on. *"Those are my prize-winning bulbs!"* She got a glimpse of a man wildly gesticulating to an official looking man holding something up in the air. 'All right!' Anneke thought. 'At last some excitement!' Johanna's eyes kept darting from where the inspector was pawing through their stuff, to the direction of the commotion. When a uniformed man started to go through her small red suitcase, Anneke's eyes narrowed, but he just looked at her drawings, and smiled. Finally, when he stamped their papers, relief was written all over Johanna's face.

"Did you hear who that was doing the shouting?" Johanna whispered to Piet they walked toward the next queue. "I think it was Kees!"

"I know," Piet answered in a low voice. "Wonder what the crazy bugger did?" He spoke to another man standing in line, "Do you know what happened over there?"

"Caught a guy hiding tulip bulbs in his *klompen*. Ha, ha, ha!" The story of the bulbs in the wooden shoes was spreading throughout the warehouse from immigrant to immigrant, and wherever it was told, peals of laughter erupted.

"Keep in line, people," crackled the loudspeaker. "Move along."

At long last all their documents had been stamped, and they were allowed to leave. But Piet said he wasn't going anywhere without Kees, so, to Anneke's chagrin, they waited some more. Finally Kees turned up.

"Thought I was done for there," he said airily. "Finally they let me go, but they confiscated my prized tulip bulbs, and," he said, "believe it or not, even my *klompen,* and how can I dig in the garden without those? It's a sad state of affairs. I practically have to enter the new country in my bare feet!"

"You're lucky they let you enter the new country at all, with or without your *klompen*, you silly bugger," said Piet affectionately. "Come on, we have to get to the train station. Don't want to miss that train. But... where's your family?"

"They allowed Lies and the kids go on ahead. We were told there was a bus provided to transport women with children under ten. They might even be at the train station already."

They left the dock area and started the trek up the flights of stairs which zig-zagged up the side of the cliff; a grouchy Anneke dragging her small red suitcase and banging it noisily on each tread of the endless stairs. "Under ten!" she muttered. "Under ten gets to ride – ten and over gotta walk. If I was here"... she counted on her fingers... "four months ago, I coulda been riding. How fair is that! Who made this stupid rule anyway?"

Finally they crossed a steel overpass and found themselves at the railway station. Lies was waiting on a bench, a cone of French fries in her lap, kids clustered around like seagulls. She was so relieved at the sight of her husband that she started to cry. *"Mijn God!* I thought they'd arrested you! *Mijn God, mijn God!"*

"Nou, nou, meid," said Kees, shushing her, clucking her under her

chin. "Everything is fine! You knew your Keesje would come through!"

Lies flared up, "You are crazy! To take a chance on going to jail over those bulbs! To try to get away with that! Crazy!" but she smiled through her tears even as she scolded him.

"Mo-om, I'm starving!" whined Henk. "Can we get some fries?"

"Not a bad idea," said Piet. "It's already late in the afternoon, and who knows when we'll get another chance to eat," and he walked over to the chip wagon. "Kees," he called over his shoulder, "can you find out where we catch the train?"

The group was happily munching fries when Kees came trailing back. Lies took one look at his long face, "What's wrong?"

"Well…" he said slowly. "Seems we've just missed our train by half an hour."

"Gone," Lies snapped, "and we missed it. And all over a bunch of lousy tulip bulbs." She glared at her husband while Johanna started to cry.

"What the heck!" said Piet frowning. "When is the next train?"

"That's the problem. Not for a long time. But," said Kees with a trace of his usual optimism, "all is not lost. They told me at the station, and I think I understood them correctly, that there is a local train soon that'll get us to the next city. Might have said something about it not being very fancy though."

They were in the process of boarding the railway car… when

Johanna halted in the doorway. She stared at the bare wooden benches, pot-bellied stove and rough bearded men, and said, "We are not getting on here! Find another train, Piet! This is just too… too…. primitive!"

Henk was trying to see around his mother. "Wow! Those men, are they miners? Are they from the gold rush?"

"Come on Johanna!" said Piet. "Don't be so particular. Just get on so we can get moving. Do you want to spend the night at the station? Come on now!" He took her by the elbow, and she grudgingly boarded.

"Not fancy! Not fancy! Should be in a museum! What kind of a backward country is this anyway? What are we doing here?"

"Johanna, shush!" said Piet. He muttered, "Bloody good thing these folks don't speak Dutch."

Kees, carrying one of his brood, was already on board, closely watching the bearded men and listening to their talk. "*Les bûcherons*," he now turned to inform the others. Henk looked at him quizzically. "Lumberjacks!" Kees announced, and Henk's eyes lit up. Kees told the boy, "You remember those huge rafts of logs we saw," and Henk nodded eagerly, "well these men were out in the bush cutting those trees. Arms on these guys are like tree-trunks themselves." Henk took a seat as close to *les bûcherons* as possible.

Johanna found empty seats at a goodly distance, let out a sigh, shook her head, draped her coat carefully over the bench before she sat. But she quickly got back up to help Lies arrange blankets and coats to bed down the little kids. The men sat down across from them. Mieke was the last to enter the train. Flounced down the aisle and found a solitary corner from which to ignore everybody.

Kees squirmed around, trying to get comfortable, "You'd think we were in the church," he complained, "sitting in the pews."

"Not that you'd know much about that, you heathen," said Lies. "The number of times that man goes to church in a year; I swear I can count on the fingers of one hand."

"That's because your family went to church not once, but twice every Sunday. Obviously you did enough praying for the both of us!"

Clanging, chugging and screeching, the train finally started up and eventually pulled away from the city. They watched the scenery – on one side flat fields and a sparkling river, on the other farms, and hamlets consisting of a handful of houses clustered about a church. Anneke and Henk looked for the cowboys of the wild-west movies they'd seen, but to their chagrin, they saw only farmers with tractors, or at best, draught-horses. They turned back to the lumbermen, who were passing a jug around, seemed to be telling stories, and would break out in raucous laughter.

Kees peered intently when he saw plows turning soil. "The soil here looks a lot like home. Different wherever you go in this country though," he told Piet. "Prairies, mountains even! But here it's dark, rich loam from river deposits. Looks like excellent soil for farming!"

"It does," agreed Piet. "It's too bad you don't have your tulip bulbs any more. It would be interesting to see how well they'd grow here."

"Yes, it is a shame. But I might not be completely stuck." He reached over and picked up the baby's teddy bear. "Feel!" he said to Piet.

Piet felt the lumpy filling. "You've got to be kidding!" and he roared with laughter. He sat back against the wooden bench, lit a cigarette, contentedly blew a smoke ring, "Well," he said to the world at large, "here we are.... at last. Enroute from Quebec City to our new homes. What an adventure!"

"The English writer," said Kees, "Charles Dickens, he called the Quebec Citadel, the 'Gibraltar of the Americas.'"

Piet shook his head in wonderment, "How do you know these things?"

"Did a lot of studying up on Canada before we emigrated. In fact, I had a whole extra year to study up on the country. Right Liesje?"

"Never mind about that!" snapped Lies. "You don't have to talk about that right now!"

Kees just grinned.

"Ignore him," said Johanna. *"I'm* glad you came the year you did, or we might never have met!"

"Thanks, Johanna." She was quiet for a moment, then said softly, "About that citadel, there *is* something very special about it. When we docked in Quebec, Johanna, I was already asleep. But I was so eager for the new country that the next morning that I was on deck at daybreak. A mist hung over the river. I looked to where the city should be, and the lower part was completely shrouded in fog. My eyes moved up, and… this fortress emerged from the mist, as if it were floating on clouds. It was… like a vision. It was…. mystical." Lies furrowed her brow, searching for words, "I felt like I'd found the holy city, you know from that song, 'Jerusalem! Jerusalem!' I almost expected a choir of angels, singing, 'Hosanna, in the highest!' And I thought, 'This is a sign. We are doing the right thing. I'd never been sure about it up until that point, not with feeling guilty about leaving my mother. I'd never been sure, until I saw that image, right there where our boat was docked, where we were about to put foot on dry land. It took a big load off my mind, Johanna, to see that." Johanna gave her friend a hug.

"Wanna play a game?" said Anneke to her brother "I'm gonna count all the yellow houses. What colour you want?"

"Blue! And I'm gonna time us. Ten minutes! See who gets the most. Da-ad!" he called over. "Can we borrow your watch?"

Ja, but be very careful with it!"

Their eyes glued to the landscape, they counted softly to themselves. "Time's up! Whatdaya got?"

"Fourteen yellow."

"I win!" said Henk. "I got fifteen blue." Anneke squinted at her brother. Of course! Didn't he *always* win? How did she know he wasn't cheating? He'd called time just after they went by a bunch of blue houses, and *he* was the one with the watch. Henk saw her expression. Smirked. Anneke's eyes narrowed further.

The baby was whimpering, and Lies picked him up and unbuttoned her dress. Little Frankie latched on, sucking noisily. From the corner of his eye, Piet watched.

"Cheater! You're nothing but a cheater!" came Anneke's voice.

"Ha, ha, ha, ha!" taunted Henk.

"Piet! Get over there. Straighten them out before they disturb the entire train."

"Well," Piet said mildly, "I don't really think they're going to disturb those lumbermen a whole lot," but he went to the kids.

Johanna, mouth pursed, shook her head. "Lies, you're lucky yours are still small. Except for that little guy eating, they're all sound asleep. Just look at them," she said, gesturing the children, sleeping in various strange postures on the benches. "Sleeping like little angels. No pestering or fighting," she said, glaring in the direction of her own brood. "But I don't believe how they can sleep on those wooden benches with the jostling of this train. Well, maybe after being tossed around on that boat for ten days, they don't even notice the motion."

"Now Johanna," said Piet, returning to his seat, after scolding the kids and retrieving his watch. "Aren't you exaggerating just a bit? The boat ride wasn't *that* bad!"

"Wasn't that *bad!*" she said, her voice rising. "Wasn't that *bad!* I was sick the whole time! Probably lost ten kilo on that trip!"

"Well," said Piet, his eyes twinkling, "you do take pride in your slim waist!" Johanna just glared.

Piet was fastening the watch on his wrist. "Nice," said Kees. Had it for long?"

"Ten years."

"Was it a gift?"

"Yes. But not for me," he sighed. To Kees' questioning look, he replied softly, "I'll tell you about it some time."

They train ride went on for hours, with stops at every whistle-stop and hamlet along the way. It was getting dark, and the temperature began to drop. The children watched in fascination as the lumbermen men started up the pot-bellied stove by chucking in newspaper and wood. Then the men in their red-plaid lumberjack shirts stood around it smoking their pipes, and passing a jug back and forth. They became more and more boisterous, singing rollicking songs in some unintelligible language, stomping their feet to the beat. Finally, the train stopped in the dark in the middle of nowhere, and the lumberman got off. The train started up again with a bang and a clatter, and still they could hear the men singing outside. Then... it was still.

Henk had watched the men wide-eyed and was disappointed when they departed. But then he looked around the area where they'd been partying - noticed something tucked away in a corner, and quickly put it down his knickerbockers. Then with the quiet, and the heat of the stove,

Henk and his sister dozed off.

The train came to a grinding and screeching halt. Kees, who was looking out the window, announced, "Montreal. The end of the line. Come on folks, we need to change trains!" They departed the rattling old railway car, small sleeping children slung over their shoulders. There was a half-hour wait in the station, and while most made use of the facilities, Kees went exploring. He came back waving a brochure at Piet, who was standing in the doorway smoking. "Wait till you see what we're boarding!" Kees told Piet. "It's called, 'The Canadian,' and it says here it's 'The first and only all-stainless steel dome stream-liner in Canada.'"

"What?" laughed Piet. "We're going from the oldest to the newest?"

"That about says it," Kees smiled broadly. "Don't know for sure if that was the oldest train, but this is certainly the newest. Went into service April 24, 1955, so just 20 days old. Isn't that unbelievable? And it's fast too, Piet. In just 3 days you can get from Montreal to Vancouver."

"Potverdomme!" exclaimed Piet. "So it would take another 3 whole days to get to the other side of this country?"

"Just a tiny bit bigger than Holland, right?" grinned Kees. "What did it take to get across the country over there? Maybe 3 hours?"

"What a vast country! A country to lose yourself in," Piet mused. He puffed on his cigarette, added, "Don't tell the women about the new train. I want to see Johanna's face."

It was worth seeing! As she boarded, her eyes went wide at the modernity, the pastel colour scheme, the chrome, and the comfortable seating. Johanna sighed with contentment as she sank back in her seat. Anneke and Henk were bouncing up and down in their seats, and as they did so, something jiggled in his knickerbockers. He pulled it out. Took a swig. Went into a coughing fit. Piet came over to pound him on the back, and saw the brown jug in his hands – smelled it – and confiscated it. Took it back to Kees, poked him in the ribs and held it under his nose. Said with raised eyebrows, "Look what *we've* got."

Soldiers boarded, and Henk's eyes were riveted on their uniforms, their badges, their caps. They motioned him over, gave him gum, joked with him in English. Henk sat squashed between the soldiers, happily grinning, no clue as to what was being said. Johanna was frowning. "I don't like that," she confided to Lies, "I don't like it at all, my son hanging out with soldiers, but what can I say? These are *Canadian* soldiers, the heroes who liberated us. I can't very well tell him to stay away from them! That boy," she said shaking her head worriedly, "has always been fascinated by anything military. Even at the age of two! One day I was outside hanging laundry, and he somehow managed to slip out the garden gate and come back carrying a shell! Proud as could be! 'Mama! Look! Bomb!' I was terrified! Thank God I didn't scream, or he might have dropped it and blown us to smithereens. I said as calm as I could manage, 'Henkie. Put your bomb in mama's clothes basket so it doesn't break.' His favourite word was 'No,' but for once he did as he was told. I snatched up the basket and ran like the devil to the open field behind our house. There I left it, laundry and all, as Henkie screeched to high heaven!" They laughed, shook their heads.

"Mind you, it came in handy in '45 when he and Mieke were watching Canadians bivouacked nearby, and a Canadian soldier saw these hungry little Dutch kids, and gave them a big pot of oatmeal, with *real* milk and brown sugar, to take home. Mieke still says it's the best thing she's ever tasted."

Lies grinned, "Maybe that's how he got hooked!"

Johanna smiled along with her, then her face changed, "But I find it scary, his fascination. Just look at him up there! I came to Canada to avoid another war... and then my son goes looking for one!"

When the soldiers stretched out to snooze, Henk came back, and finally all grew quiet. Piet sat back and watched the stars in the black sky. They passed a small town. The main street was perpendicular to the tracks, so he could see all the way down it, and he wondered about the people who lived there – and what it would be like for *them* to live in that place. And he saw the occasional lit window of an isolated cabin, and marveled at how far from their neighbours these people must live, and he mused about the size, the immense vastness of this great land. He shifted in his seat – felt something hard against his hip – retrieved the jug - and took a swallow. His entire body shivered, Wow, that stuff had punch! He poked Kees in the ribs. Said softly, *"Hier, jongen,"* and handed him the jug. In the dark silence of the ultra-modern railway car, the two men sipped the lumbermen's moonshine.

"Haven't seen so many soldiers in a long time!"

"*Ja,*" said Piet, settling back in his seat, taking another swig of moonshine. "At least these are the good guys."

'Right. Do you remember what a hell of a shock it was when when the *Moffen* invaded? I remember it like yesterday! I was a in my upstairs bedroom at my parents' house when the storm troopers came marching up our road. Heard them before I saw them."

"In no time, they invaded the Philips Factory. German inspectors snooping around. They knew what we made because we shipped all over the world, and they wanted our electronics for their for their radar, and their tanks and planes. We were screwed! They could have packed up our machinery and send it right to Germany, and us along with it! Well, Fritz Philips made a deal! Dealt with the devil, some said. Would provide such and such for the Germans, and in return could keep his factory and his workers. Made an extra effort for his Jewish workers; declared them indispensable staff. Secretly though, he encouraged us to sabotage the electron tubes bound for Germany. But oh, man, we had to be so careful with the Nazi guards prowling around!"

"So you did your bit of sabotage..." Kees said slowly, "and you helped the Germans build their tanks."

"We did do what we could," Piet snapped, "and under the noses of

German collaborators. I had a wife and children to support," he said defensively, "and you know what? If I'd been a farmer I'd have had to grow food for those Germans, and if I'd been a bartender, I'd have had to pour them beer!"

"I'll grant you that," said Kees, taking a nip from the jug and lighting a cigarette. But still…"

"Still nothing!" said Piet, his voice rising. Kees gestured in the direction of sleeping children and Piet simmered down, spoke more quietly. Repeated, "We did what we could. We were all walking a tightrope. One misstep and that was the end of you." He emphasized, "But you must know this."

Kees nodded in the dark, puffed on his cigarette.

Piet said, "The Brits found out about the electronics going to Germany. I think the Resistance kept them informed."

"Right," said Kees, and added, "I should know."

Piet seemed not to hear. Burst out with, "And they attacked! I will never forget! It was Saint Nicholas Day, a Sunday, in 1942. All over the city, kids were out on the sidewalks playing with toys they just got. Our Mieke was on the street parading her doll in the pram I'd made her. Suddenly, the air-raid sirens started shrieking. I ran into the street, grabbed Mieke and rushed my family into the WC."

"Johanna was terrified, crouched in the corner covering the kids with her body. We heard the droning of heavy bombers, heard the whistling of bombs and the deafening explosions and the rattattat of anti-aircraft guns. The children screamed in terror! From our tiny bathroom window, I could see the Philips Complex, with Germans silhouetted on the roof of the light-tower, shooting at the British planes. One plane was hit, lost control, and plunged into a section of factory, leaving only its tail and a wing visible. The Tommies were shooting back now and dropping phosphorous bombs. I saw a German burst into flames, go sailing off the roof, burning all the way to the ground. And then another one flew off the roof in flames, and another. It was like a macabre display of fireworks." Piet shivered. "Then there was so much smoke I couldn't see the factory, and still the bombs kept dropping."

"When it stopped, I went outside, and everywhere there was smoke and fire and devastation and people walking around in a daze, while others cried out for help. I tried to help. Did what I could. And then came the sirens of fire trucks and ambulances... Many houses had been hit, and even a hospital. You'd wonder how they could hit a hospital though, Kees, 'cause there's that big red cross painted on top... but there was so much smoke!"

"There was a pub hit," Kees said. "I was a student in Eindhoven then, out pub-crawling with my friends, just enroute to the next watering hole. When the sirens went off, we were lucky enough to be right by a bomb shelter, and we dove in. We huddled down there as the bombs fell and dirt rained down on us from the shaking ceiling. We were young and half drunk and tried to crack jokes, but the whistling and roar of bombs made it impossible. Then it was still, and we crawled from the shelter. There were screams coming from a pub. *De Bonte Os* had taken a direct hit and was burning with people trapped inside. I grabbed the nearest thing at hand, a shovel, and tried to get to them, but my shovel burst into flames. It was the phosphorous bombs. There was nothing we could do... And the feelings of guilt..." He sighed.

"But Kees! You tried to reach them! You did your best!"

"It wasn't that so much," he said with a leaden voice. "I felt responsible because I'd radioed information to England."

"What? You helped plan the raid?"

"No. Nothing like that. The Resistance needed a radio transmitter to contact London. My uncle was in the Resistance, and I lived in his house while I went to trade-school. I was so excited when he asked! What a challenge, to secretly build a transmitter where the Germans wouldn't be able to find it! Well, I ended up building the transmitter inside the church organ at St. Josephkerk – with the blessing of the priest – from parts smuggled out of the Philips factory. Then I helped with transmissions. Radioed information about troop movements and such. In the fall of '42 they wanted Philips' data. What and how much went to Germany – that sort of thing. I knew nothing about what was planned."

The men passed the jug, and each had a good swig. Piet said, "Well thank God they planned it for Sinterklaasdag so we weren't working in the factory. As it was, there were 147 killed. Guess it could have been one hell of a lot worse yet."

Kees said, "Churchill called for a 'wizzard war' against German technology. Philips was the hub of the electronics industry. They needed to put the factory out of commission. The RAF planned 'Operation Oyster' in broad daylight so bombing could be as accurate as possible, to avoid casualties. Well," he said, shaking his head at Piet, "we know *that* didn't exactly go to plan! A fleet of 93 bombers flew very low to avoid German radar, flying into the airspace of occupied Europe over a bird sanctuary. It was the element of surprise they needed, but," Kees grinned wryly, "they surprised the birds as well, and 23 planes were damaged by bird strikes! The planes flew so low at times, that they had protection from the dykes."

"I remember hearing that," said Piet. "An old farmer was cycling home on a road on top of a dyke, and found himself looking down on a plane. Bomber pilot waved, but the old farmer ignored him, acted just like it was an everyday occurrence." They chuckled.

Kees said, "Those Germans on top of the Philips tower must have gotten a hell of a surprise when suddenly a hundred planes came skimming in over the roof-tops!"

"I heard those guys were all still drunk from partying *Sinterklaasavond*. Mighta thought they were halucinating! Easy pickings!"

"Brits lost 14 planes. Heavy losses – but then it *was* broad daylight, and they were like sitting ducks once they'd dropped their bombs. The alarm was raised, and they still had to fly all the way back over German-occupied territory and across the English Channel."

"A plane crashed in Gelderlandsplein, the park just at the end of our street. Nose-dived right into the grassy ground! Didn't take the Germans long to get there, but when they did, they found an empty wreck. The pilot had already been rescued and hidden."

"And there wouldn't have been a Dutchman anywhere near that plane to question," smiled Kees.

Piet nodded, then said, "The Tommies completely destroyed the section of the factory where the high frequency radio tubes were made. After the raid, I was put to work on reconstruction. I was lucky! The unemployed went to German labour camps. Took a half year to rebuild. Wonder," he said softly, "if the Tommies thought it was worth it." They were quiet. Sat smoking their cigarettes. "Then no sooner was the factory up and running, or there was that strike. Do you remember, Kees?"

"Think I had the *edict* memorized. All men between 18 and 35 ordered to register for transport to Germany. I'd just turned 18 and immediately dove underground. The Resistance found me a place."

"So did my youngest brother," said Piet. "Right in my parents' house. Had to keep out of sight constantly, and at the first hint of danger – into a space between the walls. Two other brothers were transported to Germany and barely survived to the end of the war, but their youngest, my parents managed to hide."

"I hid at a farm where I lived in the barn. Completely isolating at first. Thought the farmer paranoid, but I was so young then. Not sure I understood the consequences. If I'd been found, that farmer would have been arrested... maybe even shot."

"*Ja,* and I don't know how much you heard after you went underground, but those Germans became so desperate for manpower with their own men either in the military or already dead, that the plan was to transport all *our* young men en-mass to Germany. It was the last straw! We went on strike right across the country. The retaliation was brutal! May 8, the strike shut down the Philips Factory. That same day, the S.S. stalked the streets of Eindhoven. They arrested men at random. Any men. And Kees, I've never told anyone this, not even Johanna, but the S.S., they grabbed me too. I swear my blood turned to ice! They were about to throw me in the panzer wagon, but I fumbled in my jacket for my papers, and found my Philips documentation. And because I'd been working on the reconstruction, it said, '*Essential Service.*' They let me go.

Later that day, they arrested an 18-year old boy. A student. He was in the street, talking with a friend. The friend was 17, underage, and the S.S. told him to go home. Then they took the 18 year old away in the panzer wagon." Piet took off his watch and held it up while he flicked on his lighter to show the inscription. Said to Kees, "This watch, the one you were asking me about, it belonged to that boy."

'Aartje van Dijck
met je 18e jaar - 15.4.1943
Je liefste moeder'

"How did *you* get it?"

"At the end of the war, we discovered a Nazi treasure chamber in a basement vault under German headquarters. The vault was full of plunder taken from victims, and among the rings and necklaces and pendants was the boy's watch. By his people were gone. No one knew where. I took the watch for safekeeping, hoping someday to locate them. Besides, I couldn't stand the idea of leaving the boy's watch unclaimed, there, in that Nazi treasure chamber."

"But, what happened to the boy?"

"That boy was executed."

"Whaaat?"

"Intimidation to halt the strike. There were a total of 8 men randomly picked up on the street in Eindhoven. He was the youngest. They were lined up in front of the Philips factory, and in full view of the public, shot. My 10-year old nephew was out in the street playing, and he witnessed it. Johanna's father was the custodian at Philips who was assigned the task of scrubbing clean the area where the execution had taken place. Afterwards, he could never talk about the horror of it, and he was never the same. Would sit for hours without saying a word."

"And you never found the boy's family…"

"No. No matter how hard I searched or how far I looked, I could find no trace. They'd simply vanished in the madness of that war."

Kees was holding the watch in his hand. Almost seemed to stroke it.

Said softly, "That boy was my age."

Piet nodded in the dark. Said hoarsely, "Should it have been me? If I hadn't had that document, if *I* had been arrested, would they still have picked up the boy? Would *he* be alive today? I've had to live with that, Kees."

"There's no way to tell if the boy would have lived, or if they would have shot 9 men rather than 8. But I know how you feel. If I hadn't relayed information about the factory, would the RAF have attacked? Would the people in the pub still be alive? Piet, all this stuff... I had pushed it to the back of my mind. Didn't want to think about. But, here, in the dark, in the middle of nowhere, it's strange but... I can open up about it, and I... I somehow feel lighter."

"*Ja,*" said Piet, "*ja.* It is the same for me." He passed Kees the jug again, adding, "I think we needed to 'get rid of our stories,' as the Dutch saying goes." The men sat in silence and shared the last of the moonshine. Finally Piet said, "Kees, *jongen*, it's all behind us now. Everything that happened is behind us. That ship plowing through the stormy ocean took us away from it all. This train, racing though the dark night, is taking us further yet. Kees, we've left it all behind."

"Anneke! Henk! Wake up! We're in Kingston!" They gathered their things together, and there were tearful goodbyes with Lies and Kees, who'd still spend hours on the train.

"I'll miss you!" Johanna hugged Lies as if she'd never let her go.

"Come!" said Piet, "We've gotta get off. The train's going to start up again. Come on!"

"Write me!" Johanna yelled.

As the family stepped down from the train, two figures emerged from the darkness, "Welcome!" one of the men said. "I'm Jake van der Veen, and this is my son Chris." The adults talked, while Henk and Anneke stood bewildered, clutching belongings. Mieke stood to the side, as usual ignoring everyone. "Your sister Femke," Bart told Johanna, "sent us to meet you. Femke wanted to come to the station herself, but we wanted to save as much space as possible for the luggage. We've got two cars here, but the trunk won't open on one."

"Told you Pa, we should just take a crowbar to it!" said the young man. He was tall, broad across the chest, and had a thick thatch of wheat-blond hair. But..." Chris suddenly noticed the aloof Mieke, "Well hello!" With a smile he added, "I was told you were pretty, but they weren't half right!" She blushed furiously. "Here, let me carry that," and he took Mieke's suitcase. "Why don't you ride with me? Too bad it's so dark out, or I'd show you around the area. You probably have lots of questions. I am at your service *meisje*." As Mieke rode in the front seat of the beat-up '48 Ford, sun began to peak over the horizon She glanced at the handsome young man beside her, and it dawned on her, that perhaps Canada might not be such a terrible place after all.

Squashed into the back seat of the other car with her mother and brother, Anneke dozed off again. She awoke to screams, as her mother and aunt ran into each other's arms. Her father shook hands with her uncle, said how happy he was to be in Canada. Her cousins stood and grinned at her. At the house, there was food waiting, 'sandwiches,' the cousins said, and Anneke marveled that Canadian bread had the lightness and whiteness of cake. She was given 'freshee' to drink, and then a special treat, a 'popsicle' to eat outside. She thought it all very exotic! Anneke slurped down the icy treat, then yanked off sandals and socks to go running on the dewy grass, wildly chasing her cousins like a puppy let out of its travel crate.

Anneke hadn't seen the cousins since she'd waved them off the previous summer, and was was amazed to discover that, already, they had become experts on everything Canadian! They told her they spoke English so fluently that they could barely speak Dutch anymore and were only doing so now for her benefit. "You need a new name," they told her. "You have to have an English name." Anneke was far from convinced. Were they playing a joke on her? But when the issue arose the following day, uncle agreed that 'Anneke' wouldn't do to start school with in Canada. Uncle Theo thought for a moment. "Annie," he said. "You can be Annie. That's a good English name. What do you think about that?" he said, turning to her parents.

"Ja," said her father, nodding thoughtfully. *"Dat is goed."*

"But Anneke is such a pretty name!" Johanna protested.

"We have to fit in with the new country!" Piet asserted. "She's going to go to school, she needs an English name!"

Her uncle's house was so very tiny that cousin Gerda slept in a hallway. During the day, her bed folded into the wall so people could move around. Anneke heard her mother whisper that this wasn't really a house at all; it was a converted chicken coop. Anneke had to sleep at a neighbouring farmhouse, where she shared a bed with a strange girl. Abandoned, she cried herself to sleep, sobbing quietly. She no longer knew where she was, and she barely knew who she was. *"Nee!"* she told herself. *"Nee! Ik ben niet Annie!"*

Tension built in the tiny house where the two families tripped over each other, and when the crate of household goods finally arrived, Johanna was jubilant. As Piet pried off the top of the crate, his family stood ready to embrace their belongings, their connection to their old country, to that wonderful red-brick house in the Doesburgstraat. But this was much more than an occasion for nostalgia! Finally they could set up house in the new land with their own furnishings: the pendulum clock, the treadle sewing machine, the Delft-blue pottery, and the sturdy furniture from the huiskamer.

Chapter Two – In the Land of Milk and Honey

The teacher explained, demanded, questioned; her voice droning on and on as the sun beat in through high, fly-encrusted windows, and rows of hot sticky children squirmed at wooden desks. Anneke sat near the back and watched the teacher's mouth move, but she understood not a word. Anneke's entire English vocabulary consisted of the words *OK* and *no*. Both what was said in the classroom, and what was written on the blackboard, was equally incomprehensible to her. Anneke sat, from morning 'till night, feeling isolated, hot, and excruciatingly bored. She kept looking at the clock, wanting those hands to move more quickly. One thing hadn't changed, coming from Holland to Canada – at least numbers were still the same! But the simple addition and subtraction that the teacher put on the blackboard for the class to do, was much too easy for her, so even *that* was boring. Occasionally the teacher gave her some mimeographed worksheets of harder math, and Anneke would attack them with gusto, but they were too soon finished. Sometimes there was a brief respite when a child would misbehave and be scolded by the teacher. But for the vast majority of the time, Anneke sat there in a state of complete isolation, and mind-numbing boredom. But she was resolved, was absolutely determined, that when school started again in September, she would understand English, and she would never, ever, be this bored again!

As soon as they'd arrived in Canada, before they were even living in their own house, Anneke and Henk had been hustled off to school. One of the women in the Dutch immigrant community, Bets van der Ven, who spoke quite good English, translated so mother could enroll them. "Grade four," Anneke told her. "I'm in grade four.

"Annie," said Bets, "You can't be in grade four. You have to go back a couple of grades because you don't speak English. That's how they do things here." She explained, "When you learn to speak English you can move ahead again. You're being placed in grade two."

Anneke's eyes narrowed. "My name is not *Annie,* and I'm in grade *four!"*

"That's enough!" said mother. "Be polite! We're in Canada now and we have to do things the Canadian way." So here she sat in the heat with the 'babies' listening to the teacher's voice drone on, and on, and on.

Anneke had noticed Wanda Woods standing on the perimeter of the schoolyard, a large girl with greasy hair and worn print dress. She seemed like an outcast, and Anneke, an outsider as well, smiled at her, and tried to communicate through gestures. Wanda latched on to Anneke, happy for the friendship of even a mute, immigrant kid. Their houses were near each other, and one day in early summer, Wanda gestured for Anneke to come into her home, a dilapidated tin-roofed shack. "Pie!" she said repeatedly, and Anneke assumed that meant, 'Come in,' or 'Visit,' or something like that. Anneke went to step through the doorway, and her nostrils flared. The smell was incredible! Absolutely mouthwatering! Wanda's mother, dimpled as dough, was bustling about the kitchen taking things from the oven. The woman smiled at Anneke, cut a huge wedge of something steaming, put it on a plate, added a fork, and handed it to the child. Anneke's face lit up in delight! She tasted…. incredibly delicious!

"*Lekker!*" she exclaimed, complimenting.

Wanda looked at her quizzically. "Pie," she pointed out.

"Pie!" Anneke grinned, as strawberry juice dripped down her face.

Anneke invited Wanda to her home and retrieved her Dutch-English dictionary. "You," she gestured, "teach I," she pointed, "English." Wanda looked at her curiously. Anneke continued, "I… teach you… Dutch." Wanda frowned, then suddenly smiled and nodded.

"Right," she said, "we'll teach each other how to talk." They went outside, sat down on the step, and started to work.

"Fence!" said Wanda, pointing, and Anneke pronounced the word after her. "Grass," said Wanda. "Doghouse. Outhouse. Roof!"

"*Wat is dat?*" asked Anneke, pointing to an insect.

"Grasshopper!" said Wanda, but when Anneke tried it, Wanda started giggling. With a gleam in her eye, Anneke tried again. Wanda laughed harder. This time Anneke mispronounced on purpose. Wanda howled, and Anneke joined in the laughter. But when they were laughed-out, they went back at it, until finally Anneke pronounced it to Wanda's satisfaction.

"Lieveheersbeestje!" countered Anneke, pointing. *"Zeg het* Wanda, *lieveheersbeestje."* This time Anneke was the one to start giggling, as Wanda struggled in vain with the multi-syllabic word.

Every day, as she worked with Wanda to learn the language, Anneke wrote down all her new words in a scribbler. At night, in bed, she would memorize them. And although Wanda soon lost interest in learning Dutch – a language she came to consider both difficult and useless – she continued to take great pride in her role as teacher. Her first summer in Canada, Anneke spent many happy hours playing the teacher game.

The village of MillCreek was aptly named, since it was located on a creek which had once powered a woolen mill, a saw mill, and a grist mill. Settled in the early 1800's, MillCreek grew into a thriving hub serving the surrounding rural area. Doc Meacham's house and surgery was located along the main street, along with several churches, stores, and hotels. The picturesque Stagecoach Inn with its upper and lower verandahs separated by posts and fancy fretwork, had a jovial atmosphere inside, and did a brisk business. And there were carpenters and blacksmiths, a carriage painter, Annie Gunn the milliner, and Frederick Fries the shoemaker who had come all the way from Germany to ply his trade. There was even a chair and pail factory. And every day there were the sounds of clomping horse hooves and creaking wagons with rattling milk cans, as milk from farms in the surrounding area was transported to MillCreek's cheese factory.

With the advent of electricity, mills began to fall into disuse as production shifted to factories built in more densely populated areas – the cities. With this shift went jobs. Workers followed. Automobiles now made travel faster and easier and there was less frequenting of local businesses as nearby cities offered greater variety, and cheaper prices. Along with all the other villages in southern Ontario which were built around mills powered by rivers and creeks, MillCreek went into a slow decline.

A significant loss was the cheese factory. Milk from area farms was now transported by a big blue truck to the cheese factory in the hamlet of Wilton. But the chair and pail factory survived. Now called MillCreek Furniture, the factory specialized in high-end furniture – dining room suites, bedroom suites, coffee tables... and particularly cabinets. The original limestone factory was added to several times with wood-frame additions. Trucks bearing the MillCreek Furniture logo, departed the factory enroute for prestigious furniture stores in big cities.

MillCreek had one an advantage over other mill towns in that a highway ran through it – the main artery linking Montreal and Toronto. Auto repair shops, gas stations, lunch counters and motels sprang up. There was a lot of traffic in MillCreek by the mid-50's and many transports. Occasionally transport drivers lost control and plowed into the buildings along main street. Accidents in general were common... to the benefit of the local auto repair shops. The heavy traffic caused noise and fumes year round, and in the summer months, a great deal of dust, which settled on the buildings of MillCreek.

Johanna stood at her kitchen window and stared off into the distance at the parched fields beyond the dusty gravel road. She sighed. My, but it was hot! She'd never felt such heat! The children played in the woods all day, where it was cooler, but this house was like an oven! A bottle of milk, two days old, went sour. They learned to tie a string to the neck of the milk bottle, and to lower it into the cool cistern. Henk had figured that one out. And as the sun beat down mercilessly day after day, it blistered more turquoise paint from their two-story clapboard house, an old Ontario farmhouse, complete with flies and rotting verandah. Johanna hated this house! At twenty-five dollars a month, she knew it was all they could afford, but still she hated it. "As soon as we get on our feet in Canada," Piet had promised, "we'll get something better." But *when* would things get better? At the thought of her husband, a worried frown creased her face. Piet no longer wore suits to work; he wore overalls and work boots, and he came home exhausted and gray with cement dust. Because he spoke little English, the only work he could get was labourer on a construction site, hauling bricks and cement blocks at the new school being built in MillCreek. He hadn't done heavy labour since he was a young man! She worried about him, and.... and... My but it was hot! Johanna went to the kitchen sink and pumped the wooden handle until cold cistern water gurgled out. She cooled her hands, but the stench of the stagnant water repelled her. There was no way she could wash her face with it. Finally, she scooped up a ladle of drinking water, and splashed *that* on her face. Henk would just have to carry a little extra from the tap outside the school tonight. She sighed. Unbelievable, the primitive conditions here! Their bathroom was an outhouse in the back yard. When Henk told Anneke that rats lived down in the hole, Anneke refused to use it, and hopped about the house in desperation from one foot to the other, until finally Piet took charge and straightened her out and threatened to beat Henk within an inch of his life if he ever told his little sister anything like that again. And then there were the flies! Whenever the kids left the screen door open even briefly, the house filled with horrid, buzzing flies. Henk took them on as a challenge. He would grab the fly swatter (an implement she'd never even heard of in Holland) and run through the house splattering fly guts all over the walls and furniture. She didn't know which were worse – live flies or dead ones.

Johanna sank down on a chair, and conjured up another house, a red-brick row house; white lace curtains behind brightly polished windows. Friday, that was the day all the women on the street washed their windows. Her first Friday in this house she'd gone outside to wash them, and they were so grimy she'd had to take a brush to them. But as she scrubbed, the panes rattled, more, and more, and she noticed the cracked putty that held them in place was popping right out, and she worried the panes themselves would pop out next. Defeated, she went back into the house. What day was today?

Monday. It was laundry day... and she longingly thought of her washing machine, filled with hot soapy water. Johanna'd loved laundry day! Everything came out so clean and smelled so fresh. And she'd loved hanging clothes outside, especially if there was a bit of a breeze. But perhaps what she loved most of all was taking that pail of soapy water out front to scrub the sidewalk in front of her house along with all the other housewives on her street. And they would scrub, and socialize, and chatter, and gossip.

The first Monday in the clapboard house, she'd paced the floors in agitation, wanting, needing, the routine of laundry. But her washing machine had been left behind in Holland – it was too big and heavy for the crate – and they couldn't afford another yet, so dirty clothes were taken to her sister's house for washing, and her sister did her own laundry on Mondays. So Johanna did laundry when it fit into her sister's schedule, and when she could get transportation for herself and her bulging laundry basket.

Nevertheless, that first Monday, Johanna took a pail of soapy water out front, and with her scrub broom proceeded to scrub the chipped cement-slab sidewalk. The neighbours stared in wonderment at what the Dutch woman was doing, and she heard them talking among themselves, and while she couldn't understand the words, she heard the laughter in their voices. With as much dignity as she could muster, she retreated inside.

Johanna thought about the housewives from the Doesburgstraat, and tears welled up. How she missed their camaraderie! She was so lonely, so *desperately* homesick. Why oh why, had she agreed to come to this godforsaken place? Finally, she shook herself. *Everything* wasn't bad! *One* good thing had happened. She had met Detty Kuipers, housebound with two infants, thrilled to get company. Detty's house wasn't much better than Johanna's, but it did have one luxury, a small television set. Detty would stretch the rabbit-ears and tune in to their favourite show, 'I Love Lucy,' and they would roar with laughter at the bold antics of their heroine. Although they couldn't understand the words, through Lucy's gestures and facial expressions they understood what was happening. But they wanted to understand her even better, and as they strove to learn, Lucy taught them. Much of the English the immigrant women learned their first years in Canada, came from the 'I Love Lucy' show.'

Anneke pondered later that 'fuck' must have been one of the first English words she learned. She'd first heard the jeering, "Hey Dutchman, ya wanna fuck?" from an older boy as she was crossing the bridge on her way home from the store. She could feel the threat in his words, although she didn't know the meaning. She walked more quickly, but when she glanced over her shoulder she saw several boys following her. A second boy yelled, and a third, and she was running, and again heard she the first one yell, "Hey Dutchman, ya wanna fuck?" Terrified, she rounded the corner of her street, and it was only when her house came into view, that the pounding of feet behind her ceased.

"What's wrong?" asked her mother as she came through the door, sweaty and flushed.

"Boys chasing me," she muttered, and brushed past her mother to go upstairs to her room. Johanna stared after her daughter, brow furrowed.

When Anneke saw cousin Gerda the next day, she told her of the terrifying encounter. "What were they saying?" she asked insistently. "What were those boys yelling about?"

"They do that to me too," said Gerda. "Yell at me and chase me like that. Do it to all the Dutch girls. Think they figure if you can't talk good English you can't do anything back."

"But what does the word mean?"

"Neuken. It means, *neuken."*

"What!?" said Anneke, eyebrows raised, staring at her cousin. "That's the kind of stuff parents do, right? Why….. would they…. yell…. that?"

Raised in the confinement of the city, the immigrant children loved the wide-open spaces of Canada. Anneke spent much of her first summer roaming the fields and woods, playing cowboys and Indians, wearing a neckerchief, riding a stick horse. Anneke, Henk, and their cousins assumed the identities of the television cowboys they got to watch occasionally on someone's static-y TV set. Anneke was the Lone Ranger and would call out in a deep voice "Hi, ho Silver, away!" Her eleven-year-old cousin Gerda, with the peaches-and-cream complexion and the thick blonde braids, was

Annie Oakley. Of course, Anneke thought derisively. Leave it to *Gerda* to be a *cowgirl!*

Riding the range one day, Anneke and Gerda decided to pick apples for their horses and themselves in an abandoned orchard. They were crossing a field to get there, when suddenly a voice leered, "Hey Dutchman, ya wanna fuck?" Anneke felt the hair on the back of her neck stand up, and she raced for the safety of the trees. She heard Gerda running behind her, and heard boys, like baying hounds, chasing Gerda. Anneke grabbed the branches of the nearest apple tree, and hoisted herself up high.

Gerda reached the tree, made it up the first branch, screamed, "Owwww! Let me go! Let me *go!*"

"Come on Dutchman. You know you wanna fuck. Come on outa that tree!" A boy had grabbed her ankle and Gerda kicked wildly at him with her other foot. Several boys formed a laughing semi-circle around the first one.

"Haul 'er down, Chuck. Pull 'er outa that tree! Do 'er boy!" Chuck grinned lasciviously, started to run his free hand up Gerda's leg, attempting to look up her shorts.

"C'mon Chuck! Git 'er boy!"

"Awwwww!" Chuck suddenly screamed, grabbed his eye, let go of Gerda.

"Yippee!" yelled Anneke, and whipped another green apple. Gerda scrambled up the tree to join her cousin in pelting apples at the boys, who were soon in full, inglorious, retreat.

In the heat of the summer, day after weary day, Piet came home tired, blistered from the sun, caked with sweat and cement dust. Johanna worried about him, but he insisted that he was strong as a bull. "You may be strong," she said, "but you're not used to this kind of heavy work, and it's not like you're a young man!"

"Vrouwkje," he said, putting his arms around her, consoling her with a kiss, "you worry too much."

Theo told them about a job in Kingston for a live-in nanny. "Might be good for Mieke," he suggested, but Mieke didn't like the idea at all. She'd have to speak English all day and her English was not good. Her MULO report cards could attest to that.

"What!" exclaimed Piet. "Three years of English and you don't think you can talk to a bunch of children?" He shook his head, "It's time to stop moping girl. Get in touch with reality, get a job, and contribute to the family."

"But the customs, how they keep house and cook and everything, it's all different in Canada. I won't know what to do." She wasn't going to tell them that she'd miss them because she wasn't a baby and besides, she was still mad they'd taken her away from Tim.

"Mieke, you learned your housekeeping from the best," Johanna gave her daughter an encouraging look, and added with a smile, "your mother."

"You will be fine," said Piet. "You're a hard worker and that's the important thing, doesn't matter, Holland or Canada. Besides, Kingston is only an hour away."

Johanna said, "But Piet, that is so far away! And she won't be bringing home that much money."

"Not much money! We need every penny we can get right now. And she'll get free room and board there, so we don't have that cost anymore."

"Living there, in that strange house? Is that safe?"

"The parents are both lawyers. Can't get safer than that!"

The position was with Mr. and Mrs. Harvey, who both worked for the same law firm and had four children. Since the last nanny had left abruptly, Mieke was to start right away. She would have every other weekend off.

The first week. Mrs. Harvey gave instructions for lunch before she left for work, but Mieke found her hard to understand, and when she started to peel potatoes, Rita, the nine-year-old said, "No, no! That's not what Mommy said. Not potatoes, *potato chips* and ice cream for dessert," and the child pointed to the items. Mieke wasn't at all sure, so she gave in, and after the kids had polished off the chips and ice cream... she heard them giggling.

It was the beginning of a cycle. As long as Mieke gave in to their demands, they didn't cause problems. The moment she tried to exert some sort of control, they found ways to get even. She found them in the kitchen making peanut butter sandwiches, with gobs of peanut butter all over the counter. When she scolded them, a gob landed on the floor, and eight-year-old Tommy 'accidentally' stepped in it, then walked through the kitchen, across the foyer, and out the front door. Mieke sank down at the table, defeated.

Normally, thought Mieke, she was sure of herself and sensible, but here she was so frequently at a loss – didn't know the language – didn't know the customs. It was discouraging. And there was no one to talk to, not one who spoke a word of Dutch. She thought longingly of her last job, that factory job with all the other girls her age. Many nights Mieke cried herself to sleep. The one bright spot in her life was Chris, the young man who had driven her from the train station.

Weekends when she didn't have to work, Chris drove her back to MillCreek. He said he worked in Kingston and it was easy to give her a ride. She found him wonderful to talk to, very understanding. She told him she had a boyfriend in Holland, and he said that he understood, but she still had to have some fun, didn't she? Maybe she'd like to go to the movies her next weekend off – just as friends, of course.

Mieke wrote long letters to Tim, but then, she didn't have much else to do in the evenings, other than to sit gazing at his photo. She started saving money to go back to her beloved Tim from the allowance her parents gave her when she turned over her small earnings, She didn't hear much back from him though. He wrote a few notes to say, yes he missed her too, but was very busy with soccer.

One weekend Chris took Mieke to Sandbanks Provincial Park. They had a great time playing on the beach and splashing about in the lake. Then they relaxed on the blanket he'd spread across the sand. He offered to put some lotion on her back. She thought his hands very gentle.

When she couldn't find the photo a few days later, she decided that she must have lost Tim at the Sandbanks.

Johanna was in the kitchen peeling potatoes for supper when the knock came. She dried her hands on her apron and pushed open the screen door. Standing on the verandah was Klaas, the bricklayer who worked with Piet. He was sweating profusely. I....I....I....I'm sorry, Johanna," he stuttered as he stood there, head bowed, twisting his cap in his hands. Johanna stared uncomprehendingly, then felt a shiver go through her body. "I....I'm sorry. The foreman, he wanted to come himself but he doesn't speak Dutch." Johanna grabbed the verandah post for support. Klaas wiped his forehead with the back of his sleeve. "I'm sorry Johanna. I mean, I was right there. Piet, he.... he was just walking across a plank carrying a couple of cement blocks, when all of a sudden he.... he just sort of crumpled, fell down, and lay there on the ground with his face all gray and knotted up, making these awful groaning noises. I said to him, *'Piet! Wat is het jongen?*

Wat is er met jou aan de hand?' But he didn't answer me. Then the foreman called an ambulance and they came and they took him." Klaas wiped his face again, and sighed. "To the hospital. They took him to the hospital."

"Oh mijn God, mijn God!" Johanna sank down. Klaas caught her, took her into the kitchen, sat her in a chair. "I knew he couldn't keep it up! That heavy manual labour. I told him already, but would he listen! *Oh mijn God* what are we going to do?"

Anneke and Henk, boisterous and scratching at mosquito bites after an afternoon of cowboys and Indians, charged into the house to find their mother at the kitchen table, head down on her arms, shoulders heaving, sobbing. Klaas sat across from her, nervously chain-smoking. Suddenly subdued, the children looked on with fearful, questioning eyes. Klaas decided he must take charge. "Anneke, y.... you go and get your mother's friend. What's her name?"

"Mrs. Kuipers," said Anneke in a small voice.

"Right. You tell her your mother needs her. Tell her there's been an ac.... ac.... cident. Tell her that your f.... father's in the hospital." Anneke's eyes went wide. She raced away with thudding heart. Klaas turned to the boy, "Henk, you run over to your aunt and uncle's. Tell them your mother needs a ride to the hospital. That neighbour of theirs, that retired guy, he's got that old truck?" Henk nodded. "Tell them, well they'll know that anyway, but tell them she'll need s.... someone to go with her. S.... someone who can talk to the doctor. Find out what's going on. Your uncle s.... speaks pretty good English, doesn't he?" Henk nodded again. "Well then, off you go." Henk continued to stand, rooted. "Don't just stand there staring at your mother, boy. You can't do anything here. *Go!*" Henk raced off.

Theo went into the hospital with her while the neighbour waited in his rusty Ford pickup. Johanna walked into the hospital room, and felt her chest tighten to see Piet's face, ashen, on the white pillow. His left leg was suspended from a bar attached by a chain to the ceiling. Her once robust husband – reduced to utter helplessness. Johanna cried bitter tears. "Piet," she sobbed, *"Liefje, wat is er met jou gebeurt?"*

"Don't cry, *vrouwkje*," he begged. "Don't cry. I'll be OK," but he was gray with the pain. Johanna slumped down with her face on the bed. Her body shook with sobs. Piet placed a comforting hand on her head. Finally a nurse came in to say that the patient needed his rest and she must go. She saw her brother-in-law in the hall talking to the doctor. As they walked back to the car, Theo put his arm around Johanna's shoulders, and he told her what he'd learned.

"He's hurt his back Johanna. Ruptured the discs. They're going to keep him in traction. He has to stay in the hospital."

It was so hot! So very, very hot! Johanna wore a thin cotton nighty and had only a sheet covering her, yet she tossed and turned with the insufferable heat…. and with the worry. Would Piet ever be right again? He'd been in hospital for a week but didn't seem much improved. Would he be able to work again? How would they survive? Johanna stared into the blackness of the night, as she worried, and fretted, and... Something scratched her foot. She froze. Scratchy feet came running up her leg, with a long leathery tail slithering behind. She lay stock-still. Out of the darkness emerged a pair of beady-red eyes. Johanna shot from the bed and let out a blood-curdling scream! The children came running into the room, flicked on the light, and gaped with astonishment at their mother, standing on top of a chair, screaming hysterically. "Ahhhhhhh! It ran across me! I could feel its nails on my body! Ahhhhhhh! And it's tail! I could feel its tail! It *touched* me! Ahhhhhhh!"

"Calm down mother," said Henk. "What *are* you talking about?"

"And its eyes! Awful, beady, red eyes!" and she moaned, "Oh, oh, oh, oh, oh."

"*What,* mother?"

"*It was a rat! There was a rat in my bed!!!*"

With a puzzled frown Anneke looked at her mother, "A rat?" But she'd heard enough false rumours about rats. No way she was falling for that story again! "Is that all," she scoffed, and went back to bed.

School started, and Anneke was thrilled to have achieved her goal—she'd learned English over the summer and now understood what went on in the classroom. She was no longer bored —school was exciting! Anneke sat at her desk and read, "Dick and Liz played with Spot. Look Liz, see Spot run!" She finished the book, closed it, and sat back in her seat. She thought of some of the books she'd read in Holland: *De Negerhut van Oom Tom, Het Dagboek van Anne Frank, Martin Luther en de Deuren van de Wittenbergse Kerk*. OK, thought Anneke, the current fare may not be quite as stimulating, but at least I'm reading English.

Mrs. Huff was a tall, erect, no-nonsense kind of teacher who knew how to get the best out of her students. On one side of her classroom sat the grade threes, on the other the grade fours. Anneke sat with the grade threes, her reading at grade one, her math at grade six. Mrs. Huff kept Anneke busy with numerous mimeographed worksheets on vocabulary and grammar, and even kept Anneke in after school for extra assistance. Mrs. Huff said that if Anneke kept up the hard work, she would soon be allowed to cross the floor. School was a happy place; home quite the opposite. Father was still in hospital, mother cried a lot, and they had very little food.

Theo dropped by to help. Johanna exploded. "Liar! You told us it was so good here. You said there were good jobs. You lied! This is your fault! Piet crippled in the hospital, the children with no food, this rat-infested house, and it's all because of *you!* All those nice letters you wrote, 'It's so *goed* in Canada! We have such a goed *life* in Canada.' This is *your* fault! *It's all your fault!*" Theo left, shaking his head sadly. Johanna dissolved into tears.

Then, out of nowhere, food began to arrive: a huge tub of

homemade butter, freshly-baked loaves of bread, farm sausages, a burlap sack of potatoes, baskets of vegetables, apples, milk, eggs. The minister of the Dutch Reformed Church had talked of their plight in his Sunday sermon, urging his parishioners to help. Johanna was astonished, since they didn't even attend that church. She and Piet had decided right away that their family would attend the United Church of Canada and integrate into the Canadian way of life. They were opposed to the idea of a 'Dutch' church, a Dutch school. And yet, that minister had reached out to help them, and all those wonderful farmers had brought their produce. She felt so thankful! For the first time in a long while, Johanna smiled. Anneke said that the homemade butter was the best food she had ever tasted in her entire life.

Fall came, and Piet finally came home. He lay on a bed in the living-room, a sheet of plywood under his mattress. Johanna looked at him lying there, helpless, and realized that, for the first time in their marriage, it was up to her to take care of the family, to try to resolve their desperate financial situation. She would get a job. Her sister told her that rich Canadian women were glad to have Dutch immigrant women cleaning their houses, because of the Dutch reputation for cleanliness. These jobs paid five dollars a day. Johanna calculated how many cleaning jobs it would take: rent at twenty-five dollars, electricity, food, medicine… She told Piet she was going to work. He was devastated! He wasn't a man if he couldn't support his family. Johanna held firm. The other immigrant women told her of some jobs where she could start immediately.

On her hands and knees Johanna scrubbed the white marble foyer of the Richardson house. As instructed, a toothbrush was used in the corners. At last she sat back, wiped the damp hair from her face, and sighed. It was a huge house, and Colonel and Mrs. Richardson were extremely particular. Johanna stood up – put her hand on her hip and, grimacing, straightened her back. There was no time to waste. Quickly she emptied the scrub-pail and grabbed the vacuum. Even when she'd finally finished, she'd still have to walk half an hour to catch her ride back to Mill Creek.

Johanna came home from work drained and exhausted, and then she still had to cook and clean for her husband and children. He was sick and she was worn out. She told Detty Kuipers they should never have left Holland.

Anneke came home after school and cuddled up on the bed with her father. "Papa," she asked, "why *did* we come to Canada?" Piet was happy for some diversion. He'd been alone all day.

"Well, *kindje,* when we decided to emigrate, we picked Canada because the Canadians have been so good to the Dutch people. You've heard how in the war Queen Julianna stayed safely in Ottawa with the princesses?" Anneke nodded. "And how Princess Margriet was even born in Canada, and the Canadian Government said that the Queen's hospital room could be a temporary piece of Holland so the princess could be born a Dutch citizen." Anneke smiled, delighted. "And it was the brave Canadian soldiers who fought to liberate Holland, and many of them died over there. And one of those soldiers fell in love with a Dutch girl and took her back to live in Canada. The next year they sponsored her brother, and the following year another family and so on. And last year Uncle Theo's family came, and this year it's us. We're the last link of a long chain."

"The last link," said Anneke thoughtfully, "in a long chain."

"Yes," said Piet, summing it up, rather proud of his explanation, "And that's how we come to be here."

"But papa, *why* did we emigrate? I heard mama say to Mrs. Kuipers that we should have *stayed* in Holland."

An exhausted Johanna walked in the door, started to take off her coat. Suddenly she froze. "Piet!" she screamed. "Piet!" and she laughed and cried simultaneously. There he was, standing! He had tied the corset from the hospital over his pajamas, and he was leaning on two canes, but he was standing, grinning from ear to ear. She ran to him, tears streaming down her cheeks.

A few days later she came home from work to find the miracle of Piet, holding one cane only, in his other hand a cup of coffee, which he handed Johanna as she came through the door. "*Ga maar zitten,*" he said. "*Rust maar een beetje.*" She sat down, and sipped the scorched brew. It tasted like ambrosia.

The thermometer plunged. They had no clothes for the frigid

Canadian winter. The children wore layers of whatever they owned to school, and Anneke came home in tears when her clothes were ridiculed. The house had little insulation, and there was only the oil burner in the kitchen for heat, so on the coldest days they huddled close around it. Because oil was expensive, they only fired the oil burner during the day. At night, they wore sweaters and wool socks over their pajamas, and slept under blankets and coats. A glass of water left sitting in a bedroom overnight froze solidly. The pump to the cistern froze. Outside, everything froze, and there was snow, and ice, and yet more snow.

Finally, Piet was able to work. He got a job in a local factory where other Dutch immigrants worked, MillCreek Furniture. Ralph Redgrave was an older man who took a real interest in his employees, would inquire after their families and provide them with a turkey at Christmas. He was a widower, and the factory was his life. Piet started with light work, assisting a cabinet maker. It was only half days, but Johanna could tell that he felt like a man again when he came home on Friday night, looked her in the eye, and handed her his pay packet.

Once on full wages, he told her, "You can stay home now, Johanna. You've done more than enough! Stay home," he chuckled, "and be a kept woman!"

Johanna quite happily quit her job with the Richardsons, but there were other families she cleaned for; some she had grown quite fond of. Her favourite was the Johnson family. She told Anneke about them. "Dr. Johnson," she said, with a hint of pride, works at the Queens. He isn't a regular doctor like you go to when you have a sore throat. He is a doctor of phsy, syco... *ja,* I don't know how to say it, but anyway he is a very important man. A professor!" she exclaimed. "And there are three nice children, including a baby. And Mrs. Johnson! You wouldn't believe Mrs. Johnson! She helps me with my English. She's taped names to all the furniture, and the vacuum and the mop and the pail, and she's even tied a name tag to the dust cloth. Does get in the way of cleaning a bit, but she certainly means well. Not all that practical, the Johnsons. They really need me there." So she kept working over Piet's objections, and Anneke thought it nice of her mother to want to keep working to look after those rather helpless Johnsons.

One day after school Anneke was going up to her bedroom when she heard her mother's voice in the living room. "He wants me to quit," said her mother. "No way!" Anneke's ears perked up and she sat down on the stairs. "*He* wants to be the breadwinner, that's fine. He can *pay* for the bread! That leaves me with *my* money in *my* pocket. If I want to buy a dress; I'll buy a dress. If I want to save up for a TV so I can watch 'I Love Lucy' here; I'll save up for a TV."

"But Piet never says no to you, does he?" countered a woman's voice, which Anneke recognized as belonging to Mrs. Kuipers.

"No, no, he doesn't. He's very good like that. But still, it isn't the same. Of course on his salary we can't afford luxuries anyway, but that's not the point. There's a wonderful feeling of…of freedom, and…satisfaction in deciding exactly how to spend the money that I've earned with my cleaning."

Anneke was not greatly surprised, when, sometime later, a delivery truck drove up to the front door of their dilapidated house, and dropped off a brand new television.

Finally Piet felt like his old self again! It was the first anniversary of the day they boarded the Groote Beer, and in thanks for all the help they'd been given in Canada, they invited the entire immigrant community, and they drank and they danced until the old house shook! Then it was time for Piet to perform – a song of several stanzas about the comedic twists and turns that life can take. After each verse, everyone was to sing the refrain.

Piet served as his own percussionist. He stood with his legs apart on two kitchen chairs. A metal soup ladle dangled between his lower legs, held by tea towels, twisted for tension and tied around his knees. A pot-lid was at his groin, held by a cord tied around his back. Squatting bent his knees, tightened the tea towels, and slammed the ladle into the lid with a loud, metallic crash – on the first word of each line of the refrain:

"Tsjing, boem, retteketet,
Alles is comedie,
Alles, alles, alles wel!

Alles is comediespel."

The immigrants roared with laughter at every crash. The longer Piet sang and squatted and crashed, the more the pot-lid shifted, so that towards the end of the song the immigrants were doubled over with laughter, anticipating that painful moment, when the ladle would miss the lid.

Johanna was walking to the post office when she saw Mrs. Bell, the neighbour who lived just in back of them and ran the telephone exchange.
"Mrs. Verbeek, I see you had a party."
"Yes, I hef party."
"Mrs. Verbeek, what sort of food you eat at your party?"
"Peenis."
"Oh no, Mrs. Verbeek! Not penis! That is what the men have! You mean peanuts!"

Blushing crimson, Johanna hustled home.

The Verbeeks attended MillCreek United Church where Piet would belt out hymns in his broken English until Johanna poked him in the ribs. Anneke was less enthusiastic about church.

On her way to the Sunday School, Anneke kicked at bits of gravel, scuffing her freshly polished shoes. She rather enjoyed scuffing them; polishing shoes was her bother's job. She pulled open the heavy oak door, and descended into the musty-dampness of the basement - a low-ceilinged space with peeling paint. Anneke slid into the row of wooden chairs and slouched down beside Gerda. "Bo-ring," she muttered.

"Boys and girls," said Mrs. Burt, "I have a surprise for you today. We have a special guest!" She beamed through her wire glasses at the children. "This is the Reverend Alphonsus Bentley. Say, 'Good morning Reverend Bentley!'" Anneke saw a tall, thin man, in a frayed black suit.

"Good morning Reverend Bentley," the children droned.

"The Reverend Bentley," Mrs. Burt said in a conspiratorial voice, "has come to us from *darkest Africa*. He is a *missionary!*"

He spoke of his life in the jungle, of grass huts and pygmies, of charging rhinos and poisonous snakes. He spoke of baptizing the newly converted in the Congo River. "You have to be careful," he said, "that there aren't alligators around." The children were wide-eyed. And he spoke of witch doctors. "Say you get a belly-ache when you're in the jungle," he said. "If you walk into a drug store, instead of medicine bottles you'll find dried bird heads and dead rats stuck on the ends of sticks. The medicine man will tell you to boil such stuff and drink the liquid." The children grimaced. He spoke of a mission hospital for lepers. "People whose fingers and toes," and he wiggled his fingers in the air, "can...plunk! Drop off," and he bent his fingers quickly.

"Ee-e-e-e-e!" said the children.

"Lepers are cast out of their villages. It is only at the mission where they can get help," and he went into his sermon intonation, "where sick people are being healed, the hopeless find hope, the unclean find friends. The Christ who cleansed lepers on the dusty roadside in Galilee long ago, is still doing work through his followers today. But," he continued, "it can be dangerous! Why, just this January five brave missionaries were killed, and not even in Africa, but in the jungles of *America!* This is how it happened." Anneke was on the edge of her seat. "On January third, Nat Saint and his missionary friends landed their small plane in Ecuador on a beautiful white sandy beach with palm trees. They were there to take the gospel to the Aucu Indians. Now that tribe has a history of being violent, but at first they seemed friendly enough, even shared some food, helped the missionaries build a shelter. But then on January eighth, there was an ambush. The Aucu Indians attacked those missionaries, ran them through with spears, right there on the beach, and that white sand ran red with blood. Those brave men died for Christ." He was quiet, then he pointed his finger at them and his voice thundered, "Christ calls *you,* to be a witness for him." Then, quietly, "let us pray."

Anneke walked into the kitchen where her parents were enjoying a cup of coffee. She waited until she had their full attention. "When I grow up I'm going to be a missionary," she announced, dramatically.

"You going to be a *what*?" said her mother.

"A missionary!"

"Ja, maar wat is dat?" Johanna asked. Anneke tried to explain.

"Aha!" said her father. *"Een zendeling!"* and with that, her parents gave each other the isn't-she-precocious look which sent Anneke stomping from the room.

She decided to prepare for her vocation by reading the Bible cover to cover. She put herself on a schedule. Every night, upon crawling into bed, she'd read one chapter. "In the beginning," she read, "God created the heavens and the earth." By the second night Anneke was feeling quite virtuous. The third night she read about Adam and Eve being cast from the Garden of Eden. They couldn't go back because the entrance was guarded by an angel with a flaming sword. Anneke lay there in the dark, and visualized what that would look like, an angel with a flaming sword. That night she dreamt that she was being chased by a man with a sword. She ran and tried to hide, and ran again, and still he was after her! She couldn't get away! She awoke with a jolt, wide-eyed, terrified. She sought solace in prayer. She prayed mightily. Finally she managed to fall back to sleep. The following night she read how Cain slew Abel, and that when God questioned him about it he lied, saying, "Am I my brother's keeper?" That night Anneke dreamt that their house was burning down and that, while *she* managed to escape, her brother burnt to death. She awoke in the dark, shaking. She prayed for what seemed like hours, before she managed to fall asleep again. Despite the nightmares, she was determined to continue on with her Bible reading. However, the night the cities of Sodom and Gomorrah were destroyed, Anneke's entire family perished. She awoke in absolute terror.

She tried to pray. She asked God why this was happening to her. "Why are you sending me these awful nightmares while I'm trying so hard to devote my life to you? Why?" and she sobbed into her pillow with great wrenching sobs. The next night, in utter exhaustion, Anneke dozed off before she could get her Bible open. She slept like a baby.

She decided not to be a missionary.

There was a knock on the door. Johanna opened it. Looked into cornflower-blue eyes. "Lies!" she screamed. "Is it really you?" and she stepped unto the verandah, grabbed her friend, hugged her, danced around in a circle. Then they stood, looking into each other's faces. "I am so happy to *see* you!" said Johanna.

"Me too! I've missed you so much!" An old truck was parked by the sidewalk, small faces inside pressed against windows, and Kees in his leather cap seated behind the wheel.

"Come in! Bring the kids in," Johanna urged. "Piet! Come here!" she yelled over her shoulder. "Anneke!" she stuck her head in the door, yelled up the stairs. "Come see who's here. Bring down some toys!" Happily, she chattered at her friends, "How's it going in Ravensburg? Have you got a house yet? Did your furniture get there? How's your friend Molly?"

"Kees! *Jongen!* Good to see you!" said Piet, and shook hands heartily. "Lies! Prettier than ever! How do you do it?" Finally they sat down to coffee. There was Freshee for the kids.

Lies sipped her hot brew, said, "Johanna, you know I am not one to complain, but when we arrived at that station near Ravensburg, that was the worst night of my life!"

"Ditto!" said Kees, nodding. Johanna's eyebrows knit, and Piet looking very serious, asked what happened. "We got off the train in the dead of night, and there was no-one there to meet us."

"Molly was supposed to be there. Right? Your old friend? The one who married that Canadian soldier. What was his name?"

"Stanley Whittaker. But they weren't there," said Lies. "Didn't show up. Didn't send anyone else either."

"What about other people at the station?" asked Johanna.

"Not a soul!" said Kees. "Abandoned. That little station is way out in the country.

"And there we were, with five little kids, and all our suitcases, and it was so cold!"

"Oh, oh, oh!" said Johanna, shaking her head in sympathy. What did you do?"

"We started walking," said Kees, "that's all we could do! Carrying the suitcases, and the baby. As we were tromping along that gravel road, the kids soon got tired. Short legs you know. Pretty soon the smallest one is crying, and I put him on my shoulders, and then the other ones start crying, and by now even Lies is crying, and she's usually a tough cookie, aren't you hon?"

"Strange land," said Lies, "dark, cold, and we're stumbling along on a dirt road and don't know where we're going. If we froze along the side of that road, no one would even miss us!"

"Not too likely in mid-May," said Kees, chuckling a little. But he got serious again, "Anyway, we're stumbling along, and we see a light at the end of a laneway. Finally there's a farm. We go up to the door, and this man answers, "Stan Whittaker," I say. "We go Stan Whittaker," and that guy, that nasty son-of-a-bitch, points down the road, all he does is point, although he must see the state my wife and kids are in, and then he shuts the door in our faces. After that we were more discouraged than ever, but we kept trudging along in the direction he'd pointed. Finally, we walk into a village, and I spot a gas-pump, find a garage. I couldn't believe my luck that there was still someone at work there, at that time of night, and when I ask him about Stan, he takes one look at us, starts his truck, and tells us to pile in. In no time he had us at Stan and Mollie's place."

"Dat was gelukkig," said Johanna, "that he would help you! So then everything was OK? Why weren't they at the station? Did they have the wrong day?"

"I knocked on the door," Kees continued, "and Stan answered, with a bunch of little kids clustered around his legs."

"I asked for my friend," said Lies. "'Molly?' I asked, *'Is Molly hier?'* but Stan just shook his head. *'Waar is Mollie?'* I asked. He shook his head again, and threw his arms up. He mumbled something, gestured for us to come in, to sit down. Gave us something to eat and drink, and you should have seen our little mites guzzle the milk he gave them. Then we sat there staring at each other. By now I was very worried something serious had happened to my friend. Finally, he seemed to get an idea. He went to the phone and dialed, and eventually handed the phone to me. 'Lies?' crackled a voice from the other end. 'Lies?' and I was never so happy to hear my name! You know where Mollie was?" Johanna shook her head. "In the hospital! She'd just given birth to another baby. It was so wonderful to talk to her! That's why they weren't at the station. She was laid up at the hospital, and he was tied up with the little kids. Anyway, I think they just forgot about us."

"Unbelievable!" said Piet, shaking his head. "Well, at least you came out of it OK."

"Have you got a house yet," asked Johanna, "or are you still living with their family?"

"We're still living there," said Lies. "It's a big old rattling farmhouse and we've had one wing of it, but it's been way too long!" She lowered her voice, "Stan's become quite a boozer. He's either at the Legion, or bringing the whiskey bottle home. Trauma from the war, Molly says, but I think it's a much bigger problem than that. It's been ten years since the war! But Molly won't face up to it. Won't do anything about it. We have to get to get out of there!"

"Ja," said Kees, "I could smell the booze on him the night we

arrived."

"How about your job?" asked Piet. "How's that working out? You'd think that farmer could have found you a house!"

"Another disaster!" said Kees, smiling wryly. "Because we were a little late getting to Canada, well, actually a year late," he said, raising his eyebrows at Lies, "that job was long gone. The only work I've had lately was at that garage I mentioned. Hires me for odd jobs. Nice guy, but certainly isn't rich. Sometimes he pays me in cash, sometimes barter. That's how I got the use of this truck. But Piet, how is it with you? Land a decent job?"

"*Was* very good."

Kees raised his eyebrows in a question.

Piet continued, "Got a job at MillCreek Furniture. Close by, and I've always liked working with wood. Nice old guy owned the place. Any problems with equipment, you could talk to him, and he'd soon get it looked after. Christmas party for the workers' kids complete with presents and him playing Santa! That's the kind of guy he was."

"*Ja,*" Johanna added, "and Piet liked that the furniture was really good quality."

"What happened?" asked Kees.

Piet shook his head sadly, "Old Mr. Redpath had a heart attack and his son Tom took over. Fancy-dressed fellow from Toronto. Drives a red Cadillac convertible. Spends most of his time on the golf course. No appreciation for workmanship, and none for the workers. We have some of the best cabinet makers at the factory, but now he's telling them to cut corners. The bottom line is all he's interested in."

"Too bad!"

"Sure is. Jake heard him on the phone calling us 'production units,'" Piet said grimly. "We're not even people to him."

"Few things *I'd* like to call him!" Kees said. " But first things first. Piet, I'm looking for farm work, right around here."

"Here? You want to move here?" Johanna's face lit up like a Christmas tree.

"Lots of farms around."

"So, you'll be looking for a house as well," Piet suggested.

"I'm looking to buy us a little fixer-upper house. Do you know of anything around here?"

"Buying?" asked Piet. "How can you afford to buy *any* kind of house? You weren't allowed to take more than a piddly bit of cash out of Nederland, and from the sounds of it you've earned next to nothing!"

Kees pinched the rim of his leather cap. He kept his fingers there suggestively as he said, "Good thing I was with the Dutch Resistance; you learn how to hide things, especially when you *really* don't want them found."

Every Wednesday evening the Dutch immigrants went to night

school. The teacher was Mrs. Wright, pleasant and very committed to helping. She asked the class, one by one, to write their names on the blackboard. "De whole name?" asked Piet.

"Yes. The whole name. That's right!"

Piet went up to the blackboard. Wrote, 'Petrus Johannes Antonius Verbeek,' filling the entire blackboard. "Is dat enuf ?" he asked, grinning, and sat back down amid laughter from the class and an appreciative smile from Mrs. Wright.

The cedar-shake roof of the farmhouse sagged for countless years under the weight of rain and snow, until finally it collapsed into the center, where invasive trees grew until they towered above the tilting walls. Around the house, where man once strained to clear the lumbered land and till the rocky soil, the cedar bush grew back. The creek, freed of its limestone dam, burbled its way through the bush. In the orchard, aged apple trees littered their branches on the ground. The wind busied itself at the barn, ripping off weathered boards in gap-toothed patterns. Other outbuildings, chicken coops and pigsties, had long since moldered into the ground. Only the densely concrete silo stood intact, erect, defying the elements.

It was Wednesday evening, and chattering children piled into the silo, some dragging cedar branches behind them. Henk took charge. Built a pile of dried leaves and twigs, and struck a match. Carefully he added small branches, and soon had a crackling campfire going in the centre of the silo.

They'd brought potatoes pilfered from their mothers' kitchens, and they tossed them in. Then they settled down to wait, cross-legged around the fire.

"Did you see it yet?" asked Henk. He'd grown taller by his second summer in Canada. His hair was Brylcreemed, slicked back on the sides, puffed up in front. "The new movie. The one they keep talking about on the radio."

"Yeah, I seen it," said Ricky Werkman.

"Went on Saturday," Henk said. "Paid my own way. My berry money." In response to a glance from Ricky, "From picking raspberries in Bloomfield."

"Our dad took us." Ricky's family had immigrated several years ago. They owned a car. "Stood in the lineup for an hour."

Henk continued," It was fa-a-an-tastic, especially when the Sioux attached the train."

"I liked where they were gonna burn the guy," said Ricky, and his younger brother chimed in, "Burn him alive. Scorch him. Burn him black!"

"Yeah the French guy. Wasn't that great? Did you girls see it?" Henk turned to Gerda and Nell.

Nell started to sing, "Around the world...." She chuckled, "No, I haven't seen it, but I sure like the theme song." Nell was twelve. Listened to the radio. Had a ponytail. Was developing a bust. Anneke was somewhat in awe of her.

But Nell hadn't seen the movie and she had, "That guy they were gonna burn? Same guy saved the train, right? Jeepers that guy was brave! Crawled right under that speeding train!"

"Speaking of burning," said Nell, "wonder if these potatoes are done." They jumped up to look for sticks. Anneke found one, pulled her pocket-knife from her shorts and stood sharpening it. The fire highlighted her copper-penny hair.

They poked around in the hot ashes for their potatoes. As Anneke pierced one and pulled it from the embers it sizzled, and she caught the tantalizing aroma. She sat down on the ground and carved through the black crust until she reached the soft interior. Then she used her knife-blade to scoop up the steaming white flesh, and she savoured it, bit by delectable bit. She ate a second one down to its last delicious morsel. "Sure had a heck of a time getting these out of the house," she said. "I was all alone in the kitchen when I put them in my pockets. I could hear 'I Love Lucy' playing in the living room, so I knew Mother wouldn't notice me walking through, but just as I got to the door, she looked up. I dashed outside. 'What do you have in your pockets?" she yelled. I ran on down the road. *'Anneke!'* She was so mad... she left 'I Love Lucy' to come outside and holler at me!"

"How about you, Henk?" Nell asked. "Did you get in trouble too?"

"Nah," Henk replied nonchalantly. "She just looked at my bulging shorts and smiled." Anneke glowered. Then she picked up some charcoal. Drew designs on her face. Said, "I'm a Sioux warrior." Across from her, through the smoke she saw her cousin, she of the peaches-and-cream complexion and long blond braids. "Hey Gerda, you'd make a pretty good Sioux with them there braids if you weren't so blond. Want me to charcoal your braids for you?"

"What!" Gerda sputtered. "My mother would kill me if I came home with my hair dirty. Do you know how long it takes to wash? The cost of the shampoo? And then it has to dry, and then she has to braid it again … and…"

"'Does she… or doesn't she?'" quoted Nell. "'Only her hairdresser knows for sure.'"

Henk stood up, took off his shirt and said, "I'll show you how to be a warrior!" and he crisscrossed his chest with charcoal. Clothes were soon tossed in a heap as they clamored to join in, although Gerda kept any decorating well away from her golden hair.

They danced around the campfire with abandon. Sioux warriors they were, one and all! Hands patting mouths, they did the, 'Woo-woo-woo-woo-woo,' until the sound bounced and echoed on the silo walls, 'woo-woo-woo!' reverberating up through the top into the dusky sky!

It was dusk when they finally gathered up their clothes and left the silo. There'd be trouble if they weren't home before their parents. They passed the barn, and the wind blew an eerie whistle through the gaps. They crossed the ancient orchard where trees thrust broken black arms into the sky. Anneke shivered. Then she looked toward the horizon, and above the black earth the sky was tinted tangerine, then lemon yellow, lime, cerulean, and, when Anneke tilted her head way back, a deep ultramarine. Awestruck, she stood rooted. Finally, she noticed that the others had moved on. She ran to catch up; heard them laughing before she saw them. There they were, standing knee-deep in the creek, splashing each other, scooping up water and scrubbing away at charcoal. Suddenly, there was the sound of a slap. *"Creep!"* Nell screamed. *"Keep your hands off me you lousy creep!"*

Henk's voice mumbled, "I was… I was just helping you wash…"

"Bullshit!" and Nell hit him again. Anneke watched wide-eyed as Henk clambered the bank, grabbed his clothes, and disappeared into the bush.

And Anneke sat on the grassy bank, and smiled.

"Johanna, it's so exciting *meid!* How did it happen? Tell me all about it." Lies was at Johanna's house drinking coffee, had just heard the news, and shoved her chair a bit closer to her friend.

Johanna was all smiles. "*Ja*, he talked to Piet last night. Asked his permission. At first Piet said, 'I don't know. I'm going to have to think about that," and Chris looked dumbfounded, but then Piet laughed, and said, "Welcome to the family!"

"Ha, ha! Oh, but how wonderful!" Lies drank her coffee, helped herself to a *speculaaskoekje* from Johanna's cookie tin.

"So Liesje, we are having a wedding! First they save their money for their household." She added proudly, "then there will be *big* wedding!"

"They will have a wonderful marriage," Lies predicted.

"Ja," said Johanna. "I am very happy for Mieke.

"So when is it going to happen? Did they set a date? Where will they be living? Are you going to take her dress-shopping? Will there be relatives from Holland coming over? What about a cake? Who is baking that? And flowers. You have to think about flowers…"

"Have another *speculaaskoekje,* Lies!"

On the second anniversary of the day the Verbeeks boarded the Groote Beer, Mieke and Chris got married. They didn't want to get married on just any day; the date had to be special. Mieke looked petite and lovely in a white lace dress with huge puffy skirt over layers and layers of crinoline. Chris towered over his bride, in new navy suit with boutonniere in buttonhole, thick thatch of hair slicked down for the occasion. The proud parents of the happy couple posed with them for photos, everyone smartly dressed and the women in hats with little veils. A hand-lettered sign on the honeymoon car, read:

'WATCH MILL CREEK GROW!'

"Hey Rosemary," Anneke called out, "what's the matter with your dog?" Anneke was standing on the leaf-strewn lawn of her new house. She knew Rosemary from school, and had noticed her walking by in her green pleated skirt and mohair sweater set, hair pinned back with barrettes.

Rosemary trailed a red leash, on the end of which limped on obese cocker spaniel.

"Oh, hi Annie! This here's Taffy. He's got a hip problem called dis... dis... something. Anyway, I gotta walk 'im so he don't stiffen up." Jutting her chin at the house, "You livin' here now?"

"Yup," said Anneke, petting the dog.

"You like it?"

"Nope.

"How come?"

"Come here. I'll show you."

"What about Taffy?"

"Tie him up over there." Anneke indicated a ragged juniper bush. "My dog's in the house. Old Yeller. Like the dog in the movie," she said in response to a questioning glance from Rosemary. She took Rosemary into her bedroom. "Show you why I don't like this place. See that?" and she pointed to the corner, where a ladder was fastened to the wall. Above the ladder was a trap door. Rosemary looked on uncomprehendingly. "My *creepy* brother," spat Anneke, "sleeps in the attic, 'cause this dumb house only has two bedrooms. And whether he *comes* or whether he *goes*," she said in a sing-song, "it's always right through *my* bedroom. Never knocks, just goes *right through my room!*" Rosemary frowned. Sat down on the bed.

"Must be awful to have no privacy," she commiserated. "I've always wanted a brother, or even a sister, 'cause I don't like being alone much, but... well... maybe I'm lucky. Anyway," she said, watching Anneke from the corner of her eye, "I won't be getting any brothers or sisters, not unless my parents get their *sexual* problems straightened out."

"Pardon?" said Anneke, and plunked herself down beside Rosemary. "S*exual* problems?" Anneke knew *her* parents had problems, especially when they first came to Canada, and then lately around buying this house. She'd heard them argue. *"Vrouwke,* this is the chance we've been waiting for. *Five thousand dollars* for a house! We've got the down payment saved up, and the monthly payments aren't much more than we're paying now. We can *afford* this house."

"Afford to buy it. *Ja,* I know that. *That* isn't the problem. The real estate woman, what was it she called the house?" and Johanna thought for a moment. "'Fixer-upper,' is what she said. And *that's* the problem! Can we afford to *fix* it."

"You *always* worry too much. You know how handy I am. I can do a lot, and that saves money. Anyway, the only thing that needs to be done before winter is to shingle the roof. We know it leaks, so, we do something about that. Already Jake and Theo and Kees and of course Chris, have *all* said they'll help. We'll pick a nice sunny weekend, I'll get some beer in... for after," he hastened to add, "Don't want those guys falling off the roof!" and he chuckled.

"*Ja, ja,* Piet. You always make it sound so easy. Coming to Canada was easy too, heh?" Piet looked away. "Now then, you've got the *roof* figured out. But what about everything else? What about that floor? And didn't you say the windows and the electric ..."

"It will happen, it will happen! Everything will be fine and dandy. Just takes a little time. But we will *own* it Johanna. We can do what we want *in our own house!*" Anneke thought with some chagrin that her mother hadn't even brought up the lack of bedrooms. Obviously *Anneke's* issues didn't count for much!

"Sexual problems," said Rosemary, and she furrowed her brow. "Well, they fight all the time. I'll be sitting at the kitchen table doing my homework, and through the open door I can see my mother, at her dressing table, painting her fingernails. Bright red she paints 'em. Then I see my father go into the bedroom and shut the door. I hear them talking, and I think, 'Good! They're talking quietly,' and I work on my arithmetic problems. Suddenly he yells, 'You bitch! You never want it!' I hear my mother say, in a voice like she's gritting her teeth, 'Where were you last night?' and my father, he just sneers, 'If you weren't such a cold fish I'd stay at home!' Then he slams out of the house, and she goes back to painting her fingernails."

"But what does it mean?" Anneke asked, wide-eyed.

"Don't know exactly, but I know it's about sex, because I hear my father yell, 'Sex! Sex! You don't know the meaning of the word!' Plus they keep buying more and more books about sex. They have a whole bunch."

"Wow! Can you bring them over?"

"I'm not s'posed to touch them." Anneke's face fell. Rosemary quickly added, "but I'll try and sneak one over next time they're away. Maybe Saturday. I think they're gonna see the marriage counselor again. They go right after lunch."

"Oh my goodness!" exclaimed Gerda, sitting on Anneke's bed, staring at the picture in Rosemary's book, "Is that, is that..."

"Penis," read Rosemary, "the male sexual organ which ..."

"Organ!" said Anneke, "Organ! Does it make music?" and they burst into gales of laughter. "Is it found in a church?" and they laughed louder. "Do you play it with your fingers?" and they shrieked with disgust.

"Penis," said Rosemary, resuming her reading, "the male sexual organ which carries sperm..."

"Perm!" said Anneke. "Perm! Is that where they get the stuff to perm hair with?"

"Eeeeeee!" they shrieked.

"What's going on in here?" Henk stepped into the room, tall, Brylcreemed, throwing his weight around. Anneke slid the book under the covers.

"Get outta my bedroom, creep!

"Bet yer doing something yer not supposed to!" he taunted. "Maybe Mother would like to know what you're up to."

"Maybe Mother would like to know," Anneke retorted, "but Mother *is* not home. So you can tell Mother all you want." Henk merely smirked, strolled through Anneke's bedroom, and ascended the ladder. He threw the girls one last superior look before he vanished into the attic.

Anneke hissed, "He didn't close the trap door!" The girls stared up in silence. Suddenly Anneke jumped up, rummaged around under the bed and retrieved a flashlight. They dove under the covers, and soon Rosemary's muffled voice carried on, "The sex act involves placing the penis...." followed by shrieks of laughter.

At sunrise on a Saturday in October, all the Dutch immigrant men gathered at Piet and Johanna's new house, hammers-at-the-ready in toolbelts. "I want to thank you boys for your help," said Piet, addressing the half-dozen men, "and to remind you that we only have one day to do this, because *mijn vrouwke*," and he grinned at Johanna, "will not be happy if she gets rained on tonight." Johanna glared back. The men climbed up the ladders, and within minutes old shingles were sailing down. For a while, all that was heard was the protesting squeal of nails being pried from the roof.

"Piet, th- th- ere's trouble here *jongen*," called Klaas. Piet went over the peak of the roof to the back where Klaas was working.

"What's the problem?"

"L-L-Look at th-th-these boards." The exposed roof boards were green with mould, black with rot, and chunks of rotted board had actually pulled away with the shingles. Piet's heart sank! It flashed through his mind that perhaps Johanna was right about this house. There was no way to repair it without a huge expense of time and cash. He had neither. As he stood, staring bleakly, the men gathered round spoke up.

"I've got a pile of wood behind my house from an old barn I pulled down. Boards should be just about the right size. Who's brought a truck?"

"You got two-by-fours in that wood-pile of yours? I can swing by the saw-mill. Just got my car, but they can stick out the back. Anneke, you got a red scarf?"

"I'll get the nails."

When the shingles were completely stripped, the black blight of wood rot was fully exposed. Johanna stood on the front lawn, watching, wringing her hands. The men proceeded to cut out rotten sections of roof board, and even rip off entire lengths. Johanna went inside to make coffee, and when she came back out discovered to her horror that she could now look straight through the roof at the blue sky. Lies arrived, took one look at the distraught woman, and led her back inside. *"Blijf maar even binnen zitten, Johanna,"* she comforted her. *"Drink een lekker kop koffie, en laat die mannen maar werken. Ze halen her wel voor elkaar!"* The men splinted rotted trusses with new two-by-fours, drilling and bolting the wood. With the sun high in the sky, they began to measure, saw, and hammer new roof boards in place. Piet announced a lunch break, and Johanna and Lies brought out stacks of sandwiches and coffee. By mid-afternoon the carpentry was finally completed, and the men started shingling. The industrious sound of many hammers ringing out simultaneously, finally inspired some hope in Johanna's heart. That evening, as a chill October wind blew rustling leaves over the roofline, Henk was stationed on a ladder aiming a flashlight at the last few shingles being hammered into place.

Rosemary let Anneke borrow the book. Anneke kept it hidden under the mattress; read it under the covers. She hurried through the introductory chapters which contained sexual information of a general nature. One day, when Anneke had the house all to herself, with Henk at Scouts and her parents gone shopping, she sat down on the wooden chair in her bedroom and opened the book. The chapters which followed the introduction, were about various types of sexual aberration and dysfunction. One chapter dealt with the size of sexual organs, and Anneke learned that a big problem can occur if a woman has a vagina which is too small to permit a penis to enter. She wondered if perhaps that was the problem with Rosemary's parents. Then she started to wonder about herself. "What if mine is too small?" she worried. "What if there's something wrong with me?" The book said that if one could insert two fingers, there was enough room for a penis. Anneke stood up, attempted to push in two fingers, but it was very difficult, and she'd about decided that she must be one of those abnormal women, when suddenly, she felt a stinging pain. When she removed her fingers she found them covered in blood. Terrified she hid the book and dove under the covers.

She told no one.

Piet painted the newly-shingled house a sparkling white, with red trim around the door and windows, and inside, Johanna hung her starched lace curtains. After church one bright day in November, the family posed in their Sunday best in front of their new house. The photos labeled, *"Ons Eigen Huis,"* were airmailed to all their friends and relatives in Holland, so that they could see what a success Piet and Johanna had made of their life in Canada.

"I'm not doing it. It's not fair!"

"You *have* to do it," Piet said firmly. "You know very well what our situation is. We don't have income from your sister anymore, and your mother is good enough to take on extra cleaning jobs. *You*r job is to do the housework here."

Sullenly, "What about Henk?"

Johanna interjected, "Henk is a boy. He has his own jobs. He takes out the garbage, mows the lawn, shovels the snow."

"Yeah? And how much work does he *do?* What's it take, *sixty seconds*, to put the garbage out? And - then - there's - me. Every day after school I'm supposed to..." she went into a sing-song, "do the dishes and make the beds and do the vacuuming and do the dusting and peel the potatoes and..."

"Be quiet!" said Piet sternly. "It's bad enough that your mother is working so hard and coming home dog-tired without having to listen to your surliness and your complaints." With his eyes narrowed, he looked Anneke full in the face and barked, "You will *do* as you are *told!*" Anneke stomped out of the room.

Later that day, Rosemary came over. They went in to Anneke's bedroom. They sat down on Anneke's bed, and Rosemary arranged her skirt so the pleats fell evenly around her knees. "It's just so bloody unfair," Anneke fumed. "Just because I'm a girl they expect me to do housework. I *hate* housework! And I didn't *ask* to be born a girl! And I sure as heck didn't ask for that...that *brother!*" Rosemary looked puzzled. "You don't know how lucky you are," Anneke continued. "Being an only child. No one to pester you." As if on cue, Henk came into the room, smirked at Anneke, and when she looked away glowering, winked at Rosemary, who beamed back. After the trap door thumped down, Anneke continued, "You wouldn't believe what he does to me. He drops his dirty plate in the sink right after I've finished washing the dishes." Rosemary seemed unimpressed. "Yesterday, when I went in to make his bed, I practically tripped over his dirty underpants, right there in the middle of his floor!"

"Oooooow!" went Rosemary.

"Yeah! Disgusting! *That's* what I have to put up with! And he does it *deliberately.* "Well," Rosemary said, curiously, "did you say anything to him about it?"

"You bet I did! Got in a great big fight. Then I took off, went around the back of the house, sat there petting my rabbits. That's where my mother found me when she came home. Did I ever get in trouble, 'cause I didn't have the potatoes peeled or nothing. First my mother yelled at me. Then when my father came home he *really* yelled at me. *I* got in trouble and it was all because of that *creep!*" Through gnashing teeth, "And he just loves it when I get in trouble. You are *soooo* lucky!"

"Rabbits?" said Rosemary. "You have rabbits?"

"When Samuel de Champlain and his Algonquin and Huron allies met a large force of Iroquois on the lake," Mrs. Hall wrote, "both parties landed and threw up barricades of trees. The following day they engaged in battle, and Champlain killed two Iroquois with his harquebus..." Anneke tried to concentrate on the words on the blackboard. It was critical to stay caught up copying the note into one's scribbler, because once Mrs. Hall had filled all three blackboards, she would simply erase the first, and carry right on writing. Mrs. Hall, a large woman in a print house dress, brooked no nonsense. But despite her best efforts, Anneke found herself distracted. Her eyes strayed from the words on the blackboard to Mrs. Hall herself, quite specifically to Mrs. Hall's upper arm, or rather the fleshy roll which hung suspended beneath Mrs. Hall's upper arm, and which jiggled, back and forth, back and forth, with each word the teacher wrote.

"Mesmerizing," Anneke said to herself, having only recently learned the word and keen to use it. "Absolutely bloody mesmerizing."

"Annie!" rang out the teacher's voice. "Is there a problem?" Mrs.

Hall was legendary, not only for her self-propelled appendages, but for the eyes in the back of her head.

"N..n..no Mrs. Hall," stammered Anneke. "Uhhhm, there is a word I don't know," and she proceeded to spell, "h, a, r, q..."

"If you don't understand something Annie," said Mrs. Hall, "you must put your hand up. Now, who can tell me what 'harquebus' means?"

When the afternoon bell rang, scribblers were hastily stuffed into desks, and the children rushed out into the warm September sunshine. Only Anneke dawdled. Screwing up her courage, she approached the teacher's desk. "Mrs. Hall, can I talk to you?"

"That's, *may I,* Annie. *May I* talk to you."

"Mrs. Hall, *may I* talk to you?"

"Certainly."

"Last year Mrs. Funston let me do grades three and four in one year to try to get caught up to other kids my age. And, and I was hoping that…" Mrs. Hall frowned. Anneke tried again, "When my family came to Canada I got put way back with the little kids. All the way back from grade four to grade two. Just because I didn't speak English," she added with a rankling sense of injustice, "and I've been trying ever since to get caught up." Mrs. Hall put up her hand to cover a hint of a smile. "But," and Anneke took a deep breath and rushed, "if I could do grade five and six in one year, then I would be in the right grade again." Mrs. Hall looked at Anneke closely. Noted the outgrown pants, the sweater knit from odd remnants of wool, the bright, inquisitive eyes.

"The work is more difficult Annie, in grades five and six. Now," she said thoughtfully," I'm sure the arithmetic wouldn't be a problem for you, but the spelling and the grammar would! You would need a lot of extra help, and, I would be happy to provide that, but… it would mean staying in at recess, at noon-hour, after school…"

"Yes, Mrs. Hall. I would do that, Mrs. Hall," said Anneke, standing up very straight.

"There's also a large body of work in terms of Canadian history and geography. You'd have to copy a lot of notes. I just don't know…." She observed Anneke from beneath lowered lids. Anneke's eyes darted around. She bit her lip.

"I'll copy notes faster," she said quietly, looking down at the floor.

"Hmmm," said Mrs. Hall. She rested her chin on her fist, and looked down at Anneke. "Hmmm. Let me think….well….perhaps we'll give it a trial period."

"Yes Mrs. Hall! Thank you Mrs. Hall!" and Anneke skipped all the way home.

Throughout the rest of the school year, Anneke continued to put forth tremendous effort, completing the work for both grades five and six, and catching up to her age group. When she received her report card that June, she was thrilled to have graduated to grade seven.

Anneke and Rosemary took the basket of potato peelings around to the back of the house. "Can I feed them?"

"Sure. Here you go. Make sure they all get some."

"Oh! Look at those little wiggly noses. They are so *cute*! Can I hold one?"

"Want one? I'll sell you one for fifty cents. Gotta sell them anyway. It's getting more and more crowded in that cage with all those babies growing bigger and hopping around. Besides, I want to breed Daisy again."

"How do you do that?"

"I just put Sam in her cage; he hops on her back, pokes her with his dinky, and she's pregnant. In one month she has babies." Rosemary's eyes opened wide. Anneke continued, "Sam is actually Daisy's brother, so it *is* kind of disgusting what they do."

"Her brother?"

"Yeah. They were just young when I got them a year ago. I kept them together in this one cage my dad helped me build. Then one day when I came home from school I noticed a nest in the corner of the cage, and in it were tiny, pink, hairless bunnies. I was *so* surprised! I told my dad what had happened, and he said, 'Get Sam out of there!'" Anneke whispered to Rosemary, "Because sometimes the fathers will eat the babies."

Rosemary made a face like she was going to be sick, "Cannibals? Rabbits are cannibals?"

"*Do* you want a bunny?"

"Oh, I don't know. Don't think my mother will let me. Says rabbits stink."

"You just gotta keep their cages clean. Every Saturday I clean 'em. There was this one time, when Daisy's first babies were just a month old - I was cleaning her cage, and on my shovel in between the poop and the straw, were bits of pink. I didn't know what they were so I showed my dad, and he said, *'Potverdomme!'* Then he said to my mother, 'How the hell could she have been pregnant again? We took the male out of her cage the same day her first litter was born. Good God, I don't believe it!' That's when I realized that the pink scraps on my shovel were actually newborn babies, stomped and flattened by their big brothers and sisters into little pink pancakes."

"No!" said Rosemary, aghast. "Squashed babies?"

"Yeah. You know what, Rosemary? I think maybe I'm gonna be a veterinarian."

"I'm so excited! So excited!"

"What?" said Lies, smiling at her friend. "What's going on?" and she cleared a stack of diapers off a chair so Johanna could sit down.

"Mieke is going to have a baby."

"No! Really? You're going to be a grandmother? And here I'm still up to my elbows in babies myself. And you already a grandma. But I'm so happy for…"

"*Ja,*" Johanna interrupted. "She just told me about it. The baby will be born in the spring. Isn't it wonderful? Piet will be so proud!"

"Nice for that young couple," said Lies. A loud wailing erupted in the bedroom, and she jumped up, yelled over her shoulder as she left the room, "Very nice for them."

"Mr. Gordon, could I please do some extra work?" It was early in her grade seven year, and Anneke was already bored.

"Extra work? We are covering *all* the mandatory curriculum, *and* meeting the requirements of the Ministry of Education. Are *you* suggesting that's not sufficient?"

Anneke looked down at the floor, mumbled, "No sir, it's just that… well… I did grades three and four in one year, and, and then last year I did five and six, and I… I wondered… if… I… could… maybe…" and she screwed up her courage and looked up at him, "do seven and eight this year."

He glared down, "Are you not caught up to grade level now?"

"Yes, Mr. Gordon."

"Then there's absolutely no reason to prepare extra work for you. You're in the grade you're supposed to be in and you're doing the work you're supposed to be doing, and that's an end to it. I don't want to hear any more of this nonsense." Mr. Gordon was both the teacher for the senior grades, and he was the school principal. Anneke had no recourse. She had to resign herself to spending an entire year in grade seven, and *another* entire to year in grade eight.

"Are you getting dressed up this year?" asked Gerda.

"Nope." said Anneke. "Too old. Better things to do."

"Yeah me too. Like what?"

"We did treats last year – this year, we'll do tricks!"

Halloween Eve they went out at dusk. They had scouted earlier in the day to identify their targets. Their first was basically falling down already and it took little effort. As soon as it started to topple they flew out of there, then heard the satisfying crash behind them. The next one took more effort, but they put their shoulders to the task, and managed to shift and topple it, but as it crashed, lights flew on in the house and a man came running into the back yard cursing at the top of his lungs! They ran almost to the other end of the village. "I think we should go home now," said Gerda.

"One more," said Anneke. "We'll pick one that's not so close to the house." They went to the next one, set well back at the end of a long back yard, and started to push. They put their backs into it, and it went partly over, required one extra push.

"Awwww!" screamed Gerda, as a horrible stench rose into the air. "Help me!" Anneke grabbed her cousin's hands and pulled mightily to free her of the reeking mass. By now lights had flashed on in the house, and they ran like the devil was after them... or perhaps to outrun the stench.

Back at Anneke's house, Gerda stripped off socks and shoes in the backyard as her cousin brought buckets of water so she could wash the shit from her legs and feet. Johanna came out to see the commotion, stood shaking her head while holding her nose. Gerda said in a frightened voice, "They will kill me. Aunt Johanna, if I go home like this!"

"I'm glad that Anneke could babysit for us tonight, so we could come to your house for a change," said Lies.

"Wouldn't believe what Anneke and Gerda got up to for Halloween," Johanna said. "Went out pushing over outhouses! Unbelievable!" Her voice dropped, "And you know how fussy Femke and Theo are! The last one they pushed over, Gerda right fell in. Shit up to her knees! What a stink!" They roared with laughter. "Came to our house to clean up. I felt sorry for her. Knew she'd be in even deeper shit if she went home like that! Lent her a pair of Anneke's socks and shoes."

Lies smiled, "You're lucky, Johanna, that you've got indoor plumbing now."

"Yup," grinned Kees. "That could have been *your* shitter!"

Johanna ignored the comment. "I found out that, of course, it had all been Anneke's idea! Seriously, they could have been arrested for what they did! You know, destroying property! The things that girl comes up with! Oh, oh, oh! I don't know what I'm going to do with her!"

"Of course, *you* were the perfect child!" mocked Piet. "Absolutely perfect! No way you'd be messing around with an outhouse!"

"Huh?" Liesje's eyebrows shot up. "What was that?"

Johanna was pouring coffee. Stopped what she was doing. Started to laugh. "Oh, I was told to look after my little sister Femke and…" She started again. "Back in those days *we* sure didn't have plumbing, and our house itself was really just one room, with *bedsteeen* built into the walls. My parents' *bedstee* had a shelf just inside theirs over the doors for the piss pot. A new baby would sleep between them and when it got older would go in a cradle which would go on the shelf beside the piss pot. There were a couple of pegs inside each *bedstee* for our clothes – well, in those days you didn't have much anyway – one dress for during the week, and another for Sundays. One Sunday, we were just home from church, still wearing our Sunday dresses, and my mother was trying to get dinner cooked, but my little sister Femke kept getting under her feet. My mother snapped at me, *"Doe iets met dat kind!"* so I took Femke to the outhouse to play. I told her this was our playhouse; that we would decorate it. I had some pictures I'd cut from an old newspaper, and we pinned them on the walls with thumbtacks. Femke crawled up on the seat to pin a picture up really high, and was standing on the lid stretched up her tippy-toes, when suddenly, the lid tilted! Into the hole tumbled Femke, screaming at the top of her lungs! She screeched so loud that my mother came tearing out of the house, grabbed Femke by the hair and lifted her out of the shit! She dragged her to the canal and swished her back and forth, back and forth. Femke squealed like a stuck pig! When my father came home, he had to dig her yellow *klompjes* out of the reeking mess. Was he ever mad! My mother, she did her best to clean Femke's Sunday dress, but the next time we went to church, I made sure I didn't sit near that little stinker!"

The December report cards were handed out. Anneke looked at hers, and her eyes went wide! Wow! She danced home through the drifting snow. When she reached her driveway, she saw her mother's friend leaving the house. Lies was bent over a baby carriage full of little kids, pulling hats down over ears.

"Hello, Mrs. Kuipers!" Anneke sang out.

Lies looked up, saw Anneke's glowing face. "What are you looking so happy about? Had a good day at school?"

"Great day!" exclaimed Anneke. "Got my report card!"

"Oh *ja!* Let's have a look!" said Lies, and Anneke opened her report card, holding her mittened hand up to protect it from the snow flakes. The little kids in the carriage had their mouths open to catch the flakes of snow.

"Fantastisch!" said Mrs. Kuipers. "All A's! I've never seen such a good report! Come here, you," and she gave Anneke a big hug. With a grin and a wave, she was out the driveway, pushing her carriage through the falling snow.

Anneke went inside. "Mo-om!" she yelled, but there was no immediate answer. She stepped into the kitchen, heard the television on in the living room, went towards the sound. "Mom, take a look…"

"Shhhh!" said Johanna, "I'm watching this."

"I've got…"

"Not now, Anneke!" said Johanna, her eyes glued to the screen. Scowling, Anneke walked back into the kitchen. The back door banged, and Henk came in.

"Don't even bother trying to show her your report card," said Anneke, "she's not interested. She's watching some stupid TV show."

"Oh yeah?" said Henk, "watch this. "Hey, Ma! Wanna see my report card?"

"Report card?" said Johanna. *"Ja,* come here, Henkie. Let me see." Henk handed it to his mother, cozied up on the couch beside her. "Very *good*, Henkie!" Anneke watched with narrowed eyes, then wordlessly handed over her report.

"Ja, said Johanna, "very good, Anneke. She gave Anneke's report card back, and as Anneke stood there holding it, Johanna turned back to the son on the couch beside her. "An A in arithmetic, that's very good Henk! Now, you were talking about a job drawing plans for houses, so *ja*, you have to be able to measure good don't you?"

"That's right, and figure out angles, and even the strength of materials, although maybe that's more for an engineer."

"Engineer!" said Johanna. "Well, that would be something!"

"I want to be a veterinarian," Anneke said.

Johanna looked up. *"Wat is dat?"*

"Animal doctor."

"You need education for that?"

"University."

"You know we have no money!"

"What about Henk's education? If he was gonna be an engineer he'd need university. How come you don't say no to Henk?"

"Henk is a boy. He will have to support a family and needs his education to get a good job. You are a girl. You will get married and your husband will support you. That's the way it is." Johanna looked at her glowering daughter, softened her voice, tried to clarify, "Educating a girl is a waste of money. And if we had lots to throw around, that would be one thing, you could do what you wanted. *But we just don't have it.*"

"But I got all A's!" exclaimed Anneke, near tears. "My report card is better!"

"Anneke, stop it!" said Johanna.

"Look!" Anneke shouted, snatching Henk's report card from the coffee table. "Mine is better!"

Johanna snapped, "That's enough! Put that down! Henk's report card might not be all A's, but he is the one who needs the education!"

Her face hot with unshed tears, Anneke bolted.

As she plodded along lock-step with the rest of the students, Anneke looked for other ways to amuse herself. She started doodling in class. Mr.

Gordon had his favourite students, of whom Anneke was definitely not one. His pets were Amy and Susan, pretty, placid girls in pastel sweaters. They were allowed to do all manner of interesting tasks for him, stuffing envelopes, organizing books, even washing classroom windows. One day Anneke drew Amy and Susan outside on a ladder washing the school windows, with Mr. Gordon holding the ladder and looking up their skirts. "Psssst! Let me see," whispered Rosemary from the next aisle. Anneke glanced up. The teacher sat at his desk, nose buried in a book. Anneke passed Rosemary the drawing. Rosemary looked, clapped her hand over her mouth and sat with shoulders shaking. Then she reached over to hand it back, but just as Anneke put out her hand, the paper was snatched in mid-air by one of the boys. The boy broke into a huge grin, and as Anneke watched in dismay, he passed the drawing to the boy behind him. Anneke kept her eyes on her desktop, listening to the muffled snorts and guffaws as her drawing passed up and down the classroom aisles. Anneke held her breath. Suddenly, raucous laughter rang out from one of the big boys at the back. The teacher's head snapped up, and Anneke's heart sank.

"What is going on?" Mr. Gordon demanded, looking around, his glasses slipping down his nose. "Jim, bring that up here! *Now!*" Jim lumbered to the front, grinning broadly. Mr. Gordon examined the drawing. His eyes narrowed. He looked around for the culprit. Anneke sank down low in her seat. He barked, "Annie, stand up!" With all eyes upon her, Anneke got up, red-faced, to stand beside her desk. "So you're the clever artist who drew this," he sneered. "That's a week's detentions for you. Not feeling so clever now, are you?" He crumpled the drawing into a ball and contemptuously tossed it into the wastebasket. Later, Rosemary asked to sharpen her pencil. The pencil sharpener was located directly over the wastebasket. Rosemary 'accidentally' dropped her pencil, fished it out, and managed to retrieve Anneke's crumpled drawing.

Piet raised the roof once more. With the help of friends and relatives, he added a dormer along the entire front of his house, and this allowed for an extra bedroom upstairs. Anneke was thrilled! She could actually close the door of her new bedroom and have privacy from her annoying brother. Things were looking up on the home-front!

And soon things got even better! "Oh he's beautiful! Never saw such a beautiful baby!" gushed Johanna. It was a warm spring day, and the baby was on a blanket placed on their lawn under a flowering tree. Anneke was taking photos. She'd received a Brownie camera for Christmas.

"Now one where Mieke holds him up close to the flowers," Piet suggested. "That will make a nice picture."

"Now one with his oma and opa." They were dressed in their Sunday best for the occasion. Looked proud as punch as they stood close together cradling their grandchild.

"One with the four of us and the baby. Mieke, you and Chris in the middle. OK, everybody look at Anneke!"

Proudly Piet sent photos to the family in Holland. Wrote on the back of one, 'Our first grandchild. Isn't he a sturdy lad?' on a second, 'Lovely isn't it with those flowers?' and on another, 'Our Anneke took these photos.'

Chapter Three – That Perfect Lipstick

"*What* are you *wearing?*" Johanna scolded, as Anneke stood at the kitchen counter munching a piece of buttered toast. Anneke kept her back turned to the natter which was her mother's voice. She was focused on the day ahead, a most *exciting* day, her *first* day of high school. Proudly, she wore the clothing she'd bought herself with money from her summer job. Johanna glared at her daughter, shook her head. Hard to believe now, that she'd actually *recommended* the girl for that job.

"We're looking for live-in child-care," Mrs. Johnson had told Johanna who was on her knees scrubbing the bathroom floor with steel wool to remove built-up wax, "five days a week for July and August, while the new house gets completed." Johanna wiped her wrist over her forehead and looked up questioningly. "To enable *me* to keep on top of things while the workmen are…" Mrs. Johnson ticked off on her fingers, "completing the bathrooms, putting down tile, hanging drapes, painting, installing the broadloom…. Of course Carl *could* help out – he doesn't teach in summer – but you know men! He wouldn't know peach from pink. Shag from sheepskin!" Johanna smiled. She enjoyed being taken into Mrs. Johnson's confidence. "And after we move, in mid-summer, there'll still be the exterior painting, and paving, and landscaping and all those other loose ends to tie up."

Johanna saw an opportunity, "If you don't hef somebody, my Anneke is a gud babysitter. She hef a lot of ex... exp..."

"Experience," completed Mrs. Johnson.

"*Ja,* dat is it! Ex-pe-ri-en-sss." Then, with a hint of pride, "And Anneke, she can do *tekenen*, uh, making pictures *met de kinderen.*"

Mrs. Johnson nodded thoughtfully, "Well now, that sounds like a fine idea. Alicia and Eric would enjoy doing some art. Thank you for that suggestion."

As Johanna stood in her kitchen that September morning, she thought ruefully that it was a suggestion she'd lived to regret, for *that* was the summer Anneke discovered boys, and at the construction site that would become the Johnson's new home, there were indeed boys, tanned boys in tight tee-shirts, glistening sweaty boys, painting and plastering and paving; and as they plied their trade, Anneke sauntered by, hips swaying, ponytail swiveling, basking in their whistles. "Annie," Mrs. Johnson finally said, "please stay away from the tradesmen. They appear to find your presence quite distracting, and the work," and she shook her head in frustration, "is just not getting finished." After that, Anneke sauntered further a-field. She took Alicia and Eric for walks by other construction sites in the new subdivision, where she reveled in the whistles and the comments.

"Mummy," said little Eric one day after returning from a walk, "what's a b-b-bitchin chick?" Tightlipped, Mrs. Johnson handed Anneke a final pay packet, and told her that she was no longer needed. She had done quite enough. Johanna was mortified! In all these years of cleaning for the Johnsons she had established an excellent reputation, and now... ruined! And by that little tart! There was a blazing row. Piet finally intervened. Sent Anneke to her room. Made Johanna coffee. Wiped away angry tears. When the dust settled, Anneke happily went clothes shopping. She purchased a pair of turquoise pedal-pushers for weekends, two full flowery skirts to be worn over sugar-starched crinolines, three pastel sweater-sets, and one straight skirt, calf-length, tan. She showed her new clothes to her parents.

"Mooi," said her father, and smiled, but she only got a sneer from her mother. When her parents were away card-playing that evening, Anneke put on the tan skirt, posed in front of her bedroom mirror, and frowned. She opened the treadle sewing machine, turned the skirt inside out and took an inch off both side seams. Tried it on again. Found it still too loose. She lopped another half-inch off both sides. This time when she tried to put the skirt back on, she was surprised to discover that it wouldn't pull up past her thighs. Anneke stood in the middle of her bedroom, yanking on the waistband, twisting and squeezing this way and that, trying to pull it up over her hips, but the skirt would not budge. Finally, she took it off, laid it on the bed, and sat staring at it. Suddenly she had an idea, left the room, and came back with a can of talcum powder, sprinkled it liberally inside the garment, then managed to slide and wriggle her way into the skirt. She tried to walk, but found that she could only take very tiny steps and had to swivel her hips from side to side. Perfection!

Johanna glared, *"Wat heb jij met die rok gedaan?* How can you move?"

"Gotta go!" said Anneke cheerfully. "Don't want me late for my first day of high school, do you?" She smiled smugly, flipped her ponytail, and went out the door. Johanna sagged against the doorpost and stared out after her daughter swaying and swiveling her way up the gravel road.

"In sooth, I know not why I am so sad," wrote Miss McDougall on the blackboard. She was young, attractive, with long dark hair and tartan skirt, and she held a tattered copy of, "The Merchant of Venice," in her left hand, referring to it frequently. At the back of the classroom, Anneke rolled her eyes at Gerda. Boring! Different teachers, different classes, moving from room to room – at first she had found high school sort of interesting, but that interest soon faded. She saw little point in getting good marks anyway, when there would be no university for *her* at the end of it. Besides, she could pass most tests without studying. In fact, she discovered that not doing her homework added an edge, an element of excitement, to the school experience. She might as well amuse herself. Miss McDougall, just out of teachers' college, was having problems engaging the young people, and in bringing Shakespeare to life. "It wearies me; you say it wearies you," she wrote on the blackboard with her back turned to the class. Anneke gave the signal. Students at the back of the room took aim. She signaled again. Marbles shot, clattering like tiny bowling balls along the aisles to the front of the room. The teacher shrieked and whirled at the approaching racket as the class hooted with laughter. Miss McDougall broke into tears, fled the classroom. Anneke felt twinges of guilt. The principal came in, reprimanded the class severely, made them all stay in after school under his personal supervision. But neither the guilt nor the reprimand had a lasting effect. "If you prick us, do we not bleed?" wrote Miss McDougall. Anneke signaled, and a flotilla of paper airplanes thudded against the blackboard.

Piet pulled off his work-boots. His hair, his clothes covered with dust, he sat down heavily at the kitchen table. "What's wrong?" asked Johanna, pouring his coffee, "a problem at work?"

"Nothing but problems since old Mr. Redgrave died. Two guys got burnt today. Faulty torch. Dutch guys. Dirk van Oudenallen and Jan Bos."

"Oh God! How bad?"

"Burnt their hands. Bloody painful! They're off work for now. Took up a collection to help with the bills. Don't know what the doctor will cost! Johanna, their families will need food. Can you talk to the other women?"

"Of course!"

"We need some decent equipment in that factory, Johanna, but the boss only cares about making money. Tom Redgrave, he doesn't give a damn what happens, as long as the profits roll in. Doesn't replace worn equipment and blames the men when there's an accident. A guy is involved in too many accidents... Redgrave fires him." Piet sighed. Took a slug of his coffee.

Shaking her head, Johanna asked, "How can he be so different from his father?"

"Money! Anything to make money. Building new furniture wasn't enough. Refinishing antiques now in the far annex. Stripping and sanding without ventilation. *Ja,* you can see that on me, can't you," he said glancing at the sawdust his shoulder. Piet shook his head, "We need protection in that factory, Johanna, from the fumes and the dust, from the accidents just waiting to happen, and from the unjustified firings."

Johanna's look was black, "Those accidents... you should find another job!"

"Well, *vrouwkje,* I don't have much choice. I would love to go back to insurance work, or maybe even sell real estate – some job where I can be outside, use my brain a little, work with numbers. But my English isn't good enough. That's the problem with all the Dutch fellows. With the language problem, we don't have the choices the Canadians do. Bosses know that we'll work bloody hard, even in poor working conditions."

"And for less money!" said Johanna. "Don't forget to add that!"

"Ja," sighed Piet, "for less money."

"I'm going to the drive-in Saturday night," Anneke said to her mother.

"Who invited you?"

"A friend."

"What do you mean, friend? *Is dat nou een vriend of een vriendin?*"

"*Vriend*" Anneke lifted her chin.

"No you're not! You're not going anywhere with a boy. Fourteen is *much* too young! Why, I was twenty when your father and I started dating."

With a shrug, Anneke said, "*That* was the old country." She added, "They do things *differently* here."

"I have a meeting tonight," said Piet, lacing his workboots. "I have to be in Kingston at seven o'clock, so we'll need to eat as soon as I get home."

"What kind of a meeting?"

"You're not to say one word about this…" he looked at her.

"Fine! What?"

"With a couple of guys from the CCF. Just myself, Jake and Jan Bos. Jake is doing the driving because Jan's hands are still bandaged."

"What is that, the CCF?"

"*De partij van* Tommy Douglas, you know, the man who is bringing free medical care to the west. That Tommy, he cares about the working guy. Very different from the Tories in Ottawa. Why just last winter, when Diefenbaker shut down that airplane project, fourteen-thousand workers lost their jobs. Think *he* cared about those guys? The CCF, they're going to help us, Johanna. We're going to look at maybe forming a union. But it's hush-hush, because if Tom Redgrave gets wind of it, we'll get fired."

Johanna had listened with growing concern, "What? A union meeting? Get fired? Are you crazy! We can't afford to lose your pay-cheque! Risk your job? No, no, *no!*"

"*Ja,* it's dangerous right now. But if we *do* form a union, there'll be job security. Not only that, we should end up with more money in our pockets. When did I last get a raise? I started off with ninety-five cents three years ago, and that's barely gone up. With a union in place, Tom Redgrave will be forced to pay a fair wage. And the accidents! Did you *look* at Jan with his hands all bandaged? Next time, Johanna, somebody could get *killed*. Think about *that!*" Grim faced, Piet strode out the door.

"I want to be loved by you, just you, and nobody else but you…" sang Marilyn, as Anneke cuddled up against Jack, feeling the gearshift poking into her thigh. It was all very romantic! Jack was four years older than herself, out of school, and working – at least some of the time. The best part was that he had a car and could take her places. Anneke watched the screen, observed how Marilyn, a.k.a. Sugar, moved in her stilettos. I can do that, thought Anneke, I can do that walk. She felt Jack turn his face away from the screen and bury his mouth in her hair. She felt him nibbling on her earlobe, and a tingle went through her, but at the same time her earlobe did feel kind of itchy and she wasn't sure what to do, so didn't do anything and kept her eyes glued on Marilyn. Anneke stared. What colour lipstick was that? Would they have it at Kresge's?

"Without taking her eyes from the screen, she rummaged in her clutch purse, pulled out her lipstick, applied it liberally to her mouth. "Hey!" said Jack. "I was just going there," but his mouth remained at her throat, where he planted a row of small kisses, then his tongue made tiny circles. Then he was sucking at her throat, and she felt a stirring deep inside her and her head arched back, her eyes half-closed. Though her eyelashes Marilyn floated in soft focus. Anneke moaned softly, and Jack trailed his lips to her mouth, and he kissed her, softly, then more insistently. "Gotta get around this gearshift," said Jack, and climbed over to her side, tilted the seat back, lay down, kissed her again. Anneke threw her arms around his neck and kissed back, passionately. She felt the wonder of her breasts pressed hard against him, the heat of his body against hers, the beating of his heart, or was it hers or... dimly she thought, how loud the beating... thump, thump, thump... "Damn!" said Jack. "Forgot all about it," and threw open the car door causing the speaker to crash to the ground. "Damn, damn, damn!" He threw it on the seat and tore around the back of the car to open the trunk. "Sorry about that, lads. Forgot all about ya." Henk and his lanky friend Larry unfurled their limbs from the trunk space, and jumped to the ground.

"Getting hot in here," said Henk. He noticed Jack's lipstick-smeared face. "Whoo-hoo! Hot up there too!" he said, as Larry guffawed. Jack looked a bit dazed.

"I'm going for popcorn," he said abruptly, and left. Anneke sat stiffly as the two boys clambered into the back seat.

"Let's see," said Henk from the back, "whatever will I tell motha," and burst into, "Lipstick on your collar, Told a tale on you-oo…" The boys hooted with laughter.

"Bastard," muttered Anneke.

"Well now, little sister, you just better watch your tongue. If it weren't for me you wouldn't be here tonight, would ya. No way mummy would have let you go out all alone with big, bad Jack. Just looking after your interests."

"The only *interest* you have is in a free ride to the drive-in."

"You just watch you don't get a ri-ide, from *Jackie*-boy."

"What!"

"Ha, ha, ha," chortled Larry. "Ain't no pony ride Jackie'd be given ya. Ain't no…."

"Don't know that," cut in Henk. "Don't know he's not built like a pony, do ya Larry? How about it, Anneke? Is Jackie a pretty big boy?"

"Oh, shut up!" Scowling, she leaned her head against the side window. Then Anneke became oblivious to the back seat teasing, as Marilyn appeared on the screen in a silver dress which clung to her body like a snake's skin. Anneke was mesmerized. How the heck, she wanted to know, did Marilyn pour herself into that?

The girls were lying on Rosemary's pink chenille bedspread. "Big, bloody fight at my place," said Anneke. "Don't know what's going on.

Thought I heard my father say something about wanting to have a meeting at our house. Right away my mother starts shrieking, 'Are you crazy! Are you absolutely nuts!' Then the bedroom door flies shut."

"My parents fight all the time," Rosemary said. "Sex! It's always about sex. I don't think their therapist is helping much." She sat up. Bounced up off the bed. "Look at what I bought, Annie, I bought, 'Til I Kissed You' by the Everly Brothers and I bought *both* 'Lonely Boy' *and* 'Put Your Head on My Shoulders' by that *dreamy* Paul Anka and ..." Must be nice, Anneke thought, to be able to buy whatever the heck you want. No shortage of money in *that* family: both parents teachers, brand-new two-storey house with green shutters and swimming pool, hefty allowance, *and* no chores because there's a cleaning lady twice a week – thank God not my mother. "*And* I got Fabian, and of *course* I got Elvis, and ..."

"Why don't you just play them," Anneke said curtly. Rosemary started the record player, had to jump up like a Jack-in-the-box every three or four minutes to change the 45's. Anneke lay comfortably on the chenille, wailing along with her favourites – "Waterloo, Waterlooooo," and, "Poisonivyyyy."

"And I just *love* this one by Connie Francis," Rosemary gushed, "'Lipstick on Your Collar.' It's just so..."

"Skip it!" said Anneke. Rosemary looked puzzled. "My brother sang it the other day. Don't ever wanna hear it again. But look what *I* bought," she rummaged in her purse, triumphantly whipped out a lipstick. "Got it at

Kresge's. New colour that's just out. Marilyn Monroe red!" Anneke opened her compact, applied the neon-red lipstick generously, made a pouty mouth, smiled at herself. "I compared it to her poster and it is the *exact* same colour. Wanna see how it looks on *you?*"

"Dunno. Don't think my parents would let me."

"Well, they're downstairs and you're upstairs. Here. I'll hold the mirror." Rosemary peered at her image, frowned in concentration, smeared the lipstick on and around her mouth. "That's it," encouraged Anneke. "Wow! You look fantastic! Now, then, what-a-ya got to jive to?" Rosemary put on another record, and they practised their dips and twirls, and soon were dancing up a storm.

"What are you girls doing up here? You sound like a herd of elephants!" Rosemary's father loomed in the doorway, newspaper in one hand, pipe in the other. He took a good look at his daughter. "Rosemary! What have you done to yourself? You look like a harlot! I'm not having it!" Rosemary flushed, looked down at the floor. "Bad enough your mother…" he started, than seemed to catch himself. "Wash that off this instant!"

"Gotta go," Anneke said, sprinting for the door, "s'posed to be home before dark. See ya Rosemary!" She dashed by Rosemary's father, who glared after her as she ran down the stairs. Anneke slipped into her penny loafers, hurried out the front door, and nearly tripped over her dog. Old Yeller, lying on the step, looked up at her droopy-eyed, then lumbered to his feet. "Hey Yeller!" she handed him her clutch purse. Holding his head high, he proudly carried it. Old Yeller loved to carry things for her, whether a pencil case or a brown paper bag with groceries; although Anneke had discovered to her chagrin, that it was best if there wasn't meat in that grocery bag. She left the circle of light surrounding Rosemary's front step, and felt the night close in on her. How had it gotten so dark so quickly? Earlier, the sky had been overcast; now it was pitch-black. A gust of wind whipped fallen leaves against her bare legs. She shivered. "Home, Yeller. Let's go!" Purse in mouth, the dog started off at a trot down the road, with Anneke following close behind, shoes crunching gravel, eyes glued to the one thing visible in that blackness – a beacon of yellow tail. Thank God for that dog, Anneke thought, my faithful friend. She remembered when she first got Yeller. How old was she herself, eleven maybe? A neighbour had owned pedigreed Labs, bred them, and sold the pups. Somehow, the hound from down the road got over a fence and at the Lab bitch.

"Worthless mongrels! Can't sell this lot, can't even give these mutts away," the neighbour fumed when Anneke dropped by. "They're going in a potato sack, and into the creek!"

"Please," Anneke begged, looking at the ten, helpless, multi-coloured puppies, "I'm sure my parents will let me have one, and I can *find* homes for the rest. Don't drown them. Please!" But when Anneke returned the next day, there was only one lonely-looking yellow puppy nursing from its mother. Horrified, she begged her parents to let her have it, so it wouldn't be drowned as well.

"I don't want a dirty dog in my house," said Johanna. "Fur and fleas and peeing on the floor. No! Absolutely not!"

"He can stay outside," said Anneke. "In a doghouse. He'll be a good watchdog. No more worry about burglars."

"Ja, burglars I worry about," Johanna said sarcastically. "Burglars breaking in to steal our millions *is* a big problem. We have *so* much money!" Her voice rose, "Where will the money come from to *feed* that thing?"

"Baby-sitting," said Anneke. Finally her mother gave in. Anneke named the dog after a movie she'd seen.

Henk said it was a stupid name. "Who names a puppy 'Old' anything?"

"You're just jealous 'cause he's *my* dog!"

Johanna intervened, "He's not just *your* dog, Anneke. Everything is not just *yours*. He's the family dog so he's Henk's dog too."

"Oh yeah? Then why do *I* have to buy the food, huh!

"That's enough! Keep your mouth shut! If you're going to be so miserable, you're not even going to *get* a dog." So Anneke *had* shut up. Her dad helped her with the building project, and together they built a fine doghouse, large, insulated, with real shingles, and a carpet-flap over the door opening. Anneke smiled in the darkness as she thought of what a great dog house it was, and what a great dog Yeller had turned out to be. It began to drizzle.

"Go, Yeller, Go!" she yelled, and the dog sped up. Suddenly, she lost sight of his tail! Then she spotted it again, zig-zagging on the road. What the heck! Anneke peered into the darkness and saw further ahead, a small flash of white, darting, back and forth, back and forth. Oh my God, he's chasing a cottontail! Anneke scrambled to stay caught up, to shadow their twists and turns. Suddenly she tripped, went skidding on her knees across the gravel, landed in the ditch. When she raised her head, she saw only the vague silhouettes of trees. It was dead still. "Yeller," she screamed, "Yeller, come back! Yeller!" Then she remembered. "Yeller! You *stupid* mutt! My *purse!*" When Anneke stood up, she was hit with the stinging pain of gravel embedded in her knees, and she burst into tears. Sobbing, she stumbled around in the dark trying to find her purse – blood trickling down her legs, tears down her face. She wailed with the pain and the loss, and the betrayal – if you can't trust your dog, who *can* you trust? She started the walk home, slowly, painfully, checking the gravel underfoot to try to stay on the road. Without her canine protector, every creak and rustle in the underbrush seemed ominous. The wind howled eerily in the trees. Shivering, she hunched her shoulders, wrapped her arms protectively around herself, tried to walk more quickly. Then she saw it! Anneke squinted her eyes. Saw a pin-point of light.

"What the hell…?" exclaimed Henk, as he caught sight of her in the beam of his flashlight.

"My stuff!" she sobbed. "All my stuff is gone! My makeup and my… my…" she stuttered. Sniffled. "I tried to find it but it's too dark!"

"What are you talking about?"

"Yeller was carrying my purse with all my stuff and took off after a rabbit, and now all my makeup, and my autographed photo of Elvis, and everything, it's gone!" She thought she heard a faint snicker and turned on him, "Don't you laugh, you bastard!"

"Just take it easy. Go look in the morning when you can actually see something. For now, get your ass home 'cause mother's having a fit. Why do you think I'm out here?"

Early the next morning she was up scolding Yeller, demanding to know what the dog had done with her purse. She checked in the dog-house, then retraced their steps from the night before, trying to figure out where Yeller had veered off the road. Finally she managed to locate her purse, but it had flown open and the contents were scattered over the forest floor. Anneke searched for hours, and found her picture of Elvis, some money, a comb, her compact, but she never did find the lipstick, which was the exact same colour, as that worn by Marilyn Monroe.

"Jij bent gek," Johanna hissed, *"hartstikke gek.* Crazy!" She threw on her coat. She would visit Lies for the evening, return home *after* Piet had finished with his union nonsense.

"You don't understand, Johanna," he pleaded, as she stood by the door, "this is something I *have* to do. As a *man!* Stand up! Show some *backbone!"*

"Show your backbone when your children are going *hungry.* That will help a lot!"

"Johanna, if it had been up to you, we'd never have come to Canada in the first place. *En hier zitten we nou,* in our own little house. We'd never have had this, if we hadn't immigrated. And you were only too happy to send the pictures to the family in Nederland, to show how *successful* we were. Well, this business with the union, this is something else I have to do, a chance I have to take. If you don't take any chances, Johanna, you don't get ahead."

"Our own house! *Ja,* this is our own house. *You* have the union meeting, *in our own house."* Johanna's voice was rising. "If the boss hears about this union meeting *in our own house,* you lose your job, and then maybe pretty soon we don't *have our own house!"*

"He *won't* hear about it. We're being very careful with the unionization process."

Ja, you know how to talk good, Piet. *"Big* words! Big *man*! Men! You're all the same. Start a big fight, and it's the women and the children who suffer. Just like it was in the war. The men, they make the war and the women and the children…"

"Oh, for God's sake, Johanna, there's no comparison, and there's no talking to *you!"*

"Fine! You do what you want *anyway."* Snarled, "I'm *going!"*

slammed the door shut. Nonplussed, Piet watched her leave, pulled the curtains closed against the darkness, against the possibility of prying eyes, filled the kettle with water, then lit a cigarette, blew out the smoke, and watched the blue-grey smoke-rings drift lazily towards the ceiling. He sighed. Women!

"I'm at my wit's end, Lies," said Johanna, setting down her coffee cup. "Piet is acting crazy. He's having a secret union meeting at our house. Tonight! I tried to warn him about getting fired, but there's no talking to him." Johanna was sitting on Lies' lumpy couch, with Lies nearby in a wicker rocking chair. All was quiet except for the hum of the oil burner and the sucking noises from the baby at Lies' breast.

"A union meeting? At your house? Well you just stay here with me, Johanna."

"Why does he do this, Lies? Why have it at *our* house? Why this *risk*? Why…"

"Johanna, that's just the way they are. My Kees is no different. Crazy enough to cross the ocean for a new life, they're not gonna shy away from risk once they're here."

Johanna sighed, "I suppose you're right…."

"There's nothing you can do to change these guys. But Piet's an intelligent man. He'll be careful who he brings into your house." She put the baby on her shoulder to burp it. Thought of something. Chuckled. "Let me tell you about Kees. Doesn't like his job working for somebody else! The other day he talks about starting up our own business raising produce on those acres out back. The two of us out there in the vegetable patch. Naturally I don't want to lose his wages, not with a house full of little kids. I say, 'Kees, with a baby coming every year, I don't know what kind of shape I'm gonna be in for working in that market garden,' so, and this is the good part, Johanna, he says to me, he'll start using *kapotjes*."

"That's a big change, isn't it?" Johanna grinned. "When was the last time? On the ship? Didn't work so well that time did it... when the kids blew up the condom like a balloon? Better make sure Kees buys more than one this time," she grinned.

"No kidding!" Lies put the baby to her other breast.

"Your children are still so small, Lies. My Anneke, is a *big* problem! Around the house, she always has her nose in a book. If I want the dishes done, I call her, three, four times, then I *scream! Then* she's all insulted that I yelled at her. Last *week* you should have seen her! Came home after dark, knees all skinned up, blubbering like a baby. Next day she figures she's all grown up again and wants to go on a date. That boy she sees is Canadian, so we know *nothing* about him." Shaking her head, "What can we do, lock her in her room? I try to talk to her, and she treats *me*, her *mother*, like *I'm* an idiot. Absolutely infuriating! It's a wonder I haven't *killed* her yet! Be thankful your children are small!"

Lies bounced the baby, "*You're* not turning into a terrible teenager yet, are you?" kissed its fat cheeks, propped it up on the couch near Johanna, walked to the television set. Soon the words, 'I Love Lucy,' scrawled across the screen. The women put their feet up.

The kettle was whistling when the men began to arrive – one at a time so as not to attract attention. Piet was pleased that there were three new men, including a couple of Canadians. "Tanks for coming fellows. Take a chair. Coffee?" Piet put a spoon of Nescafe into each cup, poured in the boiling water, set out milk and sugar. "Our friend from the CCF shoult be here at any moment. Wat did you say, Dirk? You were a member of the Labour Party in Nederland? *Ja,* dit is about de same ting." There was a knock at the door. "Come in, come in." Piet vigorously shook the hand of the newcomer, an earnest-looking young man in glasses and worn tweed jacket. "I don't see you car."

"Parked a block away. Can't be too careful. Yes, thank you, coffee." Opened his scuffed briefcase.

"Nou dan," said Piet, "dis is John Comberford, our friend from de CCF."

John shuffled his papers, "Pleased to be here tonight. Piet and Jan have filled me in a bit on the situation at the factory and," he shook his head, "well, we'll get into more of that later on. Right now, I just want to say how much I admire all of you fellows," he looked around the kitchen table, "for coming here tonight. It takes courage to stand with your brothers, and to say no," looking pointedly at Jan's bandaged hands, "to unsafe working conditions, no, to low wages, no, to unjust firings. Why doesn't Redgrave put in decent equipment, pay you a fair wage? Because to do so would reduce *his* profits. How are those profits earned? On *your* backs, with *your* sweat, with *your* blood!"

"That's right! That's how it is!"

"Yeah! That bastard. Cadillac he drives, brand new Cadillac!"

"Right, brothers," John continued, "*he* drives around in a Cadillac while *you* struggle to put bread on the table. Well, what are you going to do about it? I'll tell you the one thing you can do. You can unionize. Tell me, what does the boss do if one man," finger raised, "tries to stand up to him?"

"Ignores him."

"Gives him the boot!"

"Now tell me what the boss does if *all* of the men *together*," clasping his hands, "stand up to him?" Opening his hands wide, "Can he fire them *all*? No, my friends. He can't fire his entire work force. He is *forced* to listen. That rich and powerful factory owner, he is *brought to his knees!*" Pounding the kitchen table, *"The union makes us strong!* All together now brothers."

"The union makes us strong! The union makes us..."

"Double dating," said Anneke, "that's what they call it here. When you double-date you're never alone with a boy. No different from, say, taking your brother along."

Johanna frowned. "Who are these other people?"

"Oops! There's Jack. Gotta go!" Anneke grabbed her clutch purse and ran for the door.

"Ten o'clock! Not a minute later!" her mother yelled after her. A dust-grey Chevy rattled into view.

"Sorry I'm late, lassie. Trouble with the love-machine. Flat tire. Right front. Had to buy another." Jack reached across the passenger seat to throw open the door.

"Rust-machine more like," Anneke grumbled. As she walked around the car, she looked dubiously at the tire indicated, as shiny and bald as all the other tires on the car. Whenever a flat occurred, Jack would go to Barkley's Garage and spend the absolute minimum – two or three bucks at most – to buy a used tire. Within weeks, and sometimes days, this second tire would be as flat as the first. She stepped on the running board and climbed in.

Jack gave her a quick kiss, and started to sing her theme song, "And for bonnie Annie Laurie, I'd lay me doun an' dee, I'd lay me doun an' dee, I'd lay me…" The engine started up with a clatter which all but drowned out Jack's singing, but before heading out he carried on with the song, tilting his head this way and that, looking at her teasingly. Anneke looked into his dancing eyes and felt her insides melt. Then she looked beyond Jack at her house, and saw another pair of eyes, glaring, from behind the kitchen curtains. They left MillCreek, stopped to pick up some friends, and with the car rattling along on its bald tires, they headed east. Jack continued to serenade Anneke, while in the back seat there was much panting and rolling around, as Jack's best friend Wally made out with girlfriend Jill. The Chevy's springs were as bad as its tires, and whenever Jack hit a bump, there were curses from the back seat – Jack would grin broadly. Their destination was Watertown – across the international bridge. Anneke had never been to the States, and was thrilled with the adventure. "When we get to the border," warned Jack, "don't open your mouth. They'll be able to tell you weren't born in Canada."

"So?" said Anneke morosely. She didn't like to be reminded about her slight trace of an accent.

"You're *not* Canadian are you, so you need a passport. You *got* one?" Anneke frowned. Shook her head. "Then you'd better be quiet, lassie, or they'll toss you in the brig!" Jack grinned, but she could tell he meant it. Anneke felt both excited and terrified at the thought of entering a country illegally. At the border, Jack distracted the guard with jokes. Anneke was asked only one question – was she born in Canada.

"Yes," she lied in her best English. The guard let them go. In Watertown they drove around sight-seeing, then the boys had a beer in the bar, while Anneke and Jill checked out clothing stores for bargains. "Do you believe these prices? Wow! Not even half what we pay at home! Look at this angora sweater!" The girls were well padded with skirts and sweaters when they piled back into the car.

"Anything to declare?" asked the Canadian border guard.

"No sir," said Jack politely. "We just drove into the States to look around, sir, and while it is a lovely country, it really can't compare to Canada, can it, sir!" Anneke had a hard time keeping a straight face. As the Chevy pulled away from the border crossing, the girls were tugging and twisting in their seats, taking off their extra layers.

"Oh, oh," said Anneke. "I forgot to remove the tags from the stuff I bought. Glad they didn't search me!"

"Aye," said Jack. "You'd have landed in the brig twice over. The illegality that goes on around me. It's simply shocking!" He stuck his hand in his leather jacket. With a flourish he pulled out a mickey. "Cherry brandy," he said, "to soothe my frazzled nerves." He took a sip, grinned broadly, passed it to Anneke. She gulped, choked, doubled over coughing, while the back seat hooted with laughter. "That's not coca-cola you're drinking!" said Jack "You're supposed to *sip* it!" Anneke scowled, thought the damn stuff tasted more like cough syrup, but took another swallow. This time she did not choke. She felt the brandy burn all the way down her throat and into her belly. From her centre, the warmth radiated throughout her body. Anneke relaxed. Felt wonderful. Put her head back on the seat. Smiled sublimely at Jack.

It was well after midnight when Anneke got home. She tried to sneak in, but Johanna heard her, followed her into the bedroom. Anneke quickly jumped under the covers, clothes and all. "You don't have to pretend you're asleep. I heard you come in! Where have you been 'til this hour?" Anneke kept her head under the blankets so Johanna wouldn't smell her breath. "Answer me!" Johanna screeched. "Answer me!" Anneke kept mum. "That's it! The next time you're late that door will be locked and you won't be getting in. I've had it!"

"Brothers," said John, "last week you talked about the problems at MillCreek Furniture. Tonight, I'd just like to start by emphasizing that, under the law, you have the right to do something about the situation. Under the law, you have the right to organize yourselves into a collective bargaining unit. Under the law, you have the right to form a union."

"Wat is our next step?" said Piet, handing John a coffee.

"Thanks. First, you need a show of hands to make sure everyone is in favour."

"Brodders?" said Piet, using the union language he'd picked up. "Do you want a union?" All hands shot up. "Dere you go, John," Piet said with satisfaction. "Everyone!"

"The next question is *which* union. *My* union is the United Auto Workers.... You didn't know that Jan? You thought it was the CCF? No, no, that's a political party. It's easy enough to confuse, because there's a lot of overlap between the party and the unions."

"*Ja*," said Piet, "de CCF is de party voor de working people!"

"Right! Anyway, the question is whether you want to join the UAW, or if you want to take a closer look at, say, the Steelworkers or the Metalworkers – I can certainly put you in touch with those guys. I don't want to sway you fellows either way, so I'm just going to step outside, have a cigarette, and leave you to hash it out. If you *do* want to go with the UAW, I've got membership cards right here in my briefcase, and we can start signing guys up."

"Before you go out," said Piet, "can you tell us how dat works, de membership cards?"

"Happy to. Ontario Legislation states that, in order to unionize a worksite, you first have to get 55% of employees to sign membership cards for a specific union. I want to warn you," said John, looking around the table, "that, when you're doing this, getting these signed, you have to move cautiously. If you talk to the wrong guy, he's going to squeal to the boss and you can be sure that Redgrave would move heaven and earth to prevent the factory from being unionized. Now, the law says that you *cannot fire* a man for union activity. However, you and I both know, brothers, that if a boss really wants to get rid of you, it's not that hard to find an excuse. Should this occur, the union will fight for you, but these things can be very messy! So be careful, take your time, sound each man out, and when you're sure, then, and only then, do you mention the union. On the other hand, it is critical to talk to enough guys to get at least 55% of the workers signed up. Piet, did you manage to get a list of employees?"

"Right here. I had a hard time getting it. Den I said it is voor de

Christmas party."

"Good man," John chuckled. "Right then, when you have enough guys signed up, you apply to the Ontario Labour Relations Board for certification. Once certified by the OLRB, the union becomes the official bargaining agent for the worksite."

"Phew!" said Jan. *"Dat was een mondvol!"*

"A mouthful? Yes, I know! But any of the unions will help you with the process." John opened the door, "Let me know what you decide. Take your time." He stepped outside and lit up.

"Well, men," said Piet, "Wat do you tink? Find out about de different unions, or go met the UAW?"

Sam Simpson, one of the younger guys, spoke up, "My brother is with the UAW in Woodstock, and Eric says it's a good union, well-run, democratic – none of that top-down bullshit."

"Isn't it one of the biggest ones?" asked another. "Should be able to really help us out."

"That's right," said Sam, "lots of help. And., uh, in the States, I hear there've been problems with some of the other unions – illegal stuff, but the UAW – clean as a whistle."

"Like this John," said Jan, "out having a smoke or a piss or whatever the hell he's doing." They laughed. "I trust that guy. I say go with who you trust."

Dirk said, "I don't know a damn thing about one union being better or anything like that, but I've had enough of the shit at the factory, and if we can go with the UAW right now, no more pissin' around, let's get the hell on with it!"

"Well said, brother!"

"You're right, Dirk, absolutely right!"

"OK. Sounds like we are ready to vote," said Piet. "Brodders, do we join de UAW?"

All hands shot in the air! The men jumped up, chanting, "U-A-W! U-A-W! U-A-W!" as they stomped their feet on the floor. John stuck his head around the door. Broke into a huge grin.

"Rosemary, would you like to see if we can make this water any more palatable?" Anneke enunciated each syllable of the last word in her most proper English.

"Huh?" said Rosemary. The girls were in the hallway at the start of Monday lunch. They'd been making faces as they sipped water from paper cups. The drinking water for the small, rural high school was brought in, a pail at a time, and dumped into the tin water cooler. It tasted tinny at the best of times, but was particularly foul-tasting after it sat stagnant all weekend.

"Your parents are at work, right, your house is empty? There must be something at your place..." Anneke paused meaningfully, "we can pour into this water to improve it. Wanna go see?" Rosemary had a puzzled look on her face, but she nodded. She liked hanging out with Anneke. Life was never dull. In the kitchen of Rosemary's house they found an empty milk bottle. Anneke carried it with her into the living room. She noticed an entire wall of book shelves, "That where those sex books are?"

"Nah, they keep those in their bedroom."

"Too bad!" She examined the other side of the room, "What's this?"

"My dad's liquor cabinet. Can't touch that! He marks the bottles. Know exactly how much is in each one. Think he does it for the cleaning lady."

"Marks them does he? Hmm." Anneke looked thoughtful. Examined a bottle of Scotch. Turned it this way and that. "Well, if he can see the marks, so can we. We'll just remove a little hootch from this bottle, and add a little water."

Rosemary looked horrified, "He'll kill me!"

"He won't notice the difference, and even if he does..." Anneke jumped up into an oversized armchair, tapped a pretend cigar with one hand, sipped from a pretend glass with the other. In a gravelly voice, "They're just not making Scotch the way they used to. I swear they're watering it down. Damn Scotsmen! Cheap bastards!" Rosemary grinned and helped Anneke pour a few inches of precious Scotch into the milk bottle. Anneke frowned, "That's not enough!"

"Not more out of *that* bottle!"

"No, no, no. We'll add some from the *other* bottles – gin, vodka, brandy... what else is in that cupboard?" Finally, the milk bottle was full.

They topped-up each liquor bottle with tap water, before returning it to the cabinet. The milk bottle was placed in a brown paper bag, to be smuggled into the school. While Rosemary stood guard, Anneke dumped the purloined alcohol into the water cooler. She filled a paper cup. "Might I offer you a drink of this fine water, Rosemary?"

"Don't mind if I do," sipping, nodding, "yes, excellent water!"

Anneke tasted it, smacked her lips, "Superb, I say!" Her cousin came out of the bathroom, "Hey, Gerda, would you like a drink of this fine water? It is particularly tasty today." Gerda looked mystified, but accepted the cup, sipped, and grinned. "Johnny, want some of this fine water?" Students came *flocking* into the hallway. Anneke counted twenty lined up at the water cooler, cups in hand. Others, who'd obtained their drinks, were standing around the hallway, sipping from cone-shaped paper cups, discussing flavour and aroma. Just as Anneke was beginning to wonder whether the cooler might run dry, the principal came upon the scene.

"What's going on here?" he demanded of the sipping students. Anneke tried to melt into the woodwork. Mr. Witherspoon frowned, lifted the cooler lid, sniffed. His eyes grew wide. He stepped back into the staff room, and Anneke could hear him say, "You're not going to believe this…" Within seconds, a custodian arrived, and removed the water cooler.

Afternoon classes began. "The following students are to report to the office immediately," boomed Witherspoon over the PA system. Anneke shrank down in her seat "Ricky Jones, Butch Anderson, Jimmy Lemoine…"

The principal was rounding up the usual suspects. Anneke held her breath as she waited for her name to be called, "Tommy Burk, Keith Baker…" Finally the list came to an end. Anneke exhaled. Then she realized, that not only had *her* name not been called, no *girl's* name had been called at all. There'd been only *boys'* names on that list. *Only boys were being questioned!* Anneke pondered this, then decided that the principal must consider girls incapable of the villainy of the water-cooler caper. *She* was in the clear. She relaxed, looked around the classroom, and noted with some modicum of pride, that due to her efforts, her classmates were exceedingly jolly that afternoon.

Piet opened his lunch pail, took out the thermos and poured himself a coffee. He walked across the dusty shop floor and stepped over the sill into the crisp November air. "Damn!" he heard. "Damn, damn, damn!" Frank Steed, a huge, rough-looking workman in greasy overalls was down by the river, madly flicking his lighter, unlit cigarette dangling from between his lips. Piet paused, then strolled over and lit Frank's fag. The big man grunted his thanks, sucked the smoke deep into his lungs, drawled, "If this wasn't my *lucky* lighter I'd throw the damn thing in the river!" He looked at Piet, "All through the war, I kept it right here," patting the pocket over his chest. "There was this one time, we was fightin' the Krauts. It was fierce! Guys going down all 'round me. Then I get hit! I'm lying there, checking myself for damage, and all I can find is a rip in my uniform, here over my heart, and a dent in my lighter. Woulda been killed if it weren't for this lucky lighter. Too damn bad it don't work half the time."

"Let me have a look," Piet examined it. Finally said, "I tink it is the flint. Because of dat dent, you need a flint dat is smaller. Maybe I hef one here wit my smoking stuff." He dug deep in his pocket, pulled out a tiny flint, inserted it, and flicked the lighter. It flared up instantly.

"You fixed it!" said Frank, "My lucky lighter! Bitchin! How much for the flint?"

"Dat is OK. It is not very expensive."

"No, no. With the wages at this place, you can't afford to give nothing' away."

"De wages here...*ja....wel*...." Piet scratched his head. Glanced at the men by the factory door. Lowered his voice, "Some of de men, we have been talking, uh, talking about de wages. If you are interested, I hef some paper for you to look at."

Frank's eyes narrowed, "What? You talkin' union? I don't hold with none of that commie crap!" He spat on the ground. Barked, "I didn't fight no *Krauts* to let no *commies* take over!"

Piet felt the ground sink from beneath his feet.

Head bowed, Piet walked home from the factory. He kicked at the gravel on the road. How could he have been so stupid! Why did he not find out more about that man, *before* he opened his mouth. But, Piet shook his head, the guy really was *eigenaardig*, highly peculiar – one moment friendly – the next practically looking under rocks for communists. And his eyes! Slits they became! Venomous slits. Piet had *tried* to cover his tracks. "Frank," he'd said, "my English is not so *goed*. We talk about *wegen*. Uh, in English, *wegen*, dat is uh, weighing. You know, on de scale!" Frank's face twisted cynically. Piet continued, "*Voor de* Christmas party. To see who is de fattest one to play de Santa Claus. How much you weigh, Frank?" He'd blathered on, hoping to throw Frank off the scent. "We write it down. On a piece of paper. How much de men, dey weigh. Den the fattest one, dat is de Santa Claus. Hey Jan!" he'd called over, "how much you think Frank weighs?" Jan started to walk towards them. Piet slipped a code-word into his prattle, *"Gevaar,"* he said in a low voice, and repeated it once, *"Gevaar!"*

A full moon glistened on the snow-capped tombstones in the old country graveyard. The moon also shone on the '47 Chevy, parked on a service road in the middle of the cemetery. Sad old songs emanated from the 'rust-machine' and wafted among the tombstones, "And for bonnie Annie Laurie, I'd lay me doun an' dee…" Jack liked the atmosphere in the graveyard – liked to sing his melancholy tunes there. "Little Rosa was her name… and though she's gone you see … She's still the world to me… that little girl of mine." Anneke sat on the passenger's side with an old quilt wrapped around her legs. She gazed out over the tombstones, listened to the mournful songs and felt tears on her cheeks. Jack looked at her quizzically, took her face in his hands, wiped away the tears with his thumbs, and kissed her gently. He quoted:

"O Death! Thou tyrant fell and bloody!
The meikle devil wi' a woodie
Haurl thee hame to his black smiddie
O'er hurcheon hides..."

"What the heck?" said Anneke.

"Robbie Burns," explained Jack.

"Well, all I understood was, 'death' and 'devil'."

"According to Burns, the devil has a big club and drags you over hedgehog hides."

"That can't be comfortable! I had a hedgehog once. Very prickly! He was about this big," she said, cupping her hands together as if holding an apple. "Had to leave the little guy behind when we emigrated." She added sadly, "Wonder where Klaasie is now?"

They sat quietly in the moonlight which streamed into the car. Anneke saw a small broken tombstone leaning against the trunk of a pine tree, and was concentrating on trying to decipher the inscription, when she felt Jack's eyes on her. In a hoarse voice he said, "You've got a bonnie set of paps there lass."

"Huh?" said Anneke, turning to look at him.

"There," he said, dropping his eyes to her chest, grinning. Anneke frowned, thought for a moment, then gave a slight, almost secretive, smile. She *was* pleased with her breasts. Why, earlier that year, the grade nine boys had voted her 'girl with the best body.' Of course it hadn't been an official poll, hardly sanctioned by the school, yet.... "Bonnie set of paps," Jack murmured, climbed over to her side, and started to kiss her. She smelled the male smell of him, felt his arms encircling her, his warm mouth on hers, and she clenched his neck, and she kissed him hard. The kiss went on and on, then she felt Jack's hand moving on her sweater, felt his tentative touch – his hand on her breast – a pleasurable, yet scary sensation. He hadn't done that before! Should she let him? Would he think she was cheap? Would he think she was cold if she didn't let him? It sure was exciting! Her eyes were wide! Jack looked into her face, cupped her breast, and squeezed gently. Anneke breathed more quickly. Jack teased the point of her bra with butterfly strokes of his fingers. Her nipple stood up and reached the summit of her Maidenform. Anneke moaned softly. Now she felt a hand on her other breast, and as both breasts were molded, massaged, manipulated, Anneke's neck arched back, her mouth opened and she moaned deeply. Jack clamped his mouth over hers and stifled her moans. There was a deep stirring inside her, and she pushed her breasts forward for more touching and he shoved a hand under her clothes and she groaned, and she pushed him away.

"I think," she said, although she could barely speak, "I think, we should go."

Jack scowled, sat back, observed Anneke in the moonlit car, then reached over to cup her breast once more, and said resignedly, "OK." The car started up with its usual clatter. Jack put it in gear, started to drive off. Thump, thump, thump, went the left rear tire.

"Not another one!" exclaimed Anneke. "Don't tell me!"

"Sorry lass," said Jack, grinning ruefully. "Wee problem with the love-machine."

Anneke stood in her driveway and watched Jack's Chevy rattle off into the wintry night. What a bright night it was! In awe, she looked up at the full moon. She glanced at the roof of her house where moonlight glinted on snow. Her eyes moved down the building, and she noted with consternation that all the windows were black. How late was it, anyway? On the ground, over by the doghouse, there was some movement. Old Yeller emerged, his fur burnished gold in the moonlight. Anneke felt the greeting of the dog's warm tongue, and suddenly realized what a cold night it was. She gave Yeller a quick pat on the head, walked swiftly to the back door, turned the doorknob and pulled. Nothing happened. Oh, oh. She rattled the knob. Nothing. My God, mother had made good on her threat. Never thought she'd really do it, thought Anneke. Never thought she'd really lock me out if I came home late. What the hell am I supposed to do now? I could pound on the door, but they wouldn't answer it, and even if they did, I'd just get in worse shit. Besides, I wouldn't give them the bloody satisfaction. What a thing to do, when I'm only just a little bit late. Anneke's crinolines and bobby-socks were doing little to keep her legs warm, and she hopped from one foot to the other. Maybe I can sneak in, somehow, she thought. There must be another way to get into this house. Quickly she walked to the front. The front door was seldom used and highly unlikely to be unlocked, but still... She twisted at the knob. It didn't budge. The windows. She'd seen her mother slide up the bottom panel of the kitchen window just a few days ago when Henk had burnt the leftovers he was trying to reheat. Yes! If I can just find a stick to pry that window open. She looked around the yard, was pleased to find an old railway spike. Metal! Even better! She attempted to wedge the spike in the crack under the window, but the window did not move, and all she succeeded in doing was creating a hole in the bottom of the slightly rotten frame. *That* would make her popular with her father! The other windows. Anneke circled the house, trying every possibility. Finally, shivering uncontrollably, she found herself back in the driveway by the back door. In a last desperate attempt, she lobbed gravel at Henk's second floor bedroom window. She looked up, hoping for his window to open, for his light to go on. To her dismay, there was no response. His window remained black. Anneke stuck her freezing fingers under her armpits and hopped up and down madly trying to allay the shivering. What to do? Where to go? There was nothing open in Mill Creek this time of night – the soda bar, restaurant, even the gas station had closed hours ago. Well, she thought, it would serve mother, it would serve the entire family right, if she froze to death. In the morning they'd find her frozen corpse. It would be just like the story of the little match girl. Then they'd feel bad, then they'd feel sorry for how they'd treated her! Old Yeller had followed her around patiently, watched her attempts at break-in with interest, but now tired of waiting, walked to his doghouse, lifted the flap with his nose, and started inside. Anneke caught a glimpse of straw bedding. Must be cozy in there, she thought enviously. The flap fell back over the opening, and Anneke was left alone, freezing, as clouds drifted across the face of the moon.

Johanna awoke with a start. In her nightmare, her children were lost and crying out to her, and she was trying to find them, but it was snowing so hard that she couldn't see them and could only hear their voices, calling, calling…. She sat up. Looked at the alarm clock. Three a.m. She jumped out of bed, and pulled on housecoat and slippers and went upstairs to check the children. She opened Henk's bedroom door. He was sound asleep, snoring lightly. Tenderly she pulled the blankets up to tuck him in, and closed the door quietly behind her. She opened Anneke's door. Johanna's mouth dropped open. The bed was empty! Unslept in! My God, Anneke hadn't come home! Her fourteen-year-old daughter was still outside in the dead of night! Johanna dashed back to her husband, "Piet! Wake up! Anneke is missing!" Piet's eyes opened, but his face was twisted with sleep, and he stared uncomprehendingly. "Get up Piet! Anneke is gone. You've got to find her!"

Piet snapped awake. "Did you check with Henk? Maybe he knows something." Piet went in. Prodded his son.

"What? Huh?" Henk mumbled. "Isn't she in her bed?"

"No she isn't!" Piet snapped. "When did *you* get home?"

"I dunno. 'Bout midnight maybe. Thought she was in bed."

"So," said Piet, "let me get this straight. When you got home, you locked the door?"

"Yeah. That's what I'm s'posed to do," mumbled Henk, rolling onto his stomach.

"You idiot!" barked Piet. "You didn't check your sister's bedroom? Your sister wasn't home yet! You locked your little sister out! Stupid.... stupid.... ass..." muttering and cursing, Piet left his son's bedroom, ran down the stairs two treads at a time, threw on a coat and boots and went out into the darkness. Johanna was already out there.

"Anneke. Anneke! *Anneke!" T*he panic was palpable in Johanna's voice as she paced madly up and down the driveway in her housecoat and slippers. "*Oh mijn God, mijn God*! She is dead. I know she is dead. Three in the morning, Piet, and still not home."

"She *might* have come home, Johanna, you don't know that," said Piet. He was wearing his coat over his pajamas, but in his haste had forgotten to button it. "If her brother hadn't locked her out she might be in bed right now. That *idiot!"*

"Henk thought she was already in bed when he got home. He just locked up like he's supposed to. Not his fault. *Her* fault! She *should* have been home by then. *Oh mijn God! Mijn God.* Where is she? Where *is* she, Piet? She could be dead in a ditch. She could be murdered. Murdered! Just like that girl in the paper. That Lynn...."

"Harper," Piet finished. "But they got that boy, Johanna. That boy is in jail." He tried to reassure his wife, but was worried himself. The moon came and went behind dark clouds that threatened snow, and as Piet searched in the uncertain light for signs of his daughter, he kept seeing Frank's snake-like eyes. "I'm sure Anneke is fine," he told his wife. "She's been out late before."

"Late, yes. But not this late! It's the middle of the night, Piet. She should have been in bed hours ago! I *know* something happened to her. I know it! Something terrible. Like that Harper girl. Dragged into the woods. Strangled! That happened here. Right here in Canada!"

"Canada is a big place, Johanna. It happened a long way from here. And that boy, that Truscott boy, he's in jail. You don't have to worry about him anymore."

"Don't have to worry!" Johanna's voice rose dangerously. "Maybe not that boy they got in jail. Maybe *another* boy. Maybe that boy with the awful noisy *car.* Maybe *that* boy!" With a sob, "She is dead, Piet. I know she is dead. Call the police. Call them now, Piet." As if on cue, Old Yeller poked his nose from his doghouse, pushed the flap aside and crawled out. Johanna stared blankly. He came to her, seemed to sense her distress, licked her hand in sympathy. Johanna looked down, laid her hand briefly on his golden fur, reached up to wipe away tears. From the corner of her eye she saw the flap move again. Out poked Anneke's head. Johanna's eyes became as big as saucers. The girl crawled from the doghouse, stood up, yawned and stretched. Johanna started to scream. She screamed at the top of her lungs, then she cried, then she screamed some more! Windows lit up in neighbouring houses.

Piet stood rooted, silent, shaking his head.

"*Rik,*" said Lies. "Clubs are trump, and I'll take along the ace of hearts." "Got it," said Johanna. "All right! Let's beat these men!" Piet and Johanna were at the van Berkels for their usual Saturday night card game, *rikken,* a game from the southern part of the Netherlands, somewhat similar to euchre. They were playing at the kitchen table, basking in the warmth of the oil burner, surrounded by a blue haze of cigarette smoke. On the oil burner a coffee percolator hiccuped – Kees preferred 'real' coffee – refused to be won over to the modern convenience of instant. In front of the oil burner was an empty drying rack – Lies had quickly whisked the drying diapers into the bedroom when the guests arrived.

Lies slapped a trump on the three cards already played. "My trick," she said, sliding the cards towards her. She played a nine of hearts, "For my partner," she said, and Johanna took it handily with her ace. "How is it now with Anneke?" asked Lies, as Johanna was about to come back with a small club.

"Anneke?" said Johanna, her hand stopped in mid-air. "Anneke!" Her voice rose. "Unbelievable, that girl! Absolutely unbe-*lie*-vable! Missing, the other night. Three in the morning and she's nowhere to be found. We're outside looking, and I'm going *crazy* with the worry. Do you know where she was?" Lies shook her head. "She was in the...the...the..." Johanna sputtered with indignation, "doghouse! Came crawling out with the dog. Did you ever *hear* of such a thing!" She glared across her cards at Lies. There was dead silence. Lies turned to Kees, their eyes met – and they *exploded* in laughter. Lies guffawed until the tears ran down her face. Kees leaned back in his chair and roared. Even Piet smiled. Chagrined, Johanna spat out, "Well I'm glad you think it's funny! I was never so worried in my whole life. I said to Piet, 'Piet, call the police! Now!' You know, that girl is so contrary, she would never have come out of that doghouse if I hadn't mentioned the police. That girl would still be in..." An infant's wail interrupted Johanna's rant.

Lies stood up, put down her cards, wiped her eyes, "Don't know when I've last had such a good laugh! Laughed hard enough to wake the baby! I'd better go and see to that little bugger before he wakes up the rest of the kids." She walked around the table to where Johanna sat scowling, bent down and gave her friend a quick hug.

"Sorry *meid*. Couldn't help myself. Come, help me with the baby. It's like you said the other day – I'm lucky mine are still small." Cheerfully she added, "My time will come!" Still scowling, Johanna followed Lies from the room.

Once the bedroom door had closed, Kees asked, "How is it going with the union?"

"Not bad, not bad," said Piet, nodding thoughtfully. "We've got about forty-five percent of the guys signed up, and we need fifty-five. We're getting there! Only thing is, there's that guy Frank I told you about, nasty piece of work, stirring up trouble. Him and his friends, whispering, calling us reds and commies *just* loud enough for us to hear."

"What's his problem with the union, anyway? His wages would go up too, right?"

"Part of it is just commie fear-mongering, like we were still in the McCarthy era or something. More worrisome though, is the rumour that's going around, that if the UAW comes in, Redgrave will simply close down the factory and everybody will be out of a job."

"Who started *that* rumour?"

"Good question! That young guy, Sam Simpson, he told me some interesting information the other day. Said Frank's wife's name, before she got married, was Redgrave. What does that tell you! Those guys are in bed together."

"Then you know where that shit is coming from, don't you? Straight from Tom Redgrave's ass! For God's sake, watch your back!"

"Oh, I am. I'm being damn careful, *now!* I sometimes think though," Piet sighed, "what the hell am I doing? Still kinda new to this country – what – yeah, about four and a half years now. But I was always into politics back home, well, everybody seemed more involved there. Don't know if it was because it was such a small country that it was easier to feel you made a difference – I mean here the distances are so enormous! I don't know. I think too that it was the voting system there, where every vote counts, *evenredige vertegenwoordiging,* that really got people involved. I was driving somewhere with John Comberford the other day, was trying to explain the Dutch voting system, but I had no idea what it's called in English."

"Proportional representation," Kees said promptly. Piet looked impressed. Kees explained, "Read what I can to improve my English. Lots of magazines at work. Took a couple home in my lunch-pail. Lies likes to read too. When she can find time," he chuckled.

"So that's what it's called. I'll try to remember that! But back to Comberford – he's been just great! Lots of help there. The only thing is, Kees, with going to these meetings now, I just hate it that I always have to ask somebody for a ride."

"You know what the answer is – get your own car! Heard of one for sale, '38 Plymouth, good sturdy car. Belonged to an old farmer just died. Pretty old, but he kept it in the drive-shed and only drove it to church on Sundays, so it's low mileage. The widow's asking $175., but it's rusty, so you should be able to get it for less. You're good at body-work, so, if you do decide to get it, you could even work on it in that building I've got back here, that old garage – just bring some wood and fire up the pot-bellied stove. Don't wanna wait though, if you *do* want that car. It's a good deal. It'll go quick."

"Two problems, Kees. Number one – Johanna – sweet-talking her. Number two," Piet grinned sheepishly, "I don't know how to drive!"

"Not a problem! Not a problem! I can teach you to drive, and as for Johanna…" The bedroom door opened.

"Ye-e-e-s…" said Johanna suspiciously. "Talking about me?" She strutted through the door, followed by Lies, who was cooing to the freshly-changed babe-in-arms. The women sat down at the kitchen table. Lies pulled a breast over her low-cut blouse, held the baby to it. The infant sucked noisily. Piet watched covertly.

"That's right," said Kees, smiling at Johanna. "I *was* talking about you. I was just saying to Piet how attractive you look tonight. Would you like a cup of coffee, Johanna?" he asked, standing up. "Or maybe something a little stronger?" He dug around in the back of a cupboard, pulled out a bright yellow bottle.

"Oooh, my favourite!" said Johanna. "Advocaat!"

"Just for you, *meid!*" said Kees genially. He poured the thick yellow liquid into shot glasses. Passed them around.

All four raised their glasses, *"Proost!"* They returned to their card game, with Lies simultaneously feeding the baby, playing cards, drinking advocaat, and smoking cigarettes. A fierce wind now whipped snow against the rattling window panes of the small, wooden house.

"*Smaakt goed!*" said Johanna, savouring her drink. "*Lekker borreltje* to warm my insides before we head out into that snow."

"I'll drive you," volunteered Kees. "Don't want you out there in that blizzard."

"That's OK," said Piet. "It's only a kilometer. We're used to walking."

"You're tough, Piet, I know that," said Kees, grinning, "but I don't want this lovely lady getting frostbite on her nose."

Piet and Johanna got out of the car and stepped through their back door. From the living room they heard the blaring of the TV and the bickering of their children. "Good!" said Johanna with satisfaction. "Both home."

"Of course they're both home," said Piet. "They're grounded."

"You're lying!" Anneke exclaimed. "He is so Scottish."

"An act," said Henk. "He's no more Scottish than you are. Don't think he knows what he is. The people he lives with are Scottish. He tries to fit in. He's just a foster kid."

"He's no kid! He's eighteen!"

"Yeah, but he's been there since he was twelve. Paying room and board since he was sixteen. I'm told he gets nothing' for nothing'. They're not his family. He's not Scottish."

"Recites Robbie Burns," Anneke almost wailed.

"Phony son-of-a-bitch isn't he?" said Henk. Anneke landed a kick. They were sitting scrunched up on opposite ends of the couch. Henk kicked back. Anneke yelped.

"Enough already!" scolded Piet. "To bed, both of you!" He turned off the TV. "Coffee?" asked Johanna.

"*Ja,* a nice hot cup of coffee before we go to bed."

Johanna stood looking out the window at the falling snow as she warmed her hands on her coffee cup. "I hate to think of Kees having to drive back home in this blizzard."

"Maybe," said Piet, seizing the opportunity, "maybe, it's time to get our own car."

"We can't afford it!"

"We can buy a fixer-upper. Kees knows of one. Needs body work, but has a good engine. Best of all, Johanna, it's cheap. Maybe $150. What do you think?"

"We've been getting along fine without a car."

"We have not been getting along fine! This isn't Nederland! You can't ride a bicycle here. There's too much snow, everything is too far away, and besides, when they see an adult on a bicycle here, they look at you funny. Johanna," he said persuasively, "wouldn't it be nice to have a car to go for a Sunday afternoon drive…"

"Or," said Johanna, put in good humour by the advocaat, "to go shopping in Kingston."

"Or, for bragging photos to send to Nederland," kidded Piet.

"Or to go to the hairdresser in style," countered Johanna. "But," her face darkened, "how secure is your job right now, with this union business?"

"It looks good for bringing in the union, and that means a contract, *and* job security, *and* maybe a raise. Even if the very worst were to happen," Piet said seriously, "then a car would provide transportation to look for another job. Johanna, we can't go wrong buying a car."

The whistle blew and the factory streamed empty of workmen. Piet stepped outside carrying his lunch pail, into the last rays of the setting sun. He walked quickly towards the parking area at the back of the factory. He was thinking of the meeting that he was going to in Kingston, and of how convenient it was to have his own car – Piet pursed his lips to whistle – and of how he was enjoying the work on the car. He'd been sanding rust and patching holes and painting on a basecoat of red oxide paint. The car was looking great! Whistling 'Solidarity Forever,' Piet rounded the factory corner – and came to a shocked standstill. On the side of his '38 Plymouth was written in bold white letters, 'BETTER DEAD THAN RED.'

"The official part of the meeting won't start for another fifteen minutes," said the president, speaking into the mic, "but I want to share with you a newspaper clipping about what's happening in Woodstock, Local 636.

Might be something we'd wanna implement here. Snot-nosed young president out there, name 'a Bob White, getting incredible press coverage. He's letting the Red Cross use their union hall for blood donor clinics and…." The talk continued, but John Comberford, on the podium with the rest of the executive, no longer listened. Piet had entered the hall. With one look at Piet's face, John knew there was trouble. He rushed down to talk to him.

"Piet!" he said, in an urgent whisper. "Piet! What's wrong?"

Piet sighed, looked at John, "my car…" he said dully, pointing to the street.

"What? Accident?" Piet shook his head.

"At the factory today. After work I come outside and dere was writing, words, on my car. It said….." He stopped. His face was bleak.

"What! What did it say? Come on, show me." He grabbed Piet's arm and led him outside. A streetlamp cast its dim yellow light on the '38 Plymouth. The words were clearly visible, 'BETTER DEAD THAN RED.'

"My God!" exclaimed John, "Unbelievable!" Men going into the union hall, noticed the car, the commotion, came over to find out what was going on. Piet told them of the situation at MillCreek Furniture, the opposition to the union and the intimidation. The faces of the men hardened.

"Bastards!" one man spat.

"Fucking union busters!" said another. George Williams, a bearded man in checked hunting coat, and toque, examined the lettering on Piet's car, went to his truck for sandpaper, and started sanding. Others pitched in to help. As the crowd of unionists grew, there was angry muttering, and offers of advice, support, retribution.

George looked up from the sanding, "If you want a bunch of us guys to come out there, we'll be at those factory gates tomorrow. You are not alone, brother!"

"That's right, Piet!" said John. "You're *not* alone! He clamped his hand on Piet's shoulder, spoke with intensity, "Don't let them get to you! We *are* winning! We just need another *handful* of union cards. That's why they're upping the ante. Because we are so close!"

"Dey attack my car, John," Piet said miserably. "What next? My family?"

"Tomorrow," said John, "tomorrow I will call the Ontario Ministry of Labour, to tell them to get somebody the hell out to that factory. Union-busting is illegal, Piet, and we *will not stand for it!*" Piet nodded agreement but his face remained bleak. "Tell you what," said John, "that meeting can carry on without me. *You* are more important. When the guys are done with your car, I'm taking you to the Portsmouth for a beer."

They took a table in a secluded corner of the old tavern, under smoke-stained ceiling beams. Through the small-paned windows, they could see the frozen expanse of Portsmouth Harbour, and beyond that, the formidable limestone walls of Kingston Penitentiary. They sat in companionable silence, drinking their beer. Finally, Piet began to speak. "When I saw dat writing on my car, it was like I looking at *een, een, hakenkruis, ja*, I don't know how to say dat word in English." With his fingertip he drew a symbol on the table top. John looked, tried to comprehend.

"Swastika?" he asked. Piet gave a slight nod. "How do you get swastika from, 'Better dead than red?' One has to do with the Nazis, and the other comes from the McCarthy era. I don't get it!"

Piet drank deeply of his beer. He sat with his head in his hands. He looked up. "Five years, we live under de Nazi boot. Five years we hef to listen to Goebbels." He looked at John. "You heard of him?"

"Yeah, I think so. Wasn't he the Nazi Propaganda Minister?"

"Right. Near de end of de war, Goebbels, he tell de German people, *"Lieber tot als rot."* Piet looked at John, but. John still looked rather uncomprehending. "Joseph Goebbels, he talk about de Russians, *marcheren* into Germany. He want de Germans to fight to de dead.

"Really! Is that where that slogan came from? I thought McCarthy made it up."

"No," said Piet. "Goebbels. In 1945, Goebbels, he was in Hitler's bunker."

"The bunker where Hitler killed himself?"

"*Ja*. Goebbels was dere, with his family. When de Russians coming close, Goebbels and his wife, *dey* kill demself – but first, dey poison all dere children, six little children, from four to twelve year old. *Lieber tot als rot.*"

With dawning horror, John said slowly, "Better dead, than red."

Driving home, Piet felt somewhat better. The support of the guys at the union hall had been great, and talking to John had helped. The man was a good listener. He sure couldn't talk to Johanna about this stuff. Not that she'd be home tonight. Whenever *he* went to a union meeting, *she* was off to see Lies. Henk was away, too. Cadets. Marching around in the Drill Shed with puttees on his calves. Damn things were always drooping down, tangling up. Piet thought that there must to be a real art to the wearing of puttees. He pulled into his driveway. "Papa!" Anneke came running out before he'd even turned off the engine. "It's Yeller! Come quick!" Piet hurried inside, found Yeller lying on the kitchen floor, chest heaving, tongue lolling out, eyes rolled back in his head.

"What happened? Hit by a car?"

"No," said Anneke, distressed. "Wasn't hit. We were coming back from Rosemary's and there was a man at the end of our driveway. Yeller barked and the man took off, but he threw something, and Yeller started eating it. I tried to stop him, but he ate it so fast!"

Piet could barely get the words out, "This man, what did he look like?"

"Big. Rough looking."

"Right," said Piet bitterly. "Right." Gently he asked, "And Yeller?"

"Started staggering around. Gagging. It was just awful, papa! And then he started to shiver, so I kind of dragged him into the house. I didn't know what to do! There was nobody home." Piet nodded sympathetically. "Then I got him inside and he made this gurgling sound like he was choking, and then he...he...he kind of collapsed on the floor. He hasn't moved, papa, he looks so *awful!*" Anneke burst into tears. Piet stood in the middle of the floor, rubbing his hand over his forehead, his eyes closed. He let out a deep sigh. Pulled himself together.

"Kindje," he said, and put his hand on her shoulder, "you did a good job bringing him inside. Now, we have to make sure that he's kept warm. Can you find an old blanket?" Anneke ran from the room. Piet inspected the dog, noted the pale gums, the limp body. Anneke came running back with a blanket she'd pulled off her own bed. Together, father and daughter tenderly tucked it over and around the dying dog. Anneke sat on the floor stroking Yeller as her tears dripped down on the dog's golden fur. Piet, at the kitchen table smoking, watched his daughter. He marveled that Anneke, the difficult teenager, was suddenly Anneke, his little girl.

"Papa," she called. He walked over, placed his hand on her hair. She looked up through tear-filled eyes. "Can't just let him die, papa! Isn't there anything else we can do?"

"Well," said Piet, suddenly pulling on his coat. "I don't know if it'll help, but, I'm going to go see Bob, the neighbour you got Yeller from. He's a dog breeder. Maybe he knows something." Piet left. In a matter of minutes he was back, carrying a thin brown medicine bottle. Anneke watched him come through the door. Looked eagerly at the bottle.

"What is it?"

"Activated charcoal. Helps absorb the poison. Bob says it's worth a try." Piet crouched down by the dog. "All right, Anneke," he said, as he raised the dog's muzzle. "Can you pour in just a tiny bit at a time?" Anneke nodded. Carefully poured some medication down the dog's throat. "Wait a moment. Wait for it to go down. OK, now, a little bit more." Anneke poured another tiny amount. " That's it." Piet gently laid the dog's head back down.

"Will it work?"

"I don't know, *kindje*," he answered. I sure *hope* it does!" Piet sat down heavily. Looked at the limp dog, the disconsolate child, and lapsed into self-recrimination. If he hadn't tried to bring in the union, if he had been more careful, if he hadn't talked to Frank. If…if….if! The dog was dying, the child heartbroken, and it was all because of him. Caught up in his own dark thoughts, he didn't hear the door open, and was startled by Johanna's yell.

"Who let that dirty dog into my kitchen?"

Tearfully, Anneke turned to face her mother, sobbed, "Yeller's poisoned! Dying! I let him in the house 'cause he was dying!"

"What!" Johanna shrieked. "Poison! *Poison!*

"Johanna," said Piet, "if you're going to scream, get out of the kitchen. Things are bad enough in here. We don't need your racket!"

"*Poison! What* poison? I can't leave this house for *five* minutes before you...."

"Out!" he snapped. Johanna's eyes narrowed, and she opened her mouth to retort, then she thought better of it, clamped her jaw shut, and left the room.

Piet turned to his daughter, said gently, "All right, *kindje*, let's try to give him just a little bit more."

Piet tossed and turned. Got tangled in the bed clothes. Got cursed by his wife. Finally he sat up on the side of the bed, stuck his feet into his corduroy slippers, and in the darkness felt his way down the narrow, wooden stairs. He opened the door to the kitchen and saw to his chagrin that he'd forgotten to close the curtains. His child was asleep there, and *he'd* left everything wide open. He noted the moonlight pouring though the side window, and followed it to where it created a pool of golden light on the linoleum floor. In the centre of that light lay Anneke, hair a burnished copper, curled on a blanket with Yeller, arm protectively around the golden dog. Piet stood watching, a lump in his throat. It was like a scene in a Rembrandt painting, he thought, with the child and dog in that golden light, and all around them, the darkness. He went over to check on Yeller, crouched down, gently ran his hand over the fur. He looked into the dog's face, hoping to see the eyes open, head lift up, tongue lick a warm greeting, but there was no response, the dog lay inert. Grim-faced, Piet walked to the kitchen counter, lit a cigarette and sucked the smoke deeply into his lungs. His mind raced back over the events of the day, the vandalizing of his car, the poisoning of the dog, and he felt a rage build inside him. *Die vervloekte vent, bastaard, schoft!* Furiously he ground his cigarette butt into the ashtray. He could kill that bastard Frank! He shook his head to try to clear it, then he climbed back up the stairs. He let out a deep sigh, and crawled back into bed with Johanna.

Wide awake again an hour later, Piet decided that he might as well stay up. He threw on his clothes and went downstairs to make coffee. Anneke raised her head, said in a drowsy voice, "How late is it?"

"Only five-thirty. Go back to sleep, *kindje*."

"Can I stay home from school today, papa? Please? To look after Yeller?" Piet heard the pleading in her voice, noted the circles under her eyes.

"*Ja*," he said, "that's OK." Whatever the outcome with the dog, the child was in no shape for school. "For one day. You can stay home." He knew there'd be hell to pay. Johanna would disagree. But then, Johanna always disagreed with him lately. Anneke lay back down, cuddled the dog, closed her eyes. Piet sat at the kitchen table, brow furrowed, drinking coffee as the cigarette butts piled up in the ashtray. Finally, he got up, pulled on his heavy coat, steel-toed work boots, and the soft leather gloves from his white-collar job in *Nederland*, and he left the house. A yellow disc of moon hung low in the sky, the snow crunched under his feet. He wondered if his ancient

Plymouth would start. After several tries he managed to get it going, but as he drove, the windows kept fogging up, and he went very slowly, peering ahead, trying to keep the car on the snow-packed road. Finally, when the windows had cleared somewhat, he saw the unlit factory up ahead, looming darkly against a pale tangerine line of horizon. Piet pulled up by the sidewalk in front of the building and waited in the car, lost in his dark reverie. That man, that evil man! *Die duvel!* Piet could taste the bile in the back of his throat. He *must* keep himself in check. He knew he must *control* himself, yet.... He would stand up to that man, *confront* him, *force* him to admit what he had done, *expose* the devil. 'Better dead than red' was the slogan Frank had put on his car... Goebbels slogan... Goebbels... the war... the occupation... the evil all around him...

Once more it was 1943. Piet was behind the house, working in his vegetable garden. Suddenly, a woman's voice screamed from across the hedge, "Piet! Piet! They've taken Aartje!" He looked up to see his neighbour Goske, her face anguished, her hands wringing her apron. "The S.S., they took Aartje!" and she began to wail. Piet jumped over the hedge. Took her in his arms. Tried to quiet her anguished cries. He knew she had no husband to turn to. Koos had died in the bombardments. Goske lived alone with her young daughter and teenaged son. And now that son had been taken. Piet put his arm around her shoulders and led her though the wooden gate to his house, settled her in a chair in the *woonkamer*. Johanna, hearing the commotion, came racing down the stairs from where she had been cleaning, gave Goske a handkerchief, brought coffee. Finally the sobs subsided. Her head in her hands, Goske took a deep breath, "I'd been to visit my mother, so I waited for Aartje at the gate of the lyceum, to walk home together. And we were just walking along the Beukenlaan, near the Philips Factory, when he saw a friend of his, another student. 'Mum,' he said, 'I want to talk to Joost for a minute. I'll be home soon.' He gave me a peck on the cheek and ran over to his friend. I heard them talking and laughing. Suddenly I heard the roar of an engine, and a black car came racing up the street. It slammed to a halt beside the boys, and two S.S. jumped out and demanded Aartje's papers. His papers are in order, Piet. He's going to school. He's a good boy, Piet! He wants to be a teacher. Why would they take him?"

"Did they say anything?"

"I couldn't really understand them. I ran over! They talked half Dutch half German. Joost they let go. But Aartje?" Goske thought for a moment, then said slowly, "Something about the factory. Something about the strike. '*Aansporen,*' they said." Piet didn't question her further. Tried not to let the dismay show on his face. The boy *hadn't* been picked up for deportation to the German labour camps. He'd been arrested for for sabotage, for inciting the strike. "I'm so scared for my boy, Piet! Can't you do something?" and she burst into tears again.

"I'll do my best," he promised. He went to see his brother-in-law, Theo, who had worked for the police, and had connections. Theo confirmed that in retaliation for the strike, the Nazis had made arrests. "But the boy had nothing to do with the strike," Piet protested. "There must be a way to straighten this out!"

"You don't understand," said Theo. "The Nazis don't care about that! They don't know who is responsible, so they arrest randomly, to make an example, to intimidate." Theo sighed, added in a halting voice, "They took them to the Philips Factory. The word is that... they took them there to... to shoot them."

"No!" Piet cried out. "No! I've got to get over there. He's just a kid! He's got nothing to do with the factory! He's got nothing to do with the strike! I've got to tell them..."

"Piet!" Theo grabbed him by the arm. "Don't even think about it! If you go over there, if you speak up for him, they'll arrest you, too."

"No they won't, Theo! They stopped me earlier in the street today, but I'm 'Essential Service' so they let me go," and he tried to pull loose from Theo's grip.

"'Essential Service' be damned! They sure as hell won't let you go a second time! Don't be a total fool!" He shook his head, "Piet, I do not want to be the one to tell Johanna!" At the sound of his wife's name, Piet stopped struggling – almost went limp. Theo continued sadly, "Piet, getting yourself killed won't help Aartje, it won't help his mother, and it sure as hell won't help Johanna... or your children."

The lights came on in MillCreek Furniture, but Piet didn't notice. Workmen started to pass by on the sidewalk, but Piet was oblivious to their glances, to their words of greeting. Then a burly man in a red plaid jacket came into view, and Piet jolted to attention. It was him! Frank! *De duvel!* He came lumbering along the sidewalk with Harvey, one of his cronies. As they came near, Frank gestured at Piet's car, poked Harvey in the ribs, shook with laughter. Piet stepped out of his car, and planted himself firmly on the cinders of the sidewalk. His chin up, his voice tightly controlled, he stared Frank in the eye, and demanded, "Did you poison *de* dog *van* my little girl?" Frank's eyes shifted, then he looked over at Harvey, and he smirked. Piet struggled inwardly, but his voice did not waver as he repeated, "Did you poison *de* dog?" Frank gave a slow wink at Harvey, then he dove at Piet, ramming his shoulder into Piet's chest. Piet shook from the blow, but his feet remained rooted. Again, he started to say, "Did you..." but Frank's fist silenced him, and Piet tasted blood. He tried to remain focused, to repeat the question, but *Piet's* fist, seemingly of its own volition, flew forward and smashed into Frank's jaw, crashing the big man to the ground. Workmen ran over to see him sprawled in the snow. Piet looked down at his nemesis, and felt tremendous satisfaction, mingled with shock – he didn't know he could fight! This wasn't him. Hit someone? Not since he was a kid. But he had to admit it felt damn good.

Frank started to rise, slowly drawled, "Why you commie bastard..."

"Look out, Piet!" someone yelled. There was a flash of metal. As

Piet jumped back, a knife slashed through his pant-leg. Piet aimed a kick, heard a crunch of bone, a squeal; saw a knife go sailing off into the snow. Swearing profusely, Frank sat on his haunches, his right hand cradled in his left.

Piet stood over him. Grimly he said "I teach you to poison *de* dog *van* my little girl" and then he walked away. He walked around the factory to cool off, stopped to tie his handkerchief around the gash in his leg, to stop the blood trickling into his boot. Finally he went inside and started to sand the chair he'd worked on the day before. He doubted he'd be there long enough to finish the job. At any moment, he expected to be called to the office, to he terminated.

"Piet!" called a voice from behind him. Oh, oh, he thought. I guess this is it. He turned around. There were a handful of workmen, whom he recognized vaguely from the far end of the factory, the area where Frank worked. Momentarily Piet froze. Then a hand was extended, an open hand, not a fist. Surprised, he took it. A small bespectacled man said, "Hell of a job, Piet! That Frank's been pushing people around long enough, and any guy who'd poison a kid's dog, why he's nothing but low-down scum! Just the other day my kids were watching 'Lassie'..."

"That guy Frank is so low..." cut in a second man, "why he's lower than whale shit!"

"No, no, "said a third, "that guy is so low, he can look up a snake's asshole and think it's the North Star!" The men roared. Slapped each other on the back. Even Piet had to smile.

Then his eyes went wide, as the bespectacled man came back with, "Where are those union cards, Piet?"

It was a couple of hours before he was called to the office. Must have taken that long to get Redpath over there. 'Fighting on the job,' said his pink slip, 'Dismissal effective immediately.' Piet walked out the factory door with leaden legs, wondering how he was going to break the news to Johanna.

She was standing with her coat buttoned up ready to go out when he walked through the kitchen door. Surprised, she asked, "You home already?"

"Thought I'd come home for a cup of coffee," he joked feebly, trying to delay the inevitable, but Johanna quickly spotted his torn and bloody pant leg.

"*Mijn God!* What happened? *Kom hier.* Let me see that. Accident at work?" Piet remained mute as she dashed off for the first aid kit. He sat on a kitchen chair as she cleaned and bandaged the wound, nattering the whole time, "You should look for another job, Piet. That factory is *too* dangerous. And you're *not* going back to work today. You might get dirt in the wound. Get blood poisoning. Stay off your leg and give it a chance to heal. Now, *don't* move out of that chair. I have to go. Lies is expecting me for coffee." She was gone.

Anneke waited for the door to close. Then she looked up at her father, a knowing, questioning look. "Papa, how *did* you hurt your leg?"

"A knife," he said tonelessly, and pursed his mouth. Her eyes went wide. "Don't want to say any more about it now. Haven't told your mother. There'll be big trouble!"

Taking advantage of the peace and quiet, Piet read the Whig Standard, Dutch/English dictionary by his side. In the commotion of the night before, he'd missed his evening routine. While he read, Anneke was trying to dribble milk down Yeller's throat with an eye dropper. It wasn't going well. There was no swallowing, and most of the milk dripped onto the floor. Piet tried to distract her, "BB had a baby," he announced. Anneke looked up. "Yesterday. Baby boy. Nicolas. By her second husband."

"Jacques Charrier," said Anneke promptly. Piet looked impressed. "An actor. They met when they were in a film together."

"Newspaper reporters all over the place," Piet continued, "and photographers, wanting to take the first picture."

"*Is* there a picture?" asked Anneke, and started over to look, but there was knock on the door. Anneke opened it, and an excited John Comberford blew into the kitchen with a gust of wintry air.

"You wouldn't believe the state of that factory, Piet! All hell breaking loose!"

Astonished, Piet looked up from his paper, "Wat's happening?"

"Let me tell you," said John, seating himself comfortably at the kitchen table, and launching into his tale. "First thing this morning I was over at the Kingston Office of the Department of Labour, talking to Hugh O'Donnell. He's a solid, seasoned kind of guy I've dealt with before. I told him about the situation at MillCreek Furniture, about how you're trying to unionize and had a death-threat painted on the side of your car, and Hugh was concerned enough to drive right out to the factory with me. Damn lucky he was available! Piet, you wouldn't believe what we walked in to. I've never seen anything like it!"

With a puzzled frown, Piet said, "Wat..."

"Wild-cat strike. Over your termination. The men knew it was a crock of shit! That fight took place on a public sidewalk, not in the factory. There *was* no 'fighting on the job'. And the other guy, Frank, *he* didn't get a pink slip. Not that he can work anyway," John chuckled, "with that broken hand. Piet, the reason you got fired, was your union activism. Your firing," said John, glaring, hitting his fist into the palm of his other hand, "was a case of out-and-out union busting!"

"Firing?" Anneke suddenly spoke up. "My father got fired?" Surprised, John looked over at Anneke. She was on the floor with her dog. He hadn't noticed her there.

"Anneke," he said gently, "your father, why, why he's quite a 'cause celebre'." Anneke looked puzzled. "The men at the factory," John explained, "were so upset over his unjust firing, that they refused to work. Picture this, Anneke, this morning I went out to the factory with Hugh O'Donnell, he's an official with the Ministry of Labour, and we went right into the section where you father works, and," John shook his head with amazement, "it was like walking into a museum."

"What?" said Anneke, scrunching her face, "museum?" She thought of her most recent trip to the factory to deliver a thermos of coffee, of the clattering, pounding, whining ear-splitting racket, and of the shouting men, and of the dust, so thick in the air you could taste it – and she wondered how a factory could possibly be like a museum.

"Absolute silence!" said John. "It was so quiet in that factory, at first we thought there was no-one there. We couldn't see very well, the power was off, so there was just some diluted light filtering in through those grimy windows. We walked in to the middle of that huge shop. Suddenly we spotted them. It was eerie! They had laid their tools down on the shop floor, their torches, and rasps and sand-paper, and..." John took a breath, "and they were standing beside their tools, in that ghostly half-light, in their dust-covered work clothes, with the dust thick in their hair, and on their faces – those men, they were standing like statues. Hugh and I, we just looked at them, couldn't believe our eyes! No one said a word, we looked at them, they stared back at us. Suddenly, into the midst of this, walks a man dressed in suit, waistcoat, and silk tie.

"Tom Redgrave," Piet told Anneke.

"He looked pretty annoyed at actually having to deal with something at the factory. Told the men to quit screwing around and get back to work," John continued. He turned to Piet, "You'd have been proud of those guys! No one budged. They remained immobile as marble, and that really seemed to tick Tom Redgrave off! He started cursing, and he knew some mighty colourful language. He finally told them that they had exactly sixty seconds to pick up their tools, or they were fired, every last one of them! He started a count-down. By then, Hugh had seen enough! He walked up to Tom Redgrave, flashed his credentials, and said in his low, gravelly voice, 'Mr. Redgrave, I'd like a word with you please.' Well," said John grinning at Piet, "when Redgrave saw Hugh was with the Ministry of Labour, he actually tried to intimidate him! He rose up to his full height, and looked at him through slitted eyes. 'Perhaps you are not aware,' he said haughtily, 'that the MPP is a fellow golfer and close personal friend of mine.' That was a big mistake! Nobody tried to intimidate Hugh! He roared back, 'And is that close personal friend aware of the working conditions in this factory?' He pulled out his notebook, 'I've got some questions for you, Mr. Redgrave.' He conducted a thorough investigation, interviewing both workers and administration. Then he wrote a rough draft of his report. He went to see Redgrave in his office, and read him the riot act. Told him he was facing huge fines for union-busting, for flaunting the Labour Relations Act. In the end, Redgrave was only too happy to rescind the firing."

"Wat is dat? Rescind?"

"Means you're not fired anymore," said John, grinning. "No more holidaying, loafing about! By the way, how *is* your leg?" Piet looked surprised. "Yeah, yeah, I heard you got cut."

"It is OK. Johanna put a bandage on it."

"How did she take the news of the fight?"

"Hmmm," said Piet, with a sidelong glance at Anneke.

"Hasn't told her yet," said Anneke, with a conspiratorial smile.

Piet turned to John, reached out his hand, "I want to tank you," he said simply, but with obvious emotion, "*dat* I hef my job back."

John swallowed, "You're welcome. Now then, Hugh is still over at the factory tying up loose ends. Doesn't want another labour disruption breaking out the moment he leaves. Looking at some safety concerns too. Didn't like the look of that dust. In fact, Hugh said it's unconscionable that there isn't proper ventilation. Also concerned about storage of combustibles." Piet nodded slowly, frowned. "Well," said John, "the *union* can help you with that."

"Ja," said Piet, "if…"

"Oh," said John, "I didn't tell you yet, did I? The union is *in!"*

"Wat!" exclaimed Piet. "You are kidding!"

"No, I'm not! More than fifty-five percent of the workforce has now signed a union card. In fact, the percentage is well above that, and the cards are continuing to come in! Of course these signed cards still have to go to Toronto for ratification by the Labour Relations Board, but I'm sure there won't be a problem."

"Dat is fantastisch!" said Piet.

John turned his attention to Anneke, asked gently, "How is Yeller?"

Anneke's eyes filled with tears. John got down on the floor. Stroked the dog. Spoke softly to the child.

Suddenly, the door flew open! "Fight!" Johanna screamed. "You were in a fight! A common brawl! I thought I married a man with a little bit of class, and it turns out you're nothing but a...a...." Her index finger shook in Piet's face. Anneke watched, intrigued – usually it was *she* who was the object of her mother's ire. John, embarrassed, kept his eyes glued to the dog. "And you got fired! Fired!" Piet tried to speak, to explain, but it was impossible. Johanna screeched, "And why? Why? Over that blasted union business! Because you wouldn't listen to me! I told you, you would get fired! I told you and I told you, and..." As Johanna went on and on berating her husband in a voice loud enough to wake the dead, only John noticed the pricking up of one golden ear.

"Such a sweet child," said Piet. He examined his hand, finally tossing the king of hearts on the table. "You wouldn't believe the way she took care of that dog. Barely left Yeller's side."

"Sweet, *ja*, for a day or two," grumbled Johanna, playing the ten.

"Didn't last, huh?" chuckled Lies, slapping her ace on top.
Kees topped it with a trump, hauled the cards towards him. *"Hoy!"* objected Lies, but Kees just grinned.

Johanna shuffled the cards, continued, "Lasted as long as that dog was sick. When the dog bounced back, Anneke bounced back, right back to her old behaviour – running around with the boys, skirts so tight she can barely walk, big mouth when I say anything to her. Don't know *what* I did to deserve that girl!"

"Wasn't there a time you were pretty good at *kattekwaad* yourself?" Piet asked. Outside it was snowing heavily, but it was warm and cozy in Lies and Kees's little house. The aroma of the coffee perking on the oil-burner mingled with that of their cigarette smoke.

"Oh," asked Lies with a smile, "what kind of trouble did Johanna get into?"

Piet said mysteriously, "Had something to do with a little mouse."

Johanna wrinkled her brow. "Mouse, mouse..." Suddenly she smiled, "Oh, right! At the Philips factory! You know, I started working there at 14, putting filaments in bulbs and then testing them. It was piece work. I remember well that you were supposed to test the light bulbs one by one, but I found a way around it and would test them en mass when the boss wasn't around. That way I made as much a 28 gulden a week! The pay went to my mother, and let me tell you she was pretty happy with me. I got an allowance of 2 gulden. I liked it at Philips! We were all young girls together, and it was fun to talk, and to joke; but there was one girl, Marta, who was kind of snooty and didn't want to associate with the rest of us. So I decided to teach her a lesson. In the area where we worked we all had to wear lab-coats, and when we were done we hung them on hooks with our names over top. One day, I put a dead mouse in the pocket of Marta's lab-coat. She put it on, and when she reached into her pocket and touched the mouse, she started to scream at the top of her lungs! Everybody came running. I went the other way but still I could hear her screaming and screaming! I was terrified! They finally got the doctor to come and give her a shot. I was so scared they'd find out it was me. A good thing they never did, or they would have fired me, and then my mother would have killed me."

The roared with laughter. Kees said, "Johanna, I didn't know you had it in you! That deserves *een borreltje, meid!*" He went to the kitchen counter, pulled out a bottle, and started to pour. "Piet," he called over his shoulder, "you don't know what's happening at the Stagecoach Inn, do you?"

"Walked by there the other day," said Piet, joining his friend at the counter. "It's still got that 'condemned' tape around it. Was talking to one of the neighbours. Told me the owner, Bob McMillan, tried to get insurance money but the company won't pay because they claim he caused it himself."

"Why would they say that?" asked Kees and he took the drinks to the women who were still talking about Femke. "Wasn't it just the snow that caused the roof to cave in? Unless they're blaming him for not shoveling it."

"Oh," smiled Piet, "I think there's a bit more to it than that. Bob wanted to turn the building into a restaurant and *ja,* the building itself would draw people."

"Right. With those two levels of verandah running along the front, looks like something out of the wild west. So what happened?"

"He wanted a huge dining room, so he went in with some of his buddies and started removing interior walls. Suddenly there was this tremendous creaking and grinding, and they ran like hell as the beams crashed down! They'd removed load-bearing walls! Idiots! Didn't take the insurance adjuster long to figure out what happened. Bob'll be lucky if they don't go after him for attempted fraud."

"Can you get Bob's phone number? Ask him about salvage," urged Kees. "I need more lumber for my greenhouse. Come on out here. Take a look at what I've got my hands on so far," and he led Piet into a back room with some windows stacked against a wall. He quickly asked Piet, "And the union?"

Grinning from ear to ear, Piet said, "Ratified by the Ontario Labour Relations Board!" Jubilantly, he added, "It's legal, Kees! The union is legal! Tom Redgrave can't touch us now."

Anneke sat alone, scowling. Through the high classroom windows she saw drifting snow. From beyond the school walls came muffled sounds of student laughter. Snowball fight, no doubt, and here *she* was, stuck in detention, again! She sighed. Mr. Regamey approached. From the corner of her eye, she observed him critically. He was youngish for a teacher, tall, with a worn tweed jacket and ridiculous bow-tie. He walked by her desk, sat down on the desktop directly behind her. She felt a hand on her shoulder. Anneke froze. "Annie," he said softly, "if only you would co-operate, you could do very well in music class. You have so much potential Annie. You just need more cultural *exposure*," he drew out the 'o' sound. "You should be going to concerts, not sitting *here* after school. I want to help you Annie," and he gave her shoulder a little squeeze.

Anneke's eyes went wide. What was he doing? He was the teacher! He stood up, told her to finish her work, and went back to his desk. Feeling alone and vulnerable, she worked madly to complete the homework she should have finished days ago. Notes, notes, notes. Where did they go on the bar? Anything to get out of here! After half-an-hour, he came back to check her work. He leaned on her desk, put his arm around her shoulders. "Good girl," he said softly, "you've finished. Don't things go much better when you cooperate? Yes, indeed. You're done for today." Anneke tried to scramble out of her desk, but she was wearing her tightest skirt, so movement *was* difficult. "Are you having trouble?" He reached down, put his hands on her waist, hoisted her to her feet. His large hands almost encircled her, and he kept them there as Anneke stared, wild-eyed. But he didn't notice her expression – his eyes were not on her face. Slowly, deliberately, he trailed his fingers up her back. Then he seemed to shake himself, gave her ponytail a playful twist and said. "There's a good girl. Off you go! I'll see you tomorrow." Anneke left the classroom, and ran home as fast as her skirt would allow.

After that, she made sure she had her homework done, *still* he kept her in after school, sat on the desk behind her. "You have so much potential. You just need some extra attention, don't you?" Anneke played at being mute. "Have you been practicing your violin? We're so fortunate at this school to have these stringed instruments. Donations from alumni. Provide a wonderful opportunity. Why don't you get your violin and play for me." Anneke was afraid he would help her out of her desk again, so she quickly got to her feet. She could feel his eyes on her as she walked across the room to the instrument cupboard. She took out her violin, her bow and a music stand, and started to play, trying hard to concentrate on the music and to block the teacher from her mind. Suddenly she felt him near her! With a caterwauling screech her bow slipped. "Let me help you," said Mr. Regamey, moving close behind her. "Here, I'll hold you steady," and he put his left hand on her waist. "Now, I'll help you with your bow work." He cupped his right hand over hers, and made the bow sweep back and forth, back and forth across the violin. "You see, Annie, it's all in the rhythm." Anneke tried to focus on the music, on her notes, but she was only aware of his body against hers, the thrusts of the bow. Finally he stepped away from her. Said hoarsely, "You can go now Annie. Leave the violin. Go. We'll practice some more tomorrow."

"I don't know what I'm gonna do," Anneke said to Gerda, "if we didn't have music last period I just wouldn't go to his detentions. But I'm already in the room. There's no way to get away from him."

"Maybe you should tell your mother."

"Are you crazy? I can hear her now…. *Probleem met de* teacher?

De teacher *is niet het probleem. Jij bent het probleem.* You are *always* the problem.' That's *exactly* what she'd say. No way I'm telling *her!*"

Every day she had music detention so he could 'help' her. Every day he got more physical, more persuasive, "To truly appreciate the violin, you must hear it played by professional musicians." He smiled coaxingly, "Wouldn't you like to go to a concert? The Kingston Symphony is playing this weekend!" Anneke didn't know what to say, what to do. She did know that she felt incredibly uncomfortable.

She said in a small voice, "I need to go to the washroom."

"Little break?" he said. "That's fine." Anneke walked through the hallway into the bathroom. Shook her head to clear it. Tried to figure out a plan. She'd just, she'd just walk right by the classroom and, and just keep going. Tomorrow she'd plead ignorance, forgetfulness. Anneke stepped into the hall. Nearly bumped into Regamey. Oh my God, he was waiting by the bathroom door!

That night, Anneke tossed and turned. What to do, what to do… The next morning she was walking to school with Gerda. Kicking at the snow, pretending it was Regamey, she said, "Do me a favour…"

In detention that afternoon, Anneke again said she had to use the washroom, and again he followed her into the hall to stand by the bathroom door. Anneke went inside, locked the toilet cubicle and opened the small bathroom window. She climbed up on the toilet-seat, and whispered as loudly as she dared, "Gerda, are you there? Have you got my boots and stuff?"

"Roger," said Gerda, standing in the snow. She watched her cousin's head emerge from the tiny window, then half her body, then…

"Dammit, Gerda, I'm stuck!" said Anneke, as her hips wedged. "Shit! Help me!" Gerda grabbed her hands, braced her feet against the brick wall, and pulled! Anneke popped like a cork, and they tumbled into the snow. She yanked on her boots, and they ran down the road laughing hysterically, picturing the teacher waiting, and waiting, outside that bathroom door.

The next day Anneke was afraid to go to school, but the teacher didn't speak to her. In fact, he didn't speak to her again for the rest of the year.

Spring was in the air! Jack's '47 Chevy rattled along country roads, where unfurling buds painted a soft green haze across a winter landscape. Pockets of snow lingered, punctuating the dark undergrowth.

The occupants of the Chevy were caught up in their own spring fever. Wally and Jill were making out on the back seat, panting and rolling around, and cursing when the car hit a bump. In the front, Jack filled his lungs with sweet spring air, then sang, "Little Rosa," as he shifted gears from his position on the passenger's side. Anneke was in the driver's seat. She controlled gas, clutch, and brake, and it was she, who steered the car around the countryside.

Anneke loved driving, and she felt pretty proud of herself, that Jack would trust her with his prized possession. Must care for her a lot, to let her drive his car. Only problem was, she was wearing her full skirt with the sugar-starched crinolines, and it was hard to see her feet. They approached a stop sign. Jack instructed, "Slow down, slow down. OK! Clutch!" Anneke managed to stomp her feet on the appropriate pedals, Jack negotiated the gear shift, and the Chevy came to a gear-grinding halt. Curses rained from the back, but Anneke was oblivious. They were off again. "Clutch!" said Jack, "Gas. Just a little bit! Clutch!" He shifted, she pedaled, and the car proceeded to jerk down the road. Finally they were rolling along smoothly once more, and Jack resumed his singing, "Little Rosa…"

"How about speeding it up a bit," came a voice from the back. "I need a fag, man. Can't wait all day to get to Deseronto! Common, pedal to the metal." Anneke glanced at Jack, but he merely grinned, so she pulled out to pass the farm truck ahead. She pulled back too quickly into her own lane, and the truck beeped angrily, and a clenched fist waved from the driver's window.

"You cut him off!" said Jack. "My God, you cut him off!" He laughed nervously. Anneke didn't know what she'd done, or what it meant to 'cut someone off,' but soon Jack resumed singing, and all was well with the world. Contentedly she drove along, past barns and farmhouses, and newly-pastured cows.

"Turn!" shouted a voice from the back. "That's the road we need! Turn!" Anneke pulled at the steering wheel, and the car veered right. Too much so! They were heading for the ditch! Jack grabbed the wheel, jerked it back. Anneke tried to slam the brake but hit the gas, and with a sickening thud the Chevy crashed into a tree! Shaken, they climbed out. Steam poured from the staved-in hood. Jack stood, looking at his car, eyes like saucers.

"I'm sorry!" sobbed Anneke. "Sorry, Jack. Sorry!"

Jack went into the trunk. Grabbed a crow-bar. Tried to pry the hood open, but it was impossible. "Gonna get a tow-truck," he said in a monotone, and started walking down the road. Then he stopped, turned, looked back at Anneke, "You weren't driving," he said. "I was!" Anneke blinked, uncomprehending. Jack disappeared around a turn of the road.

"Insurance," Wally explained. "You don't have a license, do you? Wouldn't be insured."

"Can't have a license," sobbed Anneke miserably, as she stared down the road after Jack. "Just fourteen."

"*Hoy!* Kees," shouted Piet, as he walked along the trail to his friend's market garden.

Kees was on his knees, planting seedlings, "*Hallo!*" He stood up, his hands and knees dirt-encrusted. He stretched his back. Sat down on a log and lit up a cigarette. "What's new?"

"Well," said Piet, joining his friend and lighting up. "You were talking a while ago about salvage from the Stagecoach Inn." He blew out some smoke, "I finally got hold of Bob. Asked about the lumber. He said, 'Give me a couple hundred bucks and just get that mess cleaned the hell out of there!' Sounded pretty pissed still. Good for us though. Dirt cheap! I need lumber for a garage – have car, need garage, right?" he grinned, "and you were talking about your greenhouse? Don't know if you need a *lot* of lumber for that, but…"

"I also need to put an addition on my house."

Piet looked quizzical, "What? Another addition?"

Kees looked down at the ground, but a smile curled around one corner of his mouth, "Uh, yeah…. another ankle-biter on the way."

Piet snorted. "I thought you were using *kapotjes?*"

"Ja, in the house. But we don't have them out in the field do we?'

Piet laughed, "You dog, you!" He looked at Kees, with more than a hint of admiration,
"Can't believe Lies puts up with you!"

A smile tugging at his lips, Kees looked off at the horizon. Said softly, "Kinda how things started off between Liesje and me."

"What are you talking about?"

"I was an *onderduiker* at her father's farm from '43, slept in the hayloft, and did whatever work I could. At first, it was a miserable existence. I felt like I was in jail – never being able to go anywhere, never able to see any friends. Mind you, by then most of my friends were in hiding anyway…

or in the labour camps. But I grew to like growing things, and was in the vegetable garden as much as possible, always on the alert of course. My life changed completely when Liesje came home to the farm. She'd been working in Amsterdam, but by the fall of '44 things were increasingly desperate there. Her mother sent food packages, but they didn't always get through. Her father decided that she should come back to the farm."

"Suddenly I had this gorgeous girl bringing me my dinner every night. My God! She had this sort of musky smell, and as she came closer, the hair on the back of my neck would stand up!"

"Was that all that stood up?" asked a grinning Piet.

Kees ignored him. "She might have looked wonderful, but she was in foul humour! Was pretty ticked she'd had to leave her life in the city. But when she discovered I was an Amsterdammer she became friendlier, and we did a lot of talking... pubs, mutual friends... I hadn't even seen a girl for over a year! I remember like yesterday the first time I kissed Lies. Oh, it was sweet! But when she let me lift up her blouse and touch her breasts, her soft, soft breasts, oh, oh, oh, I thought I was in heaven!"

"Phew!" said Piet, and "weren't you afraid her father would catch you?"

"Terrified," grinned Kees. "But you know I was always on the alert anyway. And I suppose it added spice, the very furtiveness of it. One day when she brought me my plate of food I could see she'd been crying. A friend in Amsterdam had been shot by the Germans. She set my plate down, but she didn't join me, stayed standing. 'Kees,' she said, 'we could both be dead tomorrow. In this war, all we have is today.' She had a strained look on her face. And then slowly, she started to unbutton her blouse, revealing those gorgeous breasts, and she dropped the blouse on the hay. Then she unzipped her skirt, and let it fall, and as I held my breath, she slipped off her panties. And beneath her belly I saw the dark downiness, the mystery. Lies stood there, naked, vulnerable, and incredibly beautiful. I was so young! I walked over, reached down, and cupped my hand over that wonderfully mysterious part, and as I touched her she seemed to melt in my hand. And I laid her down on the pile of clothes, and I opened her, and plunged into her. My first time Piet! Plunging over and over and oh my God! Liesje's eyes were wild, and she moved with me, every move and motion she was with me, and finally, an *incredible explosion* and Liesje *screamed* and I covered her mouth with my hand and thought she would bite me. And then... there was just the smell of the hay... and my Liesje, beneath me.

"Phew!" was all Piet could think to say.

"After that, it was still war, but the best time of my life. All day I thought of the twilight, and the feel of Liesje's body under mine."

"And... you were never caught?"

Kees sighed, "One day her father came into the barn unexpectedly, and my God, he found us at it. *Mad! Was he mad!* That was *it!* He was *turning* me in to the Germans!"

Piet grinned, "Well you *were* a bastard. He hides you, and you repay him by seducing his daughter. How did you save your skin?"

"Liesje saved me. 'But papa,' she said, bursting into tears. 'I love him. Please don't turn him in!' And he didn't. But kicked me the hell off the farm. Never forgave me either."

"Understandable, I guess."

"But you know," and Kees sniffed the air, "I can still smell the hay from our first time."

"You can probably smell the hay from the last time too if it was out here in the field!"

Kees grinned. Said, "But I suppose we'd better get down to business."

"Right! Three weeks is all the time we've got. Then the bulldozers are moving in. Think we can do it?"

"Absolutely!" asserted Kees. "When do we start?"

"Saw Jack last night," said Henk, staring at the television screen, waiting for 'Bonanza' to start. "At the drive in."

"Wasn't him," dismissed Anneke. "His car's still busted. He was at Wally's last night watching the game. Bunch of the guys were there." Anneke was curled up on one corner of the couch. Henk was on the other. Their parents were out.

"That was no guy he was swappin' spit with!"

"You lying bastard! Wasn't him! I told ya!"

Logically, infuriatingly, Henk said, "Don't care if you believe me or not, but there's only one car like his. '47 Chevy held together with binder twine. Know it anywhere."

"Binder twine?" said Anneke. "Musta got it running. Musta lent it to somebody. So bloody dark at the drive-in you can't recognize anybody anyway." She looked at Henk dismissively. "Wasn't Jack!"

"Whatever you say," said Henk, staring at the screen.

The overture for 'Bonanza' started, and Anneke sat up straight. Then, over the music, she heard Henk mumble, "Musta lent his car to some other guy who sings, "Little Rosa."

"How's the garden?" asked Piet, at their Saturday night card game.

"Great. But I'll be glad of that new greenhouse next spring," said Kees. "Not much room in here," he added, looking around the inside of his small house, "to start seedlings, and then the kids knock over the plants, and the cats shit in the flower pots."

"Good fertilizer!" laughed Piet.

Lies said, "We've got more bedding plants ready to go outside. Several flats in our bedroom. "Endive and kale and other plants that you don't see much here."

"You're growing vegetables in your bedroom?" asked Johanna, scrunching her nose.

"Yes," Piet told her, "what they do is, make *neuky* in their garden, and then they grow vegetables in their bedroom!"

"*What!*" said Johanna.

Piet laughed again, then said to Kees, "Can I see those plants? Endive, that's hard to grow, isn't it?" The men walked toward the bedroom.

"Johanna, do you have any knitting on the go at the moment?"

"Why do you ask?"

"Well… maybe you can help me do some knitting... in a new-born size?"

"Wha-at!?"

"I'm gonna break up with Jack."

"But I thought you really liked him!" protested Rosemary. "And you've been going out for ages and ages! And the spring prom is coming up. And…" Rosemary had never been out on a date. She lived somewhat vicariously through Anneke, and Anneke hated to disillusion her.

"Well, he's always out with his friends lately. It's the guys this and the guys that. Jack is just not mature enough for a real relationship."

"But *he's* nineteen! *You're* only …"

"I know how old I am, Rosemary. I don't need you to tell me that. But girls mature more quickly. As for the spring prom, I already have a date. Someone much more mature than Jack!" With that, Anneke flopped face-down on Rosemary's pink chenille bedspread.

In the background Elvis crooned, "Are you lonesome tonight? Do you miss me tonight?" and Anneke's shoulders began to shake. Tears dripped into the chenille.

"But..." Bewildered, Rosemary sat on the edge of the bed, and stared at the movie poster on her wall. Bobby Darin handing pink carnations to Sandra Dee. So romantic! The way it should be. Living happily ever after. The music stopped. Rosemary got up to change the record.

Pull yourself together, Anneke told herself. Don't let her see what a sap you are. Come on! Straighten up! "Rosemary," she called over, "you got that platter by Chubby Checker?" Rosemary turned, gave a brief, questioning look, put on the record. Anneke jumped off the bed, started gyrating madly. Rosemary joined in, and soon their twisting vibrated the house, until Rosemary's father stomped up the stairs to put an end to the racket.

"Finally, a *nice* boyfriend," said Johanna with satisfaction. "Nice Dutch boy!" She dealt. They were playing cards on Lies and Kees's kitchen table, gambling with pennies.

"Very Dutch!" said Piet, organizing his hand. "Just off the boat. *Nou dan, rik!*"

"But he's not a boy, is he? Isn't Simon already in his twenties?" asked Lies. Looking at the hearts in her hand, she announced, *"Rik beter!"*

Kees had all low cards. *"Misère,"* he outbid Lies. To win he must take *no* tricks.

"*Ja,* he's older but we know the family," said Johanna. She looked at her ho-hum hand. "*Pas,*" she said, and continued, "You should have seen him when he picked her up tonight! Wore a tuxedo, with a red carnation. Looked so good I wanted to go out with him myself!" She laughed.

"How did Anneke look?" asked Lies.

"Like a princess!" said Piet proudly. He threw down a small spade. Lies played the ten, Kees the nine, and Johanna took the trick with her king. She raked in the cards.

"Where were they going dressed like that?" asked Kees.

"The high school prom."

"Prom? *Wat is dat?*"

"Ridiculous really!" Johanna scoffed. "A prom is a dance where a bunch of young kids dress up like they're going to go visit the queen! And the prices of those prom dresses! You wouldn't believe it! Why, when Piet and I got married, I didn't pay half so much for my wedding dress! I told Anneke I could sew her a dress for a lot less money, but of course she wouldn't hear of *that!* In the end," Johanna turned to Lies, "we found some that were on sale. Bought a beautiful dress, dark blue."

"He had Theo's car," Piet said to Kees. Then explained, "Simon is Theo's nephew, on his mother's side. He's staying with Theo and Femke until he gets his own place. Takes a lot of gumption to emigrate by yourself. That boy will go far!"

"He's a worker!" said Kees. "Great help taking down that old building." The card game went on, and Kees continued to avoid taking tricks.

"And Simon volunteered!" said Piet. "Just like that. *Ja*, I know he hasn't got a job or anything yet, so not too much for him to do right now. Still, a lot of young guys wouldn't…"

"And what he did for Henk…" said Johanna, shaking her head in wonderment.

The last card was played. *"Misère!"* said Kees triumphantly. "Pay up, boys and girls! That'll be five cents each."

Demolishing that stagecoach building had turned out to be a lot more difficult than anticipated. It was a long, frame building, two-stories high, built in the old western style with two levels of verandah across the front. At the gable ends of the building were enormous limestone chimneys. After the owner of the building had removed load-bearing walls during a renovation project, the weight of winter snow had caused the building's middle to cave, snapping the centre beam. The ends of the beam remained firmly embedded in the stone of the massive chimneys.

Piet and Kees used chunks of lumber as braces to prevent further cave-ins, then began to dismantle the roof. They threw shingles and broken lumber down into the backyard, carefully lowered intact roofing planks and rafters, and loaded everything on a hay-wagon. When full, they hitched it to a tractor, pulled it to a field behind Kees's house, and stockpiled the lumber.

The plan was to clear the site as quickly as possible, and then sort materials later.

Standing on the attic floor, Piet stuck his crowbar under the lower end of a rafter, and proceeded to pry it up. It gave way with great screeching sounds of ancient square-headed nails. "Look out Kees! It's swinging loose." Kees hurried over. Grabbed the rafter. Carefully lowered it off the building. Piet had already started prying the next one.

Kees asked, "Your boy coming to help?"

"Henk's at cadets," said Piet. "Should be here soon. *Ja,* we can do with more help, that's for sure."

"You know, Piet, overall the building's not bad in terms of damage. Can't believe more of the windows aren't broken. I should have me one damned fine greenhouse!"

"Wouldn't be counting my chickens, Kees. We haven't got her down yet!" Another rafter swung loose. "Grab that, Kees!"

There was a voice from the street, "Mr. Verbeek, could I be of assistance?" Piet looked down. Saw Simon. New kid. Just over from Nederland. Spoke good English, but very formal. Must have learned it at school.

"*Fijn!* Come on up! Can use a pair of extra hands. Call me Piet! We're not so formal here."

"I never had a chance to do anything like *this* in Nederland!" said Simon enthusiastically, when he'd clambered up to join Piet. "This building is right out of the wild west!" Piet gave him a crowbar, and he started working eagerly. Before long all the rafters were down on the ground, and they were ready to tackle the beam. Simon climbed on the chimney with a hammer and masonry chisel, and set to work chipping at the mortar which held the beam in place.

Piet looked up at Simon, and said to Kees with a grin, "He'll be good for awhile!" pulled out his cigarettes, and offered one to his friend. As the men smoked, they looked down over the edge of the building at the lumber in the back yard, and discussed how soon they'd need to take the next load out of there. Henk arrived, fresh from cadets, still wearing his puttees. He climbed up to the attic, and stood watching Simon. Suddenly, there was loud creaking! Simon dove down off the chimney into Henk, and spun him out of the way, as a section of centre beam crashed down.

"What the hell!" Piet rushed over to his son, who appeared shaken but otherwise unharmed. He clamped Simon on the back, "Don't know how to thank you. That was incredible!"

"Swan dive!" said Kees, to break the tension. "Could be in the Olympics. Ever thought of that, Simon?"

Johanna arrived a short while later with their coffee. Heard the story. *"Mijn God! Mijn God!"* she sobbed, as she hugged her son, who turned red and squirmed away. Then she pumped Simon's hand in loquacious thankfulness. Finally she wiped the tears from her eyes, and poured the coffee. She cut slices of *peperkoek*. Cut Simon an extra thick slice. Invited him to Sunday dinner.

That Sunday, Anneke sat across from Simon at the dinner table. Yeller lay stretched on the floor. "What a handsome animal!" said Simon. "I haven't seen that breed before."

"This is Old Yeller," introduced Anneke. "Like in the movie. He's a Labrador, very intelligent." Henk snorted at this, but Piet glared at his son, and he was quiet.

"I can see from your dog's eyes," said Simon, "that he is smart. Eyes say a lot. And in your eyes," he said, looking at her intently, "I see love." Anneke's parents looked at him questioningly. "Love for your dog," he hastened to add. After dinner, her parents toured Simon around the neighbourhood, Henk took his BB-gun to his friend's house to shoot the birds out of the trees, and Anneke, dog at her heels, went into the living room. She took the text, <u>Invitation to Poetry</u>, from her book-bag, and got comfortable on the living room couch. Final exams were only a few weeks away, and Anneke was supposed to memorize 'Lone Dog,' by Irene Rutherford McLeod. "Hey Yeller," she said, "listen to this!"

'I'm a lean dog, a keen dog, a wild dog, and lone;
I'm a rough dog, a tough dog, hunting on my own.'

"What do you think? Like it?" Yeller opened his eyes. Wagged his tail, thumping the floor. Anneke was still amazed that her mother would actually let Yeller in the house. It was only since Yeller had been sick. "Yeah, I like it too. Especially this last verse."

'Not for me the other dogs, running by my side,
Some have run a short while, but none of them would bide,
O mine is still the lone trail, the hard trail, the best,
Wide wind, and wild stars, and hunger of the quest!'

"Good, huh?" said Anneke. She thought about the poem. She too, was an outsider. It was often uncomfortable and got her in a lot of trouble, but like the dog in the poem, she sure as heck didn't want to be part of any pack. She loved a challenge. Hmm, she thought, how would that English exam go if she *didn't* study for it? Would that make it more exciting? She dropped her poetry text on the couch. She glanced at Yeller, sleeping in a patch of sunshine, then looked more closely, admiring the wavy patterns of his golden fur, the glossy blackness of his nose, the way he rested his chin on his paws. Anneke picked her book up again, turned to the inside back cover, took pencil crayons from her book-bag, and started to draw. She roughed-in the dog's outline, then used yellow ochre, and burnt sienna pencils to create the texture of his fur. With umber and ultramarine, she gave depth to the background. Finally she added details, whiskers, sleeping eyes, glossy-black nose...

"That is an excellent drawing!" Anneke jumped! Simon was

standing beside her. She had been too engrossed to notice him. "Sorry," he said, "I did not mean to interrupt."

"s'Alright," said Anneke. "I was done."

"May I?" he asked, and took the book from her hands. "It really is very good. You know what I said earlier about your love for your dog? It is here! It shines from this page!"

Anneke smiled. Her ego was fragile after being dumped by Jack, and she enjoyed the compliment. Anyway, it wasn't fair that Jack had blamed her for the accident. It wasn't her fault! It was all due to Wally. "Turn!" he'd yelled, "Turn!" Well, she'd turned all right! Turned right into that damned tree!

"I was taught art at the MULO," Simon explained, "but I was not very good at it. We studied languages too. I decided very young that I would emigrate, so I worked hard at my English. Our English teachers were very precise and particular. They were from Britain."

"So you learned English in high school, hmmm..." mused Anneke. She thought of *her* first weeks in Canada, of the misery of not speaking the language. It must be nice to actually learn a language *before* you move to a new country.

"I was going either to Australia or Canada, both countries with lots of open space, and lots of wilderness. Then Uncle Jake offered to sponsor me, so I came here." Smiling, looking from Anneke to Yeller, Simon added, "Australia, even has wild dogs. Dingoes, they're called."

"Yeah," said Anneke. "Just read a poem about a wild dog. Think the poet might have been from Australia. Wonder if *that* dog was a dingo?"

"Perhaps," said Simon, "perhaps...." He was quiet for a moment. Then he said, "Anneke, would you do me the honour of going to a movie with me? If I can borrow uncle's car?" Anneke was shocked. She'd thought of Simon as just a family friend. Nice enough, but in an old-world, old-fashioned kind of way. But, it was better than sitting home alone. Better than moping over Jack.

"Sure!" she said brightly. "Love to go." Simon asked her parents for permission, and Piet and Johanna were all smiles, which Anneke found *most* peculiar, since they *never* liked her going out. They saw Blue Hawaii. "Love that Elvis," said Anneke, when they went out for a coke afterwards. "Dreamy! They'll be playing lots of his platters at the school prom."

"School prom?" said Simon. "Could I maybe...."

When Piet and Johanna found out Simon wanted to take their daughter to the prom, their smiles got even wider.

As they danced at the prom, he towered above her. She felt his hand warm against her back. With his other hand he held hers. Arm straight out, he propelled her around the high school gym like they were waltzing in an old-world ballroom. Anneke found it highly embarrassing. She hadn't realized Simon was such a square. Not only did he dance differently, but he was the only one in a tuxedo. The waltz ended, and Simon and Anneke sat at the paper-covered table, sipping their punch. The DJ put on another platter. "Come on, baby, let's do the twist!" blared from the loudspeakers. Couples jumped up from their seats, dashed for the dance floor, started to twist.

"Let's dance!" said Anneke, but he said he hadn't learned this at his ballroom dance class.

"We're gonna twisty twisty twisty," sang Chubby, "'Til we turn the house down."

Anneke tapped her foot on the floor, and bounced in her seat. "Ee-oh twist baby baby twist...." Suddenly, Anneke realized that she was wearing the wrong dress. All the other girls wore pastel-coloured dresses. Anneke's dress was royal-blue. That sales rack must have been winter stock! She had committed a major faux pas by wearing a winter colour to a spring prom. Wrong boyfriend, wrong dance, wrong dress – what a disaster!

When the prom was over, he drove her home, parked at the end of her driveway. Reached for her. Started kissing her. She wasn't keen, but what the heck! After tonight she was going to dump him anyway! Then he reached into the front of her prom dress, pulled out her breast, brought his mouth down over the nipple. Started sucking. This had never happened to her before! "What are you doing?"

His eyes were closed, but he loosened his mouth from her breast just long enough to mumble, "This is nice, very nice."

She didn't know what to make of it, but then she felt a tingling start deep inside her, and it really felt quite wonderful but they were in her driveway and what the hell was he doing anyway when he was supposed to be this nicey-nice guy all proper and her parents' choice and everything. A figure started coming from the house towards the car, "My father," she whispered, pulling her sweater in front of her. Simon shot up.

Piet opened the car door, "Anneke, time to come in," he said, giving Simon a cool, cynical look. Anneke bolted into the house.

"Should have known it was too good to last," lamented Johanna when a commercial interrupted 'I Love Lucy.' She sipped her coffee, lit a cigarette.

"What?" asked Lies. "Here, give me a light." Johanna reached over with her lighter, and Lies exhaled a cloud of blue smoke. Lies settled back in her ancient armchair, feet on a hassock. Her tummy strained at her dress.

"Anneke!" Johanna grumbled. "Goes out with the perfect boy. Absolutely perfect. Polite. Nice-looking. You saw him, Lies. Perfect! So what does she do? Dumps him! Won't go out with him again. Won't even say why. So obstinate! So damned difficult! And, you're not going to believe this, Lies. You know how smart she is. Report cards just came out, and," Johanna emphasized each word, "Anneke barely passed English!" She sighed. "And that's not even the *worst* of it! She failed music. How can *anybody*," said Johanna, throwing her hands up in the air, "fail music?"

Chapter Four – The Plymouth Belvedere

It was the summer of '61, and Anneke was in love! Howard was *very* handsome! He had dark wavy hair, and striking blue eyes, and he was tanned and muscular from his work on construction. He didn't talk much, so Anneke decided that he was the strong, silent, mysterious type, like the men in the cowboy movies she used to watch when she was younger. She could picture him as the Lone Ranger, with a mask and a white horse. Of course he didn't ride a horse, he drove a car, but it was the most beautiful car Anneke had ever seen, with lots of chrome, and huge fins, and a three-tone paint job – cream, peach, and grey. They'd met in the summer, and had been dating for just a few weeks when school went back in. In the afternoon of the first day, Howard pulled up to the main entrance of the school. Anneke strolled nonchalantly towards his car. As she got in, she glanced around, and could see that *all* the other girls were *green* with envy.

Her parents said Howard was too old for her. "You're only sixteen! He's a man; you're just a girl!"

"Sure," said Anneke, "It's OK if he's six years older and Dutch, like Simon, but when he's six years older and *Canadian*, all of a sudden he's too old!" She *knew* she had them. Much as her parents might disapprove of her going out with Howard, they didn't have a leg to stand on.

On a bright fall afternoon, the tri-colour '57 Plymouth Belvedere was taking Anneke and Howard along country roads to the family farm. At a blue mailbox, it turned down a laneway, and suddenly, to her amazement, Anneke found herself in a golden tunnel. Ancient orange and yellow maples flanked the narrow lane, touched overhead, fluttered their leaves to the ground. The sun filtered through the trees, filling the tunnel with hazy light. Anneke was breathless! She wanted to stay in that magic spot, with her perfect man, forever. Too soon, the car emerged into the open, and Anneke saw a clapboard farmhouse with peeling paint.

Howard parked by the drive-shed, and as they went into the house, he took in an armload of firewood. It was very warm in the kitchen; dinner was being cooked on the woodstove. A thin woman, hair pulled back in a bun, grayish apron over print housedress, was stirring a pan – gravy, Anneke thought – while a small boy clutching her apron, sucked his thumb. As Howard clattered the firewood into the wood-box, the woman glanced over briefly, then turned back to her task. Howard stayed by the wood-box, proceeded to organize the wood. Anneke frowned. Was he not going to introduce her? Maybe these farm people didn't do introductions. Maybe that was too formal. Uneasily, she remained standing in the middle of the kitchen floor. She heard buzzing sounds, noticed fly strips hanging from the ceiling, black with dead and dying flies. She looked down past the dark wallpaper, at the worn linoleum, but there too, were dead flies. In a corner of the room she spotted an old man in dirty bib overalls. He looked at Anneke through rheumy eyes, and smiled. Anneke smiled back, then turned to the small, thumb-sucking boy. "Hi!" said Anneke, but the child hid behind the woman's skirt. .

The woman pursed her mouth, "Dinner's on," she said. Anneke looked for Howard, but he'd gone over to the kitchen sink and was busily pumping water to wash the sawdust from his hands. The woman pointed, "You can sit there," she said to Anneke. The door opened, and a man entered carrying a bushel-basket of apples. The woman snapped, "Arnold! Born in a barn?" He scowled. Set down the apples. Closed the door.

Everyone sat down, and the woman placed the food on the table. They passed the serving dishes, filled their plates, began to eat.

"This beef is delicious," complimented Anneke.

"Raised it ourself," said the old man, and smiled a broad, gap-toothed smile at Anneke.

"Have you lived on this farm for a long time?" she asked, politely.

"Aw was born here," said the old man. "Born right thar in thet there bedroom. Then I brought my Betty here when we got married. Oh, she was some wonderful woman, my Betty was! She died five year back," he said sadly, and Anneke felt sorry for him, but then she noticed the other man, Arnold, glaring daggers at the old fellow. Unnerved, she decided to be quiet. No one else spoke, and, aside from the occasional prattle of the little boy being fed on his mother's lap, the food was finished in silence. Finally, the woman stood up, placed the child on the floor, and started to collect the empty plates. Anneke got up, cleared dishes, served pie, and sat back down. The woman wrapped a tea-towel around the handle of the coffee pot which had been boiling interminably on the back of the wood-stove, and poured the coffee.

"Unless you'd rather have milk," she said to Anneke.

"No, thank you, I'll have coffee," said Anneke curtly. Did the woman think she was a child? But when she tried to drink the potent brew, she had to add milk and more milk, to get it down her throat. She thought she detected the hint of a smirk on the woman's face.

After dinner, Howard offered to show her the farm, and Anneke couldn't wait to get out of there, although she felt guilty about skipping out on the dishes. She watched the farm collie trot off to get the cattle for milking. Soon, cows were plodding back along a well-worn track to the barn, the dog zig-zagging at their rear. Howard yoked the cows, pulled up a stool and milk-pail and went to work. There was the hiss of milk, the clang as it hit the metal pail, the sweet smell of the rising steam.

Anneke, elbows on a bale of hay, happily watched Howard work. His sleeves were rolled up on his tanned, muscular arms. My, but he was handsome! How she loved him! Howard, Howard, how I love you, she thought.

"Have you been milking for a long time?" she asked, trying to engage him in conversation.

"Larnt when I was eight," he said. Anneke had to listen carefully. He was mumbling into the cow.

"So…. do you do it every day?" she tried again.

"Try ta help out. Got cheap board. Arnold's gone ta the Masons."

"Off to a meeting, is he?"

"Yup."

Yes, thought Anneke, Howard was definitely the strong, silent type, and she wondered what was really going on inside his head, what he was thinking, as he sat there milking those cows. She gave a fleeting thought to the rest of the family. Sure were strange! But she'd never been around farmers, especially Canadian farmers, and maybe that's how they were. Anyway, she didn't care, that family was just the wallpaper of Howard's life – the dark, fly-speckled, wallpaper.

Finally the milking was finished. Howard separated the milk from the cream, and gave Anneke an entire jar of fresh sweet cream to take home. The cream did nothing to sweeten her parents towards Howard, and there was no reciprocal dinner invitation.

Early in November, the construction project where Howard worked, wrapped up. There was no other work in the area. This was fine from Anneke's perspective because it meant they could spend more time together. However, after a few weeks of being unemployed, Howard picked Anneke up after school on day and told her he had news. "Was in the union hall today," he said. "Job in Norbury. Gonna go. Leaving Sunday."

"Nooooo...." said Anneke. "Too far! You can't!" Tears filled her eyes.

"Hafta go," he said. "Can't live on pogey. Got car payments."

"What'll I do without you?" sniffled Anneke, but Howard just stared ahead. "I'm going to miss you so much!" she sobbed. Still, he stared out the window. Finally, he spoke.

"D'ya think..." he stammered, "I mean, will ya ma..." he mumbled, "I mean ... um." At last he got some words out, "D'ya wanna go steady?"

"Yes!" said Anneke, beaming through her tears. "Yes, yes, *yes!*"

"Thank God he's gone!" said Johanna. "Let's hope that fellow stays away."

It was Saturday night and they'd finished their card game. In the corner of the room, the small, black-and-white television flickered. They were enjoying *een borrel*. Kees poured the young Dutch gin into shot glasses, and stirred a coffee spoon of sugar into each.

Piet said, *"Ja,* let's hope so. He's far too old for her. He's been working for years, while she's still a schoolgirl." He tossed back his *borrel,* smacked his lips, said with a wry grin, "Still, you've got to give her credit. Did you know, Kees, that when we told her she couldn't go out with this guy, she accused us of discrimination? Said we discriminated against Canadians. Clever tactic, I thought."

"It's not funny, Piet!" scoffed Johanna.

Kees laughed. Stood up. "Another *borrel?*" He'd just been paid by Quattrocchi's Specialty Foods for his produce. To celebrate the success of his gardening venture, he'd splurged on the bottle of *jonge jenever.*

"Ja, lekker!" said Piet. "But I'm surprised you've still *got* vegetables to sell. Isn't it too cold?"

"Kale is better *after* the first frost," said Kees.

"A toast!" said Piet. "Kuiper's Vegetables!" They clinked glasses. Tossed back the gin. "Pretty impressive how well you've done."

"Couldn't have done it without *you!"* said Kees. "That's some mighty-fine greenhouse we built!" He walked towards the television set, "Did you see the last Wayne and Shuster Show?"

"No, I missed it."

"Hilarious!" Kees proceeded to flick back and forth between channels 7 and 11, trying to get decent reception. "They go to a school called NeckTech to learn about sex."

Piet grinned, "Well *jongen,* I don't think *you* need to go to any NeckTech!"

"That's for sure," said Lies. She leaned towards Johanna. "You know those clothes I told you I lost?"

"Ja, I remember. That was strange! Vanished right off your clothesline!"

Lies scrunched up her face, "I found them!" Johanna looked at her, puzzled, as Kees continued fiddling with the knobs of the television, his back to the room. "In the trunk of his car!" Lies said loudly. Kees turned. Grinned.

"*What* was in the trunk?" asked Piet."

"Their clothes," said Johanna. "He hid them in the trunk!"

"No," said Lies. "Not *their* clothes. *My* clothes! My underwear, to be exact!"

Piet looked at Kees, "Why on Earth," he asked, his eyebrows raised, "would you hide her underwear?"

Kees came over. "Well, friend," he said, clapping Piet on the shoulder, "it's like this. When I'm in the mood, I'm in the mood, that's why I don't like for Lies to wear underwear. She's a good sport when we're working in the vegetable garden, but next thing you know, we're driving into town, I'm reaching for paradise, and the gate is closed."

Piet and Johanna stared at him, wide-eyed. Finally Johanna said, "Kees, did you not think with the cold weather coming…"

"She's got them back!" He spoke defensively, but his eyes crinkled.

"I haven't got a damn thing!" Lies held up panties riddled with holes. "What did you have in that trunk, you son-of-a-bitch? Battery acid?"

Anneke went to see her friend. Flung herself down on Rosemary's pink chenille bedspread. "Got a letter from Howard yesterday," she said. "I was so stunned, I didn't know what I was doing for the rest of the day!"

"What..." Rosemary tried to ask, but Anneke kept talking.

"I tore up at least twenty-five pages trying to write him back. Then I started again and I knew it was now or never, so I finished it. Now the answer is on its way. The strange thing is," she said, "that I still can't believe it. I can't believe that I'm going to marry Howard Hall!"

"What!?" said Rosemary. "What did you say? You're going to do what!?"

"Marry him," said Anneke.

"You can't!" exclaimed Rosemary. "You can't get married! I haven't even started dating yet!"

"I know that," said Anneke, pursing her mouth, nodding, "I know that, but I've been dating for over two years and I know my mind!" She lifted her chin, "I'm gonna marry Howard!"

"Make him take you to the S&R," said Johanna. "He owes you!"

"You'll wonder where the yellow went...." jingled the television.

"You're right," said Lies, as she poured the coffee. She held the cookie tin out to Johanna, "You know I had some really nice sexy stuff. And then that guy hides it. And ruins it. That crazy Kees!"

"When he takes you shopping for the groceries on Saturday, you tell him you're going to the S&R. Don't take no for an answer. You're too soft met die jongen." Soft in the head, Johanna thought, for letting him get away with that sort of thing in the first place. Incredible how that woman doted on her husband! She was very fond of Lies, in fact Lies was her best friend, but sometimes Johanna had the urge to shake her!

Lucy appeared, dressed in Italian peasant costume, and Johanna and Lies settled in to enjoy the action. Lucy hoisted her skirts, climbed into a vat, and started stomping grapes, as the women shrieked with laughter. When Lucy got into a grape-flinging food fight, and was knocked sprawling into the vat, Johanna and Lies howled!

Too soon, the program ended. Wiping tears of laughter from her eyes, Johanna stood up, pulled on her coat and gloves. With her hand on the doorknob, she said, "And, Lies, never mind so much about buying more sexy underwear, the snow's about to fly, get something warm!"

"Today we start our major sewing assignment," said Mrs. Hammond, "the straight skirt! Sewing a fully lined, woolen skirt, is not a task for the faint of heart, and so that you do not feel completely overwhelmed by it, I will take you through the project step by step. Today we will trace the pattern. Tomorrow we will cut it, and the following day we will baste. All right now girls, get out your fabric, your pattern, and your tracing paper." The students proceeded to bustle about.

"Bo-ring!" said Anneke in a low voice to cousin Gerda.

The teacher glared in her direction. "Did you have a comment, Annie?" Anneke was quiet. "A comment you would like to share with the rest of the class? No? Then get out your fabric!" Anneke got up, pretended to look busy. "Your fabric, Annie, now! Where is it?"

"No time to get it," said Anneke, morosely.

"If you don't have anything to work with," said the teacher, "I'm not going to have you in here disturbing the class. Get out in the hall!"

Anneke left the room, stood in the hallway, leaned against the doorjamb. As if she would waste one second of her precious weekend shopping for school stuff, when Howard was in town! Not bloody likely! It had been their first weekend together since he'd left for Norbury, and how wonderful it had been. Dreamily, Anneke thought back.

It was already ten o'clock when he pulled into the driveway. Anneke ran out to the car, her mother yelling after her, "Make sure you're in the house by eleven!" She hopped into the Belvedere, and it smelled of Howard and she fell into his arms and he kissed her deeply, and she felt like she'd come home. She cuddled up against him, and he drove slowly to a deserted spot by the creek. A full moon reflected in the water. Blue-black cedars silhouetted against the sky. They kissed, and she wanted it to go on forever. Finally, he leaned over, reached into the glove compartment. With a shy smile, he handed her a package.

"Got ya somethin," he said. Anneke's eyes went wide. She removed the white tissue-paper wrapping to discover a velvet box, the name of a jeweler engraved on the lid. Eagerly, she opened it, found more tissue paper, and under that, an inch-wide chain-link bracelet, covered with sparkling blue stones.

Anneke sucked in her breath, said, "Wow! Beautiful!" She kissed him. "Thank you!" And she thought it was wonderful that he would buy her jewelry, a symbol of his love. And she felt so loved, and cherished, like she was in a real grown-up man-and-woman relationship. And she wondered on what occasion, or to what event, she would ever wear something quite so gaudy.

Howard said, "Made me real happy, yer letter. Wanted to git ya somethin nice."

"You made me real happy too!" Anneke responded. "It's so exciting being engaged! I haven't told my parents yet, 'cause they'd be sure to have a fit about it, but I told my friend Rosemary, and she couldn't believe it! Did you tell your family?"

"Haven't been to th' farm. Drove straight here from work – five hours – 'fraid if I was any later they wouldn' letcha out. But," he said, and he was quiet for a moment, as he looked down at the floor, "them out on th' farm, they're, well they're not really my fam'ly. I was in th' Children's Aid. When I was eight, they put me put me out there. There was Mr. an' Mrs. White, an' Arnold. Mrs. White, she wanted another young un around, 'cause Arnold, he was pret'near grown. She was real good t'me. Let me help 'r make pies. But then," he frowned and chewed his lip, "she got killed."

"What happened?" Anneke whispered, her eyes large.

"She was in the truck with the ol' man. He didn' watch what he was doin. Got charged with careless. Bad accident. Her head got cut off. Arnold hasn't spoke to the ol' man since."

Anneke's eyes were moist, as she kissed him. "When we get married, I'll be your family!"

Leaning against the doorjamb, Anneke reflected that she meant it. He'd have a real family once they were married. Thinking back over the weekend, she thought it surprising how much Howard had talked. It was the most she'd ever heard him say. However... he hadn't... done anything! With them apart for weeks, and now properly engaged and everything, you'd think he'd have tried something! Perhaps, she thought, scratching her head, he was not sexually attracted to her. Or, was it possible that he simply had no interest in sex? She'd heard there were people like that... The school bell jolted her. The classroom began to vacate. Anneke got her coat from her locker and joined the stream of students pouring outside. Sadly, there was no Plymouth Belvedere waiting in front of the school. Anneke trudged home.

At the house, chores awaited. It was Thursday, the day her mother cleaned house at the Johnsons', and Anneke was expected to cook and clean at home. However, after a hard day at school, she needed a break. She got milk and cookies, and settled down on the couch with her latest Michener epic, <u>The Bridge at Andau</u>. Absently, she fed cookies to the dog. "Hey skivvy, what're you doing on the couch?" The voice jolted her. Henk was in the doorway. "Get at your chores!"

Anneke glowered at him, "Get lost, jerk!" He smiled a smug smile, left the room, and bounded up the stairs. Michener's spell was broken, and with a long-suffering sigh, Anneke closed the book and went into the kitchen to peel potatoes. She was just putting them on the stove, when Henk clattered back downstairs, BB gun in hand. He went as far as the back door, then turned, "Hey, skivvy! How come my bed isn't made yet?"

"Make the damn thing yourself!"

"Can't do that. That's woman's work, well, girl's work, in your case. Better get at it! Don't want mummy to think you're lazy!"

"Lazy! I'm lazy! You don't do one speck of work! I gotta do it all! You good for nothing... bastard!" shrieked Anneke. Henk remained standing in the doorway, a taunting grin across his face. Anneke reached into the pot, grabbed a potato and heaved. Henk ducked, and the potato thudded impotently against the door. Laughing uproariously, he ran out the driveway. Seething, Anneke picked the potato up off the floor and threw it back into the pot, splashing water over the stove. She turned on the heat, returned to the living room, flopped on the couch, and soon lost herself in Michener's tale of courageous Hungarians facing down Russian tanks.

The stench of burnt potatoes brought her back to reality.

It was December 31st. Dawn had barely broken, and already Piet was hard at work making oliebollen for his New Year's Eve party. Piet took great pride in this yearly culinary ritual and was renowned, in the Dutch community, for the flavour of these golden globes.

With the burner on low, Piet gently warmed a bit of milk, and stirred in a package of yeast. He put flour in a bowl, made a hollow in the top, added the yeast, salt, and eggs, and stirred. He washed and dried raisons and currants, chopped apples, added *sukade,* and blended the fruit into the yeasty dough. Then he covered the bowl with a tea-towel, and set it near the oil burner to rise. Piet made himself a coffee, lit a cigarette, and stood looking out the window at the drifting flakes. There was at least a foot of newly-fallen snow in the driveway. Might as well get at it. He went into his garage to get a shovel, paused, looked around. Piet nodded to himself; he and Kees had done one damn fine job with the lumber from the stagecoach building! His garage was sturdily built, of huge, hand-hewn beams, and wide pine boards. It was large enough for his vehicle, with enough room left over for all his woodworking tools. The garage added value to the property, yet its cost had been minimal. Piet stepped outside, started shoveling. He could barely lift the shovel, the snow was so deep! Still, it felt great to exercise in the fresh air. When the driveway was half done, Piet rested, stretched his back, looked up at the sky. Peered around. Couldn't be sure what you might see up there these days! In April, a Russian had become the first man to fly in space – went all the way around the world, he did. Then, a month later, the Americans shot one of their guys up there. To top it off, that new American President said that before the end of the sixties, the Americans would put a man on the moon. Piet shook his head, and started shoveling again. Maybe a few years from now, he thought, he would look at the *moon* a little more carefully too! Finally the driveway was done, and the shovel put back. Soon Piet was dropping spoonfuls of yeasty dough into a pot of sizzling oil.

"Great balls, Piet," grinned Kees.

"L-L-L-Lekker! Echt l-l-l-lekker!" complimented Klaas, as he dipped an *oliebol* in powdered sugar, and took a huge bite.

"What are these?" asked John Comberford.

"Piet's balls," said Kees. "Piet's oily balls. Have a bite!"

"That is not correct!" said Theo. "The literal translation of *bol* is not ball, it is bulb." He turned to John, "you know," he explained, "like a tulip bulb."

"Balls to you too!" muttered Kees, and tossed back another *borrel*.

"Very light and fruity," commented Femke, as she bit into her second one, and Piet considered it quite a compliment, because his sister-in-law was famous for her baking.

"Piet, *ouwe jongen*, you've outdone yourself!" said Jan, between bites.

Like pigs at a trough, thought Piet fondly, watching his guests devour the *oliebollen*. *"Nog een borreltje?"* he offered, and poured another round.

"Enough *vreten en zuipen!*" said Lies. "Time to exercise!" She proceeded to jump up and down like an Olympic runner at the starting gate.

She was in her bare feet, wore a low-cut, red dress. As she jumped, her breasts threatened to escape. The eyes of the men were upon her. "Who's coming with me?" asked Lies, as she jumped. "Piet? Johanna? Klaas?"

"Oh, no. Not me!" said Johanna, making a face. "It makes me shiver just to think about it!"

Piet jumped to his feet. "I'm coming, Liesje!" he said, grinning lasciviously. John jumped up. Other men followed.

"Come on, *jongens!*" said Lies, jumping, bouncing. "Bare feet. Off with the socks!"

"What?" said John, standing in the middle of the floor, one foot raised. "*Why* are we taking off our socks?"

"Custom," said Piet, "New Year's Eve," and he rolled up his pant legs. John looked far from convinced, but his socks came off. The door was thrown open, and off they ran, barefoot in the snow, Lies bounding ahead like a deer! Around and around the house they ran, in the dark, in the cold, in the knee-deep snow out back. Finally, Lies bounced back inside. Then the men – feet and ankles fiery-red – stumbled in after her, as the women erupted with cheers, and hoots of laughter. The men collapsed on kitchen chairs, panting madly, dripping puddles on the floor.

Kees had remained inside, puffing a cigarette. "Crazy Lies!" he grumbled, but there was a hint of admiration in his voice.

On New Year's Eve, Anneke and Howard babysat at the farm.

Arnold had wanted to take his wife out for the evening, and had approached Howard, who had mentioned it to Anneke, who had been far from keen. After all, it was their first New Year's Eve together, and she thought they should go somewhere exciting. "Arnold's got problems," explained Howard to Anneke. "Ethel hates it on thet there farm. Says the wallpaper's ugly, an' the linoleum, an' she can't stand thet outhouse. She wants Arnold to do the place up, but he says he aint spendin' a penny 'till th' ol' man drops dead. That ol' man," said Howard, confidingly, "can cut Arnold out of 'is will any time 'e takes a notion. An' Arnold's scared Ethel's gonna git fed up with waitin', an' one of these days is gonna bugger off. So e's got a problem. Wants ta sweeten 'er up by taken 'er out for New Year's Eve. Anyways," said Howard said with a slight smile, "If we babysit, we kin have the place t'ourselves!" Anneke's face lit up. New Year's Eve alone with the man she loved. How romantic!

Howard picked her up in his Belvedere. When they arrived at the farm, Ethel was bustling about in the kitchen. She told them, "Markie's asleep. Shouldn't wake up. Bottle in the fridge if'n he does."

"Watch the ol' man!" said Arnold. "Ol' bastard's in 'is room already, but I think he mighta got hold o' some cigarettes. Likely ta set th' damn house on fire!"

Anneke and Howard went into the living room and watched the taillights of the truck recede down the long laneway. He turned on a table lamp, and a spot of dim light fell on the dark wallpaper. In a corner of the room stood a small television on a chrome cart. Howard turned a knob, waited for the warm-up. "Wan' a drink?" he offered.

"Sure!" said Anneke. She watched him as he left. Watched his powerfully-built body move across the room – six foot plus, muscular and barrel-chested. What a hunk! Then her brow furrowed. 'Moose,' she'd heard someone call him the other day. "Why?" she'd asked Howard.

"The guys. They call me that."

"Yeah, but why?"

"Dunno. Just do." Well, thought Anneke, *I'll* certainly never call you that! Howard came back in carrying glasses of amber liquid.

"Tonight," came the voice from the television, "we have a *reeeeally* big shew!" and Anneke and Howard settled down on the musty, rose-patterned couch. He kissed her, and she cuddled up against him, as they watched the singers and the dancers and the comedians. When the show was over, and Howard had gone to refill their glasses, Anneke thought to herself that it was pleasant, spending the evening like this with Howard, watching a little TV, drinking some rum and coke, like they were already married.

"Howard," she asked, while the commercial was still on, "when do you think we'll get married?"

"Gotta git me some money saved," he said. "Got me some overtime comin' up. Time-and-a-half. Sock 'er away."

"Right," said Anneke, although it was clear as mud.

"If there's welders," he continued. "They're short welders. Caint move ahead real fast when they're short."

"Right," said Anneke again. "Welders." She tilted her head and looked at him, "Howard, what is it exactly, that you do?"

"Pipefitt'n."

"Ri-i-ight."

"Tum te de dum, te de dum, te de dum," rolled the music from the corner of the room.

"Love this show!" said Anneke, happy for the diversion. "Love watching those guys tear around on their horses."

"Hard work, ranchin.'"

"And I love how they're are always joking around with each other, and ... "Her voice trailed off as Hoss Cartwright lumbered onto the screen. Turned out, that this week, Hoss was in love with Margie, the daughter of the town banker. Told Pa Cartwright he was going to marry her. However, Margie ran off with some smooth-talking dandy, and Hoss was heartbroken. In spite of everything, he went to her rescue when she was left alone and pregnant in a distant city.

After the show, as the credits scrolled down the screen, Anneke sighed deeply, "Wow, that was beautiful! That Hoss, what a guy! So genuine! So gallant! Don't you think?" Howard's forehead creased. He didn't answer. Anneke kissed him. Pressed her body against his. He kissed her back. There were stumbling sounds on the stairs. Howard pulled away. The old man, plaid robe dangling open over crumpled pyjamas, appeared in the doorway, peered through rheumy eyes at the television screen.

"Thet 'Candid Camera'?" he asked. Howard looked over.

"Yeah."

"Ma favourite," said the old man, "be right back," and shuffled off into the kitchen. A moment later, Anneke heard the back door slam.

"Outhouse," said Howard, in response to her questioning look. Howard looked up at the ceiling, said, "I s'pose I'd better go check on th'young lad," and went upstairs. The old man shuffled into the room, rubbing his hands together.

"Cold out!" he said to Anneke.

"Yeah, it was pretty cold when we came here this evening, and I imagine it's worse now," she said. "Like this program, do you?"

"Yep," said the old man, sitting down in the musty arm chair.

Howard came in. "Sleepin'," he announced. "Drink?" he asked the old man, who looked up, grinned a toothless grin, nodded, and turned his eyes back to the screen. Soon he was sipping his drink, and chuckling at the antics on the screen. When the eleven o'clock news came on, his head dropped back, and he started to snore. Howard prodded him, and slowly he got up, and shuffled back up the stairs.

Howard's eyes were now glued to the screen – the sports news was on – as if that was of the remotest interest, Anneke thought. She put her arms around his neck, and started kissing him, and he kissed back, with his eyes still on the TV screen. Anneke gave up. Sat back. Pouted. Stared at the ceiling.

"And now from the ballroom of the Waldorf Astoria, Guy Lombardo and his Royal Canadians!" Music flowed from the TV, and Anneke looked over to see a band in red jackets with maple leaf emblems blowing on brass instruments, while glamorous couples waltzed around a ballroom. Soon the countdown began, and at the stroke of midnight, there was cheering, and popping of champagne corks, while the band launched into 'Auld Lang Syne'

Howard and Anneke toasted each other with their rum and coke. "Happy New Year!" they chorused, "Happy 1962!" They kissed, and Anneke wanted it to last forever, but too soon, Howard broke it off and settled back to watch the rest of the celebrations. Frowning, Anneke reflected that, really, Hoss and Howard were just so much alike. Great guys, but probably not much into sex. Guys who maybe needed a little bit of a push to be more demonstrative, to move ahead with a relationship. After all, Anneke thought, she and Howard had been alone nearly all evening, and still there had been nothing beyond the occasional kiss, not even the least little bit of petting. Again the old doubt came up, of whether he was even attracted to her physically. She took a deep draught from her rum-and-coke, and screwed up her courage.

"Howard, how come you never, you know, try anything?" Howard's face twitched, and he stared straight ahead at the TV. Right away, Anneke realized she'd made a mistake. She'd embarrassed him. Shit! Miserably she sank down in a corner of the couch, and tried to focus her eyes on the screen.

Shit, shit, shit! One month they'd been engaged, and then she had to go and do something so totally stupid. Tomorrow he would drive back to Norbury, and that would be the last she'd see of him. Damn!

A commercial jingled on the television. Howard turned to Anneke, and kissed her. Anneke melted with relief. Then, to her surprise, he reached down and placed his hand on her breast. He squeezed and released, squeezed and released, and Anneke's mind flashed back to the cow barn. She scolded herself mentally, thought, this is Howard, the man that I love. This is wonderful; he *is* attracted to me sexually. Relax, she told herself. This is what you wanted, and she kissed him hard. Car light shone in the windows, and they sat back, finished their drinks.

Minutes later, having said their goodnights to Arnold and Ethel, they stepped out the kitchen door into the open drive-shed. Ahead of her, through the archway, Anneke saw sparkling snow and a star-lit night. She took a few steps forward, then felt Howard reach for her. He started kissing her, and then her eyes went wide as his hands were on her and …. Oh my God! He'd misunderstood! She'd encouraged him to do a little bit of petting. That was all she meant! But now…. Should she try to stop him? Embarrass him again? That would end their relationship for sure! It's OK, she told herself. We're engaged. We're getting married anyway. She looked out the doorway, up at the stars, and then….

"Impossible," she thought. "There is no way that will fit!" She was standing up against the drive-shed, her skirt was raised, and he was trying to enter her. Oblivious to the problem, he poked between her thighs in the vain notion that he was inside of her. "This is not terribly comfortable," she thought, "I wish he'd get it over with." He poked and prodded for some time, then suddenly pulled back and squirted on the ground. "Well," she thought, "*that* was rather romantic!" But she felt kind of proud that she'd done 'it'.

Anneke slouched into home form. "You're late!" said Mrs. MacDonald. "Get to the office for a late slip." Anneke slouched on down the hallway.

"Again?" scolded the attendance secretary. "Detention! Today," and handed her a slip.

"Already got a detention today," smirked Anneke.

"Then this is for tomorrow," said the secretary though clenched teeth, and she retrieved the slip, scribbled on it, and handed it back to Anneke.

Anneke took the slip in her hand. Looked at it. Then, smirking even more, said, "Already got one for tomorrow."

The secretary grabbed it back. "Sit here!" she snarled, and clicked off on her high heels into the principal's office. Anneke could hear the rumbling of voices. The secretary clicked back out, snapped, "Inside!" Anneke walked in to a large, carpeted office, picture window overlooking fields and woods. In the middle of the room, at his oak desk, sat Mr.

Witherspoon, bent over his notebook, writing. Anneke stood on the carpet, stared at his bald spot. Mr. Witherspoon continued writing for some time, as Anneke shifted her weight from one leg to the other. Finally he put his pen down. Leaned back in his chair. Put his hands behind his head.

"Enjoy school, do you?" he asked in a neutral tone of voice.

Anneke raised her chin. Looked at him through lowered lids. Remained mute.

"Well," he said, almost genially, "you seem to work hard at, uh, earning that extra half-hour every day!"

Anneke glowered darkly.

"Perhaps," he said, "you're enjoying school just a bit *too* much," and he twirled his pen in the air. "Perhaps… it's time for a break." He put the pen down, looked straight at her, and emphasizing each word, said, "One more late, Annie! One more assignment not done and you are suspended! Is that clear?"

Anneke nodded slightly.

"Pardon?" he barked.

"It's *clear*," said Anneke. Suspension would mean big trouble at home!

"Then get to class, and don't let me see you in this office again!"

A few days later, during science class, Anneke was handed a note telling her to report to the guidance counselor. "Come in! Come in," said

Mr. Hammond jovially. He was a large, robust man in a worn suit. He ushered her into his office and closed the door behind her. Anneke felt claustrophobic in the closet-like space – narrow, darkly paneled, with one small window placed up high near the ceiling. Much of the space was taken up by a huge metal desk. Mr. Hammond squeezed around it, sat. Then he waved to the wooden chair which was wedged between the doorway and the desk, and said, "Please Annie, have a seat." Anneke slouched down. Mr. Hammond leaned forward, placed his elbows on the desktop, his chin on his fists, looked at her intently, "Annie, did you ever get the results of those tests you wrote last year?"

"What tests?" she sulked.

"Do you remember," he continued chattily, "towards the end of the school year, there were those tests that all the grade tens right across the province had to write. You wrote them in the gym. Remember that?"

"Yeah, I remember. Math and English."

"Right! *Well*," his eyebrows went up, "those tests went to the Ministry of Education for marking, and copies of the results were sent back to the schools. And your results, Annie," he paused, nodding, "indicate a *very high* level of ability." He smiled at her.

Anneke's brow furrowed, "So-o-o-o?"

"Let me read you the results." He sat back, shuffled the papers on his desk, "English in the 98th percentile. Mathematics in the 97th. What that means, Annie," and he paused for effect, "is that you have the ability to go to university and become *anything* you want to be: doctor, lawyer, *anything!"*

Anneke's face lit up, "Really!" But then her face clouded over, as she thudded back to reality. "My parents don't have the money," she said dully.

"There are various ways to pay for a university education," Mr. Hammond explained, "part-time work, bursaries, scholarships…"

"Really?" She sat a little straighter, head tilted thoughtfully, "scholarships…"

"That's right!" encouraged the counselor. You have the ability, and there are lots of ways to get around the money issue. Of course," he said raised his hands, "to qualify for a scholarship you do need to get high marks, and that would mean buckling down."

Anneke nodded absently. Wow! She was *smart!* She *used* to think she was, when she was younger, but then her marks had been so bad for so long, that she'd completely lost track of whether she was smart, stupid, or in-between. "So… there *is* a way for me to go to university without my parents paying?"

He nodded. "Yes, there is a way." He emphasized, "But it's up to you, if you are willing to work hard enough to get those scholarships. You can do it, Annie. But it is your decision."

Anneke left the guidance office walking on air. All the dreams of her childhood were still possible. How incredible! Back in science class she shocked the teacher by actually smiling at him. But then, during class change, she saw the principal and the guidance counselor standing by the water cooler talking, and she was sure it was about her. And suddenly she knew what that guidance appointment had been about. Of course! Witherspoon had told Hammond to haul her in and straighten her out. 'Buckle down,' the guidance counselor had said. 'Work hard,' he'd said. And she'd fallen for it! Lapped it up! What an idiot she was! As if she could actually get into university. Why, she would do well to pass grade eleven. As a matter of fact she was pretty darned sure she wouldn't. Well, who cared! School was hell. Home was hell. The only thing that was not hell was Howard!

Howard, Howard... how she loved him!

"My family won't be home for hours," she said. "Gone to Ravensburg, got friends there." They were sitting on the couch at Anneke's house. It was Sunday afternoon. Soon Howard would be leaving for Norbury.

"Gone huh?" he said, wrapping his arms around her, and Anneke felt a wave of warmth and contentment. He started to kiss her, and she put her hand on the back of his head, trailed her fingers over the nape of his neck, and his kiss got more passionate, and Anneke reveled in her power to excite him. He took his lips from hers, whispered in her ear, "Not sendin' me back like this, are ya?"

Anneke grinned, stood up, "Come here you," and she sprinted

towards the stairs. It felt wonderfully daring, taking her man upstairs, here, under her parents' roof. Although they'd been intimate several times, it had never been in her house. At the top of the stairs she took his hand, and led him into her bedroom. She pulled the curtains closed against the bleak, cloudy day, and then, standing on the bit of carpeting on the middle of the wooden floor, they threw their arms around each other, and their bodies, their lips, pressed together, moved against each other, rhythmically, passionately, and his hand went for her breast, then under her skirt, and they threw themselves on the bed, as he pulled off her underwear, and in his haste fumbled with his belt, his zipper, and then he was on her and she felt him thrusting, trying to enter her, and again she marveled at how large he was, and she opened her legs further to accommodate him, and slowly, laboriously, he thrust his way inside. And now she moved with him, moved to his rhythm, and she felt a stirring deep inside her and it felt so wonderful, and she delighted in each thrust of his body, and then she heard him mumble.

"I have to pull…"

"No," she breathed, between thrusts. "It's safe…. this…. time of the month," and he halted for a split second and looked at her, and then he plunged on.

Johanna was making the bed when Anneke walked into her parents' bedroom. "I want to get married," she announced.

"*What?*" Johanna, fluffing a pillow, stopped in mid-air. "You want to do *what?*"

"Get married. I want to be with Howard, and he's working in Norbury, so I want to quit school, get married, and join him."

"Are you *crazy?*" Johanna shouted. "You're sixteen! I was twenty-two! Your father and I were engaged for years, saved our money, got married properly. You are just a child! What do you know? You know nothing!"

Anneke's eyes narrowed. "I know that I want to be with Howard!"

"You can't even cook a meal. Think you can run a household?"

"Yeah, well according to you I *never* do anything right anyway. Doesn't matter how hard I try, it's *never* good enough!"

"You *try!*" sneered Johanna. "I go out and work all day and come home to burnt potatoes and a dirty house. *Sure* you try! You try really hard to, to, get into *trouble!* You're nothing *but* trouble!"

"Yeah, that's me!" said Anneke cynically. "Trouble. Well, you never loved me anyway! You just loved Henk!"

In a daze Johanna walked through Lies' door, then burst into tears. Lies looked up, her eyes went wide and she put the baby down and ran over, "*Meid, meid! Was is er aan de hand?*" she asked, putting her arms around her friend.

"It's Anneke!" wailed Johanna. "Big fight today. She wants to get married. Right away!" Johanna sank down on the worn couch. Covered her face with her hands. "She can't wait to get out of the house! Have I been *such* a bad mother?" she sobbed.

"No, no. Of course not," said Lies soothingly. "You're a good mother!" and she picked up the fussing baby and took it into the bedroom. Came back out with a box of Kleenex.

Johanna wiped her eyes, blew her nose. "You know what she said to me?"

Lies shook her head.

"She said I never loved her. Said I just loved Henk. It's not true, Lies!" Johanna wailed, "It's not true!" and she rocked back and forth.

"Of course it isn't, *meid!*"

"It's not that I didn't love her," Johanna sobbed. "It's just that he needed me more."

Lies went to the cupboard. "This might help," she said, and brought out a bottle of cognac. "Kees won it in a draw at work. Was saving it for something special. But," she said, acknowledging her friend's distress, "this is special enough." She poured some into a glass, handed it to Johanna, who nodded her thanks. Lies glanced back at the bottle, "Maybe I'd better have a little one to keep you company," she said. For several minutes it was quiet, as they savoured the cognac.

Johanna, red-eyed, sniffling, said, "Lies, remember what it was like in Nederland, after you had a baby? They'd give you a glass of cognac to strengthen you."

"That's right! Almost made it worth the pain," Lies smiled.

"I remember when I was pregnant with Anneke," sniffed Johanna. "It was the last year of the war, and there was nothing to eat. Apples, that's all I had, apples. Piet got them from the farmers. Brought them home in the saddle-bags of his bicycle. Had to be careful the Germans didn't see him. When she was born," said Johanna, with a slight smile, "I called her *Appelwang.*"

"And *were* her cheeks like apples?"

"Exactly! She was such a healthy baby! Nothing like her brother. He was always sick. Bronchial asthma he had. Terrible time breathing! I was the same way myself as a child. I still remember visitors coming to the house, and my father saying, *'That* one! Look how pale she is. She won't live long!'" She shook her head at the memory.

"That's an awful thing to say in front of a child."

Johanna nodded. "So when Henkie had the same sickness, I decided life would be better for him. We had him to different doctors, but sometimes the remedy seemed worse than the cure! We had to tie him upside down in Piet's easy chair, and leave him there so his lungs could drain – poor little guy. They said removing his tonsils would help, and because of his condition, they removed them without anesthetic. Didn't make a difference with his health; just made him scared of doctors. Even after he started school he was home a lot. Whenever the weather was cold and damp, he had an awful time breathing, and in Nederland, the weather always seemed to be like that."

"But Johanna," said Lies, *"I've* never seen him sick."

"That's because he hasn't *been* sick since we came to Canada. Doctor doesn't know if it's the difference in weather, or if he just outgrew the asthma, but what a relief! All the worrying I've done! Lies, I don't know if I ever told you, but Henkie was the biggest reason I agreed to come to Canada. I was so afraid there might be another war over there. In the last one, Piet's brother Geert came back from the German labour camp with TB, and had to have a lung removed. I was terrified that would happen to Henkie, when he already had such trouble breathing."

"So Henk was sick in Nederland, and has been healthy here and grew to a strapping six feet... Hmmm," mused Lies. "Maybe it was coming across on the boat. That good sea air. What do you think, Johanna?" and she grinned mischievously at her friend as she poured more cognac.

"It did nothing for me.," Johanna sputtered. "I puked all the way!"

"Ha, ha! Don't I know it! But listen, you started to tell me about Anneke."

"Anneke could always look after herself. But, she was a handful! From the time she started crawling she got into trouble. When she was three I sent her off to school, and with her away, I could concentrate on taking care of Henkie. He was five, still at home."

"What kind of a school could you get her into at three?"

"A school run by nuns, in an old stone cloister."

"You're not Catholic!"

"No. But the nuns, they'd take the kids real young. And she loved it. Learned crafts. For her first day, I bought Anneke a new skirt, very full, and navy-blue. I always made all the clothing, so this was something special, expensive, store bought. When she came home after school, I told her to go potty. Sometime later, when she hadn't come back out, I went in to check on her, found her still sitting on the pot, but she had scissors in her hands. Weren't mine – must have been from school. 'Mama, look what I make,' she said proudly. There on the floor of the WC, was a row of what looked like navy-blue paper dolls, connected hand to hand and foot to foot." Johanna shook her head, "I may have gone a bit hysterical. I let one *scream* out of me, then I ran to the next-door neighbours. 'You've got to see this!' I yelled. 'You won't believe what she's done now!'"

"Lies burst out laughing. "Very creative!"

Johanna said with a wry grin, "Yes, you wouldn't think nuns would teach girls how to cut up their skirts, would you?"

"Makes me look at them a whole new way!"

"I bought her a pair of *klompjes* – not that people in Eindhoven wore wooden shoes much, but she looked so darn cute when she pranced off to school! One day it snowed, and she was late coming home from that cloister. Piet was home early from work and went to look for her. Well, by the time he found her she was... fine, even proud of herself."

"But..."

"She told him that the wet snow had stuck to the bottom of her *klopjes* until there was a big ball of snow there and she couldn't walk any more. She sat on the curb crying. A big boy came along and he was wearing klompen too, and showed her how to kick the bottom against the curb to knock the snow off. When Piet found her she was kicking the curb every few steps, proud as punch of her new skill."

"Lies laughed. Then said, "She walked to school alone?"

"*Ja.* Very independent. She liked to help her father do woodworking in the *schuur*. Henk, with his asthma, never went there; couldn't go near the sawdust. Anneke would hold the boards while her father sawed. Then she'd sandpaper the ends for him. Liked that sort of thing. But housework!" Johanna shook her head. "Hopeless!"

"Her sister was so different. Mieke always knew her place as a girl. Was interested in cooking and cleaning. Practical. Big help to me. And now she looks after the two little boys, and does her housekeeping with pride. But Anneke, *Anneke!*" Johanna needed a sip of cognac. "Nothing but complain! Insists it's unfair. 'Just because I'm a girl,' she told me in that snotty tone of hers, 'you expect me to do *all* the work, while Henk gets to play!' I explained to her, 'Boys do not *do* housework!' But I've had an awful time with her, Lies! I'd come home from cleaning all day, to find burnt food, dust balls under the beds, and piles of dirty dishes, and there would be Anneke, with her nose stuck in a book. She'd look up all surprised that I was home." Johanna shook her head, "How can that girl even think about getting married, when she can't do the simplest chores?"

"I suppose she thinks life will be different with her prince charming."

Johanna pulled a face, then she carried on with her rant, "But it's not just the housework that's a problem. I don't think she does a lick of schoolwork either! Her marks are terrible!"

Lies looked thoughtful, said, "Remember when she got that report card that was straight A's? What grade was she in then, seven?"

"Yes. Then there was all that nonsense about university. She was going to be this and do that. Be a doctor for the animals or save the heathen in Africa! University! 'Your father and I,' I told her, 'were both maybe ten years old when we were pulled out of school to help our families. And then *you* think you can go to university? You don't know how lucky you are to *high school!* University! Do you think money grows on *trees?*'" Johanna shook her head. "Liesje, I've tried to get that girl to face reality. Have I not done my best with her?"

Lies seemed mesmerized with the last bit of cognac, which she was swirling about in the bottom of her glass. Finally she answered, "Of course you have, *meid!*"

"Kees called to say he would be late," Lies said, "so we won't be leaving for awhile." She smiled at Anneke, "That means that you've got a little break before you start baby-sitting. Come and sit down on the couch. Would you like some Coca Cola?"

"Sure!" said Anneke. "Thanks. Are the kids already in bed?"

"That's right. The little darlings," she grinned, "are asleep." She handed Anneke the coke.

"Now then," she said, settling down comfortably in her arm chair and lighting a cigarette, "What's new with you?"

"I'm getting married," announced Anneke, "soon."

"Really?" said Lies, as she looked at Anneke thoughtfully. "Think you're ready for such a big step?"

Anneke scrunched up her face and raised her eyebrows. She liked Lies, found her to be empathetic, and she was trying hard to be honest, to reach inside herself for an answer. "Don't know about being ready," she finally said, "but Howard and I are in love and we want to be together."

"*Ja,*" said Lies, "I can understand that. Young love! It's not *that* long ago I was young. But Anneke," and she looked into the girl's eyes. "I think I know what you're going to answer, but I have to ask anyway, would it not be a good idea to finish school first?"

"Honestly, Lies," and Anneke paused. "I don't think at this point I could even pass grade eleven." She sighed, "I used to do really well at school, but then it started to seem like such a dead end. I wasn't going anywhere! And by now it's been so long since I tried, since I studied, it's been so long that I've been fooling around in class, that I don't think I could do it even if I wanted to. My mind is in such a space now that as soon as I try to focus, it just goes blank and wanders off. Sometimes I feel a bit like a zombie or something, I don't know what it is. A few weeks ago, the guidance counselor called me in, and told me I had all this ability, and everything, and it made me feel really good for a little bit, but Lies, I don't know what it is, I might have the ability, but still, I can't focus, I can't do it any more, Lies."

"Is that why you want to get married so soon, because you think you'll fail?"

"I know that if we wait to get married until I graduate, we'll wait forever!"

"Anneke, I used to be a pretty good student myself, and I discovered that how well you do in school depends a lot on the habits you get into. Right now, you've gotten yourself into some pretty bad habits. How about I give you a hand to try to turn things around? You could bring your homework over here, maybe… a couple of times a week?"

"Thanks, Lies," said Anneke. She was starting to feel guilty. Lies was being so kind, so understanding, so helpful! Anneke took a deep breath, "The thing is, Lies, that there's not much point. The thing is that… that…. I'm pregnant." Anneke looked down at the floor.

Lies' eyebrows rose. "Anneke," she said, and waited for the girl to look up, in order to give her an encouraging smile, "I'm glad you told me. But you know, you're not the first and you certainly won't be the last to get pregnant before you're married. Have you told Howard?"

"Hasn't been back in three weeks. Didn't want to tell him by letter."

"How do you think he'll take it?"

"Well, he did propose to me, Lies. That first week he was up in Norbury he sent back a letter proposing. Said he wanted to marry me! So, he should be OK with this. He'll be back this weekend. I'm gonna tell him, but I'm really nervous about it. But, we're in love, so everything should be fine. Right?"

"Of course, *kind,* everything will be fine. And your mother? Have you told her? I *think* she kind of suspects…"

"Oh, no! She's already upset enough that I want to get married right away. There's no way I'm telling her the rest of it. No *way* she's finding out!"

"But *kindje*…"

"No, Lies! *Promise* you won't tell!"

That Saturday evening, the Belvedere was parked by the creek. The car windows had steamed up earlier and were now rolled down, letting in brisk, March air, revealing Anneke and Howard, on the backseat. Howard mumbled, "That sure was good."

"Uh, huh," agreed Anneke. Contentedly, they lay curled in each other's arms. It was an overcast March night, brisk and quiet, but for the distant sound of a dog barking. Finally, Anneke broke the silence, said,

"Howard, when do you think we could get married? I miss you so much when you're away, and you're only back every few weekends!"

"Weekends are time-an-a-half," said Howard. "Good money. Bankin' 'er. Figure on gettin' married," he said furrowing his brow, "well, uh, when ya git yer grade twelve."

"Can't wait that long," said Anneke.

"Yeah, it's hard fer me too."

"No Howard, you don't understand! I *really* can't wait that long."

Howard shot to a sitting position. "Wha-a-at?" he drawled, "But I thought.... Are ya sure?"

"Yes," said Anneke in a small voice. "I'm sure." She sat up as well, backed into the corner.

"How....?"

"Dunno," Anneke murmured. "Guess there's nothing that's a hundred percent..."

"Yeah," he said, letting it sink in. "But uh, I hear that, uh, there's stuff ya can take, to...."

"I would *never* do that!"

"Yeah," he repeated. "'Course not." Then he was quiet. Anneke sat huddled in the corner, waiting. Finally he said, "Getting' cold in 'ere. C'mon, git in th' front. Start 'er up." Miserably, Anneke got out. Briefly she stood on the snowy ground, looked up at the starless sky, then she climbed into the front seat to join a silent Howard. She sat against the door, and stared, non-seeing into the dark night. Howard started the car, started backing up from their spot by the creek, and still not a word was said. Then they were driving along, yellow headlights illuminating snow-clad roads. Finally, they pulled into Anneke's driveway. Howard stopped the car and mumbled something, and Anneke had to strain to hear him, "Uh, yeah, married, uh huh, right away, yeah. Uh, ain't got much money saved though."

Anneke let out a deep sigh, "Just as long as we're together," she said, moving closer to Howard. "That's all that matters, right? I'll talk to my mother again about getting married, although the last time it ended up in a big fight. But then," she said dismissively, "she never likes anything I do anyway."

"You're gonna tell yer mother?"

"Oh, no! Not about *that!* Nobody needs to know. As soon as we're married I'll join you in Norbury, and then, when it's time for, you know, we'll have been married for months and months, and nobody will even *realize*. But," she said thoughtfully, rubbing her chin, "Soon our *engagement* won't be a secret anymore, and I could even wear an engagement *ring*, couldn't I, to school and everything, so maybe… you could…." she looked at him beguilingly.

"Git y'an engagement ring?" He smiled at her, as one would smile at a kitten that had overturned a potted plant.

It was the following Monday, and Johanna was in the kitchen doing the laundry in her wringer-washer. She enjoyed the routine of this task. She enjoyed using her skill as a homemaker to bring organization and cleanliness to her household. She enjoyed the feeling of control this gave her over her life. Johanna leaned against the washing machine, and smiled as she thought back to Nederland, where every *day* her housework had routine, gave satisfaction. In Nederland, thought Johanna, as she put dirty sheets in her washing machine, everybody knew their place, knew what was expected of them. Would Anneke have been such so rebellious if they'd stayed there? Would the girl have known her place? The children understood Canadian society better than Johanna did, and they would say things, and she would have no idea if that's actually the way it was here, or if they were just trying to put one over on her. It made it really hard to keep them on the straight and narrow. She'd worried, and worried, but what could she do? They were all in a new country. They had to fit in with the way things were done here.

In Nederland, she thought, as she went into the bathroom to get the dirty towels, she and Piet had dated by going out on their bicycles. Here, girls went out with boys in cars, and who knew what happened! Johanna thought with a wry smile, that it was definitely more difficult to get pregnant on a bicycle. Quickly she became serious again, as she thought of Anneke, out with Howard, home late. She shook her head, as she thought that it wouldn't surprise her to find out her daughter was pregnant. It would explain a lot! It would certainly explain the sudden insistence on getting married. But what a scandal it would be! And the thought of Anneke as a mother was the stuff of nightmares! Johanna sighed deeply, climbed the stairs to the bedrooms to get the rest of the laundry. She started to take clothes from Anneke's laundry hamper, when suddenly, to her immense relief, she noticed blood stains.

"I'm quitting school, and I'm getting married," announced Anneke, as she walked into the living room after school.

"No you're not!" said Johanna, decisively, as she continued her dusting. "You are staying right where you are until you finish high school. After that I will be more than happy to wash my hands of you!"

"Well you can be happy a little earlier," scoffed Anneke, "because I'm quitting now, I'm getting married, and I'm going off with Howard."

Her eyes narrowed, Johanna snapped, "You are not old enough to get married without our permission." Johanna had done her research, had obtained this useful bit of information from one of the women she worked for. Glaring at her daughter, she added with a note of triumph, "And we are not giving it!"

"Right!" said Anneke, dripping sarcasm. "You want me to run away with Howard without getting married. Is that what you want?"

"What I want is for you to behave yourself long enough to finish school!"

"You're not listening to me! I've told you that I'm leaving, now, one way or another!"

Still holding her dust-cloth, Johanna sank down into the couch, defeated. With trembling voice she said, "Is your home so terrible that you can't wait until you're old enough to leave? Is it that terrible?" She started to sob. Suddenly she cried out, "Am I such a terrible mother?" and began wailing, her body shaking with great heaving sobs.

Anneke stood rooted. Anger she could deal with. This infinite sadness spilling out of her mother, she could not. She reached a decision, "The reason I want to get married," she said in a flat voice, pausing for Johanna's attention, "is because I'm pregnant."

"No you're not," muttered Johanna through her tears. "I just did the laundry two days ago."

"Didn't want you to know, because you were upset enough already."

Johanna stopped sobbing. Looked at her daughter through narrowed, red-rimmed eyes. "How…"

"Liver," said Anneke. "Bought fifteen cents worth of pork liver. Lots of blood and gore. Yeller ate the leftovers."

To Anneke's consternation, Johanna started wailing again. But then Anneke realized that these weren't wails of sadness, they were howls of hysterical laughter.

She heard her parents talking late into the night. The next day, Johanna, dark circles under her eyes, informed Anneke that there would indeed be a wedding, and as soon as possible.

When Howard came back Easter weekend, he brought Anneke an engagement ring, with a very tiny diamond, and they went to the parsonage to talk to the minister about setting a date. The earliest opening for a weekend wedding was the afternoon of Saturday, 26 May.

Howard was invited to come to dinner after church that Easter Sunday, where a seething Piet did his best to be civil. With tension thick in the air, Howard nervously dropped food, and spoke completely unintelligibly, which only confirmed Piet's opinion that Howard was nothing but a Neanderthal, a low-life brute who had violated his daughter. Johanna did her best to steer the dinner conversation to practical matters, and they did manage to reach some decisions. The wedding would be very small, with only the closest friends and family. Invitations would be ordered right away, and sent out as soon as they arrived from the printer.

Finally, the interminable meal came to an end, and Anneke and Howard went outside. She'd been craving time alone with him, time to cuddle, time to feel cherished and loved, and she was about to get into his car so they could drive to their favourite spot by the creek, when she suddenly realized that he wasn't getting in. He was just standing there, leaning on the hood of the car. His mouth tensely set, he looked off into the distance. "Gotta head back," he said, as Anneke's eyes opened wide in consternation. "Gotta find an apartment. Aint a whole lot around."

"But, but we…"

"Cain't fit y'inta ma room at th'roomin' house, kin I? Barely got room fer me!" He walked around the car and gave her a quick kiss, then he got into the tri-colour '57 Plymouth Belvedere, and quickly drove off. A forlorn Anneke watched him leave, as she stood in the driveway, alone.

"Howard gone already?" asked her mother, with a frown, when Anneke walked into the house. "Didn't you need to talk more about the wedding? Does he even have a best man?"

"Had stuff to do in Norbury," mumbled Anneke, and she climbed the stairs, threw herself on her bed, and sobbed.

A few days later, Anneke walked into the school and flashed her engagement ring at the other girls. "Had enough of this place! Getting married!" she told them. "Going off to Norbury with Howard!" and she fancied herself quite the romantic figure, going off to be with the man she loved. She went into the office to sign her school-leaving forms, and the secretary quickly tripped around the desk in her high heels, and whipped out the paper-work. Anneke signed the forms, then went down the hallway to clean out her locker. The bell rang signaling the imminent start of classes and hordes of students entered the school, filled the hallways, and funneled through classroom doors. Clutching her bundle of books to her chest, Anneke walked out of the school, alone.

It was the morning of May 26th. Everything was being readied for the afternoon wedding. As she fashioned Anneke's bouquet of spring flowers, Lies hummed a favourite tune. Gerda and Rosemary chattered and laughed merrily, while decorating the oak pews of the church with huge bows, which they made of white crepe paper. In the basement of the church, the church ladies were busily spreading margarine on bread, making the sandwiches for the reception. As they worked, they speculated – was she or wasn't she? Johanna had told them, "What can you do, when they want to get married so young. But she's not pregnant! I just did the laundry and..." Despite this declaration from the mother-of-the-bride, still, they talked. Johanna, home ironing, worried about scandal, worried about Anneke managing in that far-off city, and worried about the slightly-used wedding dress, which she had on the ironing board. Could it be pressed to look like new? Henk was polishing shoes at the kitchen table, grumbling because this week, he had to do it both Saturday and Sunday. Piet was purchasing jenever for the house party that evening, but his brow was furrowed and his eyes angrily slit, as he thought about the Neanderthal who had gotten his Anneke pregnant, the brute, who was about to become his son-in-law.

Anneke, curlers in her hair, sat under the dryer at the hairdresser's, crying huge, silent tears. "It will be fine!" she told herself, as her tears evaporated from the heat of the dryer. "Everything will be all right!" But still she cried. It must be her 'condition' she decided, that caused this sadness, this fear, this feeling of desolation, at the thought of going off to that strange city, to go through pregnancy and childbirth, far away from all the people she knew, far from her family, her friends. How would she even know if everything was normal, she wondered, when none of the women in her life, her mother, her aunt, Lies, would be there to advise her? She tried to think of something happier, pictured the wedding that afternoon, and the reception, then the party at her parents' house, and after that, going to a motel with Howard. But then, the following day, they would leave for Norbury, and Anneke was afraid. But no matter how afraid she was of leaving, Anneke was even more afraid of staying. The tears poured out, as she thought of the unspeakable that could happen, for it had been three weeks, since she'd heard from Howard.

"You look just like Jackie Kennedy in that dress," gushed Rosemary. "Absolutely elegant!" Anneke was dressing for her wedding. She had told no-one that she hadn't heard from Howard. She didn't want people to think badly of him, or for that matter, to look down on her, and she certainly didn't want her parents any more upset then they were already! After breaking down at the hairdresser's, she had somehow managed to calm herself, by telling herself that Howard's intentions were honourable.

Must have worked late, yesterday, she'd told herself, that's why he's not here yet. Worked overtime, making extra money for us! Anyway, he'll be here for the wedding! He'll be at the church! I can trust Howard!

After all the anguish, the worry, and the stress, Anneke was calm. She was so calm in fact, that her entire body felt numb. It was almost like she wasn't even in her body any more, but was sort of floating around, looking down on herself as she was being dressed for her wedding, there, in that small bedroom, in the upstairs of her parents' house.

And dimly, through the fog of her mind, Anneke wondered if it really was her wedding she was being dressed for. From the sadness which exuded from her parents these last few weeks, from the sadness that Anneke felt deep in her own heart, it seemed they must be dressing her for her funeral! Wedding, funeral, somehow it made no difference to her!

Rosemary and Gerda were completely oblivious to Anneke's mental state. As they bustled about, they did notice how quiet she was, how still she stood on that little rug in the middle of the bedroom floor – but they put it all down to the simple fact that she was a bride. Of course she wasn't herself! This was the most important day of her life! She was simply overwhelmed by the momentousness of the occasion!

Rosemary checked out Anneke's dress, "All that lace, and those poufy crinolines! Why, you'll do well to get through the church door!"

"That dress," said Gerda decisively, "must have cost a fortune!"

And from her distant state, Anneke thought that, yes, it had been very expensive indeed! And had been worn only once. By Professor Johnson's niece.

"Pearls," said Rosemary to Gerda. "She needs pearls. Jackie always wears them." She tilted her head. Looked at Anneke appraisingly. "And they would pick up the little seed-pearls in that lace."

Gerda dug around in Anneke's box of costume jewelry, "As long as it's the Jackie Kennedy look you're after," she said to Rosemary, handing her the pearls. "As long as you're not making her look like *the other woman*."

"What!" exclaimed Rosemary, removing the Woolworth price tag before fastening the pearls around Anneke's neck. "Who are you talking about?"

"You saw her. Last week. On the news. When she sang to the president."

"You mean... Marilyn?"

"Uh-huh."

Rosemary's eyes went wide. "You mean Marilyn Monroe in that dress she wore when she sang 'Happy Birthday' to President Kennedy? You mean Marilyn Monroe in that skin-tight, skin-coloured dress with the rhinestones? My *goodness! Hardly* suitable for a bride!"

Yes, thought Anneke, especially a pregnant bride.

"Made the president's eyes pop though, didn't it?" said Gerda, grinning.

"I guess so...," said Rosemary. "But wasn't that dress *so* tight they had to sew her into it? Oh my! Think of the scandal if Anneke wore something like that!"

Scandal, thought Anneke, God forbid there should be a scandal!

Gerda said, "If we had to sew her into a dress she'd become a human pincushion and bleed to death before the wedding. Speaking of that, look how pale she is. You'd think she had no blood in her veins!"

"Needs rouge," said Rosemary, opening the Maybelline makeup case she had bought especially for the occasion. She brushed the bright pink powder on Anneke's wan cheeks.

"She's still too white. Put some on her chin and her forehead."

"Right!" said Rosemary, dabbing away.

"What do you think of that rumour, Rosemary? You get all the movie magazines. Is it true, that rumour about MM and the president?"

"Noooo!" said Rosemary aghast, stabbing Anneke with an eyebrow pencil. "Terrible, the stories they make up about famous people. There is no way Mr. Kennedy would have sex with that woman! He's much too distinguished! Besides, he's too old."

Sex, thought Anneke, sex. That's what got me into this situation. But Howard will be here soon. Everything will be fine!

"Turned forty-five on his birthday. Not that old! Mascara," Gerda ordered, "and eye shadow."

"Green or blue?"

"Blue," said Gerda decisively.

Green, Anneke wanted to scream, green, not blue! Blue is your colour, Gerda, because your eyes are blue. Mine are green! But Anneke remained mute.

Rosemary applied the eye-shadow. Stood back to look. Got out the eyelash curler. "It's just so romantic!" she oozed. "Anneke getting married and riding off with her man into the sunset! Just like in the movies."

"Which movie?" challenged Gerda. "Don't remember a whole lot of them ending *that* happily."

"Or, maybe not so much like the movies, but... maybe more like the Kennedys." Rosemary rambled, "You know what they say about the Kennedys living in Camelot and all that! Well, Anneke and Howard will have their own little version of Camelot right up there in Norbury, and there they will live happily ever after. It is just *too* romantic!"

In her mind, Anneke repeated the words like a mantra. Happily ever after. Just like the Kennedys. Happily ever after. Just like the Kennedys. Happily ever after...

It was time to go. Henk was waiting with the car. He had driven his parents to the church earlier, because everyone couldn't fit into the vehicle at the same time. The girls helped Anneke into the back seat, carefully holding up her dress to avoid crumpling it. Gerda got in with Anneke, while Rosemary, carrying the make-up case for touch-ups, importantly got into the front with Henk. Flirted, "My, you look handsome in that suit! And a boutonnière even! How suave!"

Henk drove the few blocks to the church, while the girls continued their chatter. He rounded the corner of Church Street, and the steeple of MillCreek United came into view. Soon the rest of that stately, Gothic church became visible. When they were close enough to see the parking lot, Anneke suddenly burst into tears. "What the heck!" exclaimed Henk.

Rosemary whipped around in her seat, and both girls stared at Anneke, perplexed, concerned. They looked over at the church but saw nothing unusual. Looked at each other, wide-eyed. All at once, Anneke's crying switched to manic laughter, which reverberated inside the car. Henk thought it a damn good thing the windows were closed, as he drove up to the church. Shrieking hysterically, Anneke stared at the parking lot. Parked among the vehicles belonging to the wedding guests, was a tri-colour '57 Plymouth Belvedere.

Notes

'Piet' is pronounced 'Pete.'
'Kees' is pronounced 'Case.'
'Lies' is pronounces 'Lease.'
Adding the suffix 'je' creates the diminutive or affectionate, so that 'Lies' becomes 'Liesje.'

The Dutch tend to like their compound words, such as langgevelboerderij. These can be easily broken down:
lang - long
gevel - front of building
boerderij - farmhouse (or farm)

My inspiration for this historical novel came from many sources. I'd heard from my parents about the war and the horror of the bombings, but it wasn't until recently that I realized to my shock, that the Dutch were alternately bombed by the RAF and the Luftwaffe. My uncle Robert Mulder was a fireman at Philips and told me of his experiences with the SS arrests that followed the nation-wide strike. A ten-year-old cousin witnessed the executions that took place in front of the factory.

I have been told numerous stories of the immigration experience, and although the characters in my book are fictional, anecdotes do reflect real stories of Dutch immigrants, whether it's being dropped off at a remote train station in the middle of the night with no one there to meet you, or being denied permission to go to Canada, because you mistook the emigration inspector for the housing inspector.

Thanks to everyone who shared their stories with me, with particular thanks to those who are no longer with us. Thank you for the inspiration.

Gesina Laird-Buchanan (van der Klooster) was born in the Netherlands, grew up with war stories, and recalls that as a small child she was envious of older siblings who had actually experienced all that excitement. Gesina studied art history at Queen's University and went on to teach high school art. She currently lives in a historic limestone house in Napanee, Ontario, tends a rose garden, and sculpts historical figures.